Glorious Sunset

Glorious Sunset

Glorious Sunset

Ava Bleu

www.urbanchristianonline.com

Urban Books, LLC
97 N18th Street
Wyandanch, NY 11798

Glorious Sunset Copyright © 2014 Ava Bleu

ISBN 13: 978-1-60162-670-7
ISBN 10: 1-60162-670-3

First Trade Paperback Printing September 2014
Printed in the United States of America

10 9 8 7 6 5 4 3 2 1

Distributed by Kensington Corp.
Submit Wholesale Orders to:
Kensington Publishing Corp.
C/O Penguin Group (USA) Inc.
Attention: Order Processing
405 Murray Hill Parkway
East Rutherford, NJ 07073-2316
Phone: 1-800-526-0275
Fax: 1-800-227-9604

Glorious Sunset

by

Ava Bleu

To everyone struggling to find their way and hoping for a little love and light to go along with those important life lessons, I speak for you.

Acknowledgments

This book was truly a labor of love as I navigate my own personal journey and learn the spiritual lessons of the flawed and humble. Some of us have a little further to go to reach salvation than others; we are dedicated to our path but sometimes a little wobbly on our new legs. Bear with us.

I believe in love, I believe God has a purpose for us (and love has a lot to do with it), and I believe God has a sense of humor. With those thoughts in mind this tale of miracles was born. No doubt you will recognize a fantasy or two; I play upon those familiar themes with the greatest respect to our literary legends and homage to global tall tales, Christmas stories, and spirited fables from Africa. Every culture has myths and stories passed down through the generations. No one can say how much of these stories may be true, but until someone can say with certainly what *isn't* true, some of us will choose to revel in the possibilities and, most certainly, find God in every one of them.

Thank you to my family—my heart and soul. Thank you to everyone who read my story and listened to me go on and on about this king and his endless love. Thank you to my editor Joylynn Ross for believing my little story has a place. I'm so proud to be one of the many authors on the Urban Christian line and do hope you enjoy this novel as much as I enjoyed writing it.

Acknowledgments

It may best be fitting to close this in the tone of my wonderful hero:

"I wish you pleasure and enlightenment such that your spirit will reach to the heavens with the joyful abandon and happy surrender of the branches of the magnificent baobab!"

. . . Or, happy reading.

Ava Bleu

Prologue

1600 AD: Jaha, West Africa

The acrid smell of a burning village brought King Taka Olufemi awake, sputtering, coughing, and wincing in pain as he did so. Slowly memory returned and with it the horror. He cracked his eyelids open, his eyes immediately burning with the pebbly smoke that floated in a low-hanging cloud. Pushing himself upright from where he lay causing sharp pain to streak through his torso and the agony brought his gaze down as he sucked in his breath and jerked his hands to the source. Seeing the jagged, torn flesh of the wound in his side, the rest of his memory came and with the memory:

"Oh no. No, no, no . . ."

He forgot his pain. He fought off the sway of the world as he stood, struggling to focus and see through eyes watering with smoke and something else he didn't dare identify. He didn't need to see when he could smell. He was a king and warrior; battle was in his bones and death always a close companion. He smelled both here.

He looked around. Men, women, children; the massacre was complete. Beyond the hall huts and houses of his village were blackened ash. The air still burned with the stench of fire. He couldn't understand this. In all his life he'd never seen such brutality, never known such dishonor. Still, he firmed his jaw and kept looking, turning in a wide circle until his feet staggered to a stop before his brain could even register.

His body knew how to find its heart.

He stumbled like a drunkard. When, finally, he was upon her he could only drop to his knees. Agony slammed him like a lion strike in the wild. And much like a lion strike, the blow from the magnificent body was the stunner, but then the massive teeth would rip a man's flesh from his bones as a second course. He felt the teeth ripping his beating heart from his chest and groaned with the searing pain as he admitted to the horror before him.

"Zahara." He gathered his murdered queen in his arms and breathed into her fragrant hair, tears welling in his eyes. The wrenching that tore through him was brutal; already his body ached, keenly, from lack of her. The panic began, at that moment, threatening to strip away what was left of his sanity. With the madness came the screaming, purging to the only one who could hear him now.

"I am King Taka Olufemi!" he shouted to the universe, with all the power of his soul. "You may take my kingdom, you may take my loved ones and friends, but you may not have her! Do you hear me?"

The room crackled with audible air bubbles popping all around. The sound grew in crescendo and the hall lit with a light unseen by most people. Taka had felt this sensation many times throughout his life. It was always followed by the appearance of Aniweto. Ani was his gentle-voiced friend and confidant but he was more commonly known as his guardian angel. The legend of Taka's easy communication with heaven had always been a blessed thing to him, but the blessings hadn't helped him today. Knowing the power that brought Ani into his life, he knew his words went straight on high. Right or wrong, today he would use his friend to get his point to the one who had wronged him.

"I've given our Father my allegiance and my faith, and this is how He repays me?" he said, his voice hoarse. "My tribe, my people: all gone. And all I would have asked was that you leave one person. Just one person!"

He fumbled for his sword, his mind automatically preparing for battle with an enemy, as if this enemy could be bested by a sword. He looked at it and realized the futility. He glared at Ani, and though his ego demanded it, his soul could not mask the pain. "I have nothing left to live for. In one afternoon you've taken everything from me. I'll give you the rest to complete the package!" Quickly he moved the sword around, its tip at his own stomach, the blade slicing through the skin of his damaged hands.

"Taka!" Ani exclaimed. It was his friend's voice but it was different today. It didn't happen often, but occasionally his familiar guardian would change slightly. Ani's voice would deepen in timbre and his eyes would shine with a light that told him he was visited by the Almighty through his dear Aniweto's body. As Ani had always told him, he was merely a messenger and a vessel, a tool of the Father. But Taka sometimes forgot exactly what that meant, how close and special was his relationship and his gift to reach the Almighty so easily. Today, apparently his request was beyond Ani. Through his friend he listened to a voice felt to the depths of his soul. He knew he was not only with his guardian this day, and the Father's next words confirmed that.

"I did not take them from you, son; evil did that. My pain is greater than you could know. But even still, even with this tragedy, you know better than to take what I have made. You are still here, Taka. All is not lost if you still have the will of a warrior."

Will of a warrior? Taka bent to lift the body of Zahara in his arms. His soul twisted with grief. "Here is my will, lying dead in my arms. Tell me, Great One, have I not

done everything you have asked of me? You tell me this is
my destiny, to be without her? It cannot be. I ask for only
one thing: give her back to me. With this one woman I can
pick myself up and go on. She is more than my wife; she
is my best friend. She is my reason to rise. All I need is
Zahara and I will accept whatever you have for me. I will
accept this carnage. I will swallow my tears and bury my
people without a murmur of complaint. I will never cry
again; just bring her back."

"Have you considered perhaps Zahara could not accept
this carnage? She has not years of battle, has never seen this
much destruction or dreamed she would have to survive
it. She is a strong spirit but this is too much for most of
my children to bear. Too much for all but a man weaned,
trained, and protected by his guardian angel. You are the
only one with the strength of mind and spirit to withstand
this horror, Taka. I will be here for you even when it seems
no man wants to hear your voice. I will guide you and see
you through every step and you will honor her with your
courage. My son, my heart hurts for you but it is Zahara's
time, not yours."

"I beseech you," he moaned, his hands clutching
the cloth of her garments, willing the life back into the
woman who wore them. He would put her down and
crawl on his hands and knees if that was what it took.
He would beg if that was required. He was beyond pride,
beyond rationality.

"She is already gone on, Taka. It is her time, son. It is
not yours. It is not yours."

The finality in His tone finally snapped Taka out of
his subservience. Hope died like clay drying in the sun.
He lay his wife's body down gently and stood to the
Almighty. "Then I say it is my time as well. I still control
that, do I not? Do I not?"

"Would you insult me so as to take what I have given
you in love and throw it away?"

"What of that which you have taken from me? She and I had so little time together. Had I known what was to come I would have spent every waking second in her arms, braiding flowers through her hair. We had not even created life between us yet you take her from me already?"

"The love you and Zahara shared was a gift. Two years of pure love, more than some have in a lifetime—"

"It wasn't enough!" Taka yelled, fury growing out of control inside him. Two years with Zahara could never be enough. A lifetime could never be enough. "You are a false and cruel entity to play games such as this. What is the purpose? Are we just toys? Playthings to amuse you?"

"Taka, I allow you license to speak because my love for you is great, but it is not your right to question my purpose."

"If I cannot question your purpose, if your reply to me is that I have no more right to question my existence than a child should question why he must take his sustenance every day, then it is obvious to me you have no respect for me. Perhaps you never have that you could dabble in my life in this fashion with no more care than you would have for the rubbish we burn as trash. I see now I am more disturbed by this massacre of your children than you ever could be. Thank you, Father. I have made up my mind. For this I will take from you yet another of your children!" Taka once again picked up the sword, ignoring the pain in his hands. The tip was at his abdomen and his face drawn with determination.

"Insolence!" Ani's body quivered with emotion. Ani had never raised a voice to him. The very ground vibrated with the anger of the Almighty. "Taka Olufemi, I have watched you grow from a child to a man and I have blessed you with strength and courage, pride, honor, and dignity and yet all you can see is what you do not have at this moment, at this time. You ignore all I have given and denigrate my purpose, and even my existence. You are a spoiled child, and, even worse, an arrogant, short-sighted man. I had thought you contained more. You want your queen back?"

"That is all I want. And you would never have to do a single thing for me again. You would never need to speak to me or grace me with Ani's presence. I would be satisfied never to hear the voice of either one of you again if you give me back what you have taken."

"Very well. You will not die today, Taka. But you will no longer exist as you are. You are a phantom to the world." The Almighty reached down, cupped Zahara's cheek lovingly with saddened eyes, and then removed the ruby brooch from her dress. "This token of love you once bestowed upon your wife will become your home and vessel. Zahara, as you knew her, is no more. Her spirit has already moved on and will take another form soon, and after that another, and another. You will live a life of chance, Taka. You come alive only when someone picks up this bauble and rubs life into the stone in the center. You will neither age nor grow old. You live to grant wishes to the people who release you from this stone, to watch as they appreciate what you have thrown away. Three wishes, three days. Once the third wish is granted you return to the stone."

"What has this to do with my wife?"

"This brooch will travel through the hands of men. There is no telling where it will go or how it will get there. Zahara's spirit will someday settle into the body of a woman who will share her face. You will know her when you see her, though she will have no memory of you. If she chooses to be with you, you will be able to live your life with her as a mortal man. If she denies you I will remove you immediately and you will go on to the fiery afterworld you so covet."

Taka took a deep breath, finally feeling some hope. Finally, a chance. "So I must make her fall in love with me again. That should be easy. Zahara and I love each other deeply."

"Zahara is gone, Taka. You will have to touch her spirit if you have any chance of living a life with the woman you claim to love."

Taka frowned, feeling at a loss. "Touch her spirit? That means nothing to me. Nonsense and drivel. I still have this body and this face; her 'spirit' will certainly accept me. I am her king; she will know me, despite what you say. Our love is stronger than death. Our love can survive anything. You shall see. What do I do to start this journey?"

The Almighty looked at him a long time, His face softening. Taka felt a tingling in his side and looked down. He touched the place that had been wounded and felt nothing but his own perfect skin. He looked back at the Power behind Ani who said merely, "What do you do? Thank me for my mercy, son."

Chapter 1

Present day: Columbus, Ohio, USA

Violet Jackson's company, Shades of Violet, was buzzing with activity, phones ringing and people moving around; it was crazy and manic and Violet loved it.

Her business wasn't large, but it was profitable and growing every day. She had a staff of one assistant and a multitude of interns eager to cut their human ecology teeth in a bona fide design studio and Violet was more than willing to take advantage of their free labor. It freed her up to do other things like what she was doing now: convincing someone to do what she wanted.

Violet thrust a swath of material toward a slight woman with glasses perched on her nose.

"Red?" the woman said. "I don't know."

"Absolutely, red," Violet assured her.

"Red seems so radical."

"This change in your life is very radical."

"But, what about this nice pink here?" The woman meekly held up a "candy hearts" pink paint swatch.

Violet hid a sigh and dropped the material. The thing about Columbus, Ohio was that it wasn't New York City. There were precious few people who had both the money and the desire to delve into unchartered territories. Artists with courage were always broke, unlike those rich little bohemians in New York. And the rich people in Columbus were busy trying to one-up each other by seeing which one could get the dullest dull colors they could find and calling it "classy." Sure, she liked some plain stuff too, but not all the time. The reviewers claimed it was because she was black and naturally took to reds and golds. Whatever.

She took the woman by the arm. "Doris, I love you to death but I will not do another pastel chic job for you. For some people that might work, but not for you. Red is your favorite color."

"But red walls? What will people think? I'm forty-five years old. It'll look like a hippy pad."

"It will be tasteful and classy and you will wonder why you ever hesitated."

"But—"

"Listen to me, Doris. You said you wanted to completely change that house and I don't blame you. But you also told me pastel is what *he* liked. Ivories, beiges, light peaches: those were colors he wanted, am I right?"

Doris nodded, wide-eyed.

"Where is he, Doris? Where is this man you spent your whole adult life trying to please? I'll tell you where: he's shacking up with some silicon-stuffed porn star in a penthouse with a Porsche and his freedom, that's where. So what the heck are you still trying to please him for? The kids are away at school, Doris. There's no one rumbling around in that house but you. It's pretty much the only thing you got in the settlement." *Well, that and maybe a million or ten.* But rich women loved it when you pretended they were just like regular working-class grunts. "So you tell me, who should you care about impressing now? Doris?"

Doris looked at her shyly. "Me?"

Violet held her hand to her ear. "I'm sorry, I can't hear you."

"Me?"

"You're darned right. And what has been your favorite color for only your whole entire life?"

"Red."

"Okay then. Am I going to be creating a warm, comfortable home for you with red walls that reflect the fire in your fireplace and in your soul and giving you a sense of peace and pride and confidence? Or am I going to my Rolodex to refer you to one of my associates who specialize in your ex-husband's favorite pastels?" Violet was bluffing, of course. She would no sooner turn away business than she would cut off her right arm, but bluffing sometimes worked.

Doris smiled, bashfully, and pumped her arm in the air. "I want red! Oh, I want red!"

Violet smiled. "That's all I need to hear." She hugged Doris. "Now, get out of my shop and let me work."

Doris looked at her, eyes twinkling. "Thank you, Violet. I'm so excited!" She was dreaming of her new red walls as she scurried out of the shop.

Violet was thinking of the potential of this sale. She would give Doris a redesign that would be the envy of every moderately wealthy divorcee in Columbus. And then they would all flock to her thinking that that Violet woman had some innate sense of color credited to her ethnicity. Then they would all want to do the "ethnic" and Violet would happily smother her indignation under the blanket of money and fame that was sure to follow. It was a win-win situation all-round.

Whew, that almost made up for the fact that her neighbor had stolen her paper, again. It almost made up for the fact that the cleaners had somehow forgotten to send out her clothes so the thirty minutes out of her way had been wasted. It almost made up for the fact that her hairdresser had overbooked and she was the casualty. Sure, they all got a piece of her mind but Violet got the short end of the stick. Couldn't trust anyone in this darned town. It was the story of her life.

Violet barely had a moment before the phone rang and her assistant was handing her the receiver.

"Yeah. What?" It was one of her contractors working on a house and trying to give her the shaft. It was like she had CHARLIE BROWN stamped on her forehead! "No, I told you pink marble. Look, you little twerp, if I have to come down there and kick your tail all the way to Italy, you will get that marble and have it properly laid by the opening date or . . . What? Try suing me; my lawyer is even worse to deal with. Mhmm, mhmm. I thought so. Thank you so much." She hung up the phone. It was always amazing how quickly fear could motivate the jack-offs of the world. For goodness' sake, all she wanted was for people to do what they said they were going to do! But she knew the cliché was true: if you wanted something done right you had to do it yourself.

Her receptionist handed her some pink message slips and she was about to go back into her office when the front door opened and a thin, pretty, cinnamon-colored woman ran in smiling. Her best friend, Brenda, was fifty pounds soaking wet with a trust fund big enough to cover the state of Texas. Brenda: friend and competitor with her own shop not too far from Violet's. Brenda: who'd only just last night revealed in a lavish, intimate to-do—with 200 of her closest friends—that she was engaged to none other than Violet's ex-boyfriend, Gary. Brenda: who'd put Violet on the spot, asking her to be her maid of honor while the fiancé/ex-boyfriend smirked with malice. 200 people stared with morbid curiosity and Violet managed to successfully accept the heartfelt invitation, and keep the champagne-flavored bile from projectile vomiting from her throat at Linda Blair *Exorcist* speed, at the same time. That Brenda. If Violet weren't so quick on her feet it might have been a disaster of epic proportions.

Though they were best friends, she could easily have gone a week without seeing her smiling face but Brenda was back with the timing and frequency of a bad penny. Violet seriously thought about ducking behind a bolt of fabric but her doe-eyed friend was too quick, herself.

Brenda spotted Violet and ran over on the balls of her feet, looking more like a strange gazelle than a socialite. "You'll never guess what happened!" she said to Violet.

"Umm, you're marrying my ex-boyfriend? I mean, really, Brenda, how many times do you have to say it? Do you think I forgot in the eight hours since I saw you last?" Violet tried to smile over the grimace and stamp out any trace of hysteria.

"No, something else! You'll never guess in a million years!" Brenda dissolved into giggles, only slightly less annoying than the guessing game. She was giggling so much, this had to be bad news.

Something else? What else could there be? After the engagement bombshell everything else should pale in comparison, right? Prickles of discomfort made their way over her skin. "Tell me, Brenda, before I slap it out of you."

"You know the Bickman account?"

Violet's ears perked. "Ronald Bickman? The zillionaire who is decorating his newly built five million dollar home? That Bickman?"

If Brenda's jumping up and down didn't confirm, her open-mouthed, soundless scream did the job. "I got the account!"

"The Bickman account?" Violet's skin turned icy. "The one that every designer in town is trying to get?" *The one that I'm trying to get?*

Brenda nodded enthusiastically and she jumped again, making the male interns all happy at the sight of her bouncing boobies. "I got the account!"

Violet felt stuck on phonics. "Ronald Bickman?"

"Yes, Ronald Bickman, yes! Violet, I got the account!"

Violet was silent and still for a moment, swallowing down an unexpected wave of hurt, then: "You witch."

Brenda dissolved into tears of joy and laughter, enveloping Violet in a hug. "I knew you'd be happy for me! Oh, Violet, this is going to put us on the map."

"You mean it'll put your business on the map, not mine."

"I've been waiting for something like this my whole life. And really, I have you to thank. Once he saw the Melting technique—"

Violet felt her stomach slowly slide toward the bottom of her pelvic cavity and sink somewhere underneath her intestines. "Melting technique?"

"He was looking for something different, original. And when I showed him how we could lay the patterned material on the walls and paint over them in a semi-translucent color and then apply low-grade heat, he was hooked. We used a tweed-ish material with an oatmeal overlay."

"You showed him my technique?" Violet asked. The air swirled about her head, dangerously. It was the first sign of fury; she knew it well as it was one of only two danger zones. But Brenda was her friend and her sense of loyalty was throwing her synapses all off whack. Fury had no place in friendship, right?

Brenda covered her mouth with her hand and her eyes grew large. "Oh, Violet, I haven't offended you, have I? It's just that I was losing his interest so fast I had to think of something. And it isn't like Melting is your trademark or anything. I mean, it's a procedure anyone could have thought of."

"But anyone didn't think of it. I thought of it. And patented it," Violet ground out through her smile.

"Oh God, Violet, you're not mad, are you?" Brenda had finally caught a whiff of Violet's inner fury and the water in her eyes threatened to spilleth over.

Violet could feel the eyes of her staff and customers on her. It would not do to make a scene. And what would be the point? If she ran around now claiming the Melting technique was hers, it would only look like sour grapes. She would have to find another way to handle this. She shuffled her anger beneath her pain, which was anchored somewhere underneath her stomach and intestines, and shrugged, despite the dangerous pounding of her own heartbeat in her ears. "Don't be silly. I'm happy for you."

She was the bigger person, she said to herself as she enveloped Brenda in a hug way too tight, hoping to rupture her spleen. Sometimes extra weight came in handy. But Brenda was immune to injury and pulled herself from Violet's grasp, happy again.

"Besides, this isn't just a good thing for me. Ronald Bickman could have flown in someone from New York, Milan, Paris, anywhere. But he stuck with a designer from right here in Columbus. This is going to put all of us on the map. I hear his last home was featured in *InStyle*."

Violet winced and was only half joking when she said, "Okay, stop right now or I'm really going to have to do you bodily harm."

She hadn't had a blow to the gut like this since . . . last night. And before that? Oh yes, the time she'd found out Brenda and Gary had been going at it like jackrabbits behind her back; that had nearly made her pass out. She'd always thought it was ridiculous when she'd read about women catching the "vapors" but that time she was pretty darned sure she'd caught a vapor or two. She must have caught a whole vat of vapors. She could barely crawl out of bed after that. If it weren't for the fact that Brenda was her only friend, she would no longer be a friend at all, but beggars couldn't be choosers. And the cheating thing, that was a memory best reminisced along with a bottle of tequila and a quart of ice cream at home. It had no place in the office. *No place in the office!*

"You know, I feel a little headache right here between the eyes." Violet tweaked the area of her nose in that spot, disappointed that it was actually true. It had started out such a wonderful day.

"I know; it's like my luck is incredible, right? But now I don't know how I'm going to do everything. A wedding and a contract and we're going to have to move, for sure. We need something way bigger, for expansion, you know?"

Violet covered a hiccup behind pursed lips. The hiccups were the first sign of her second danger zone: the one she was more afraid of than blind fury.

"Look at me standing around, shooting the breeze when there's so much to do. Gotta go. I'll see you later!" Brenda called happily, in her unique blustery, self-centered way. The bell tinkled behind her as her jaunty, skinny behind wiggled out the door.

It was the tinkling bell signaling the utter futility of her life that finally did it. In what "law of averages" universal theory did spoiled little rich girls always trump lower–middle class, hardworking, smart, determined, ambitious girls? *Every freakin' time.*

Violet's breath caught in a louder hiccup gasp and all eyes swung her way. *Calm down, sister.* But how could she calm down? Brenda stole her man and her contract right from under her! Her eyelid jerked ominously and before uttering another word she began a quick, stiff power walk to her office, feeling the eyes of her staff following her all the way. Shutting the door behind her, she fumbled the blinds closed, and made a mad sprint to her desk. Quickly, she procured an empty brown paper

lunch bag from her hidden stash as the gasps erupted
from her in progressively louder, stronger increments.
Finally, Violet plopped into her chair, leaned her head
between her knees, and pressed the opening of the bag to
her face with trembling fingers. She let loose, breathing in
a huge amount of air so quickly stars swam in front of her
face, exhaling just as violently. The brown paper balled
up tight and then expanded on her exhale like a crazed
balloon as she gave in to the hyperventilation.

What was the matter with her? Brenda was a twit. Why
did she let her upset her? So what if she had Gary? He
wasn't any prize. So what if Violet had once thought he was
the one? Didn't mean anything. So what if Brenda passed
her technique off as her own? Didn't mean anything. So
what, right?

She was working that bag like an accordion. After a few
minutes her lungs had relaxed, along with her shoulders,
neck, and stomach; and she lifted her head, sighing as
her body relaxed into the chair. She balled up the bag and
tossed it into the trash, allowing her brain to take over
now that her silly emotions were in check.

She breathed her relief. Thank goodness she'd made it
into her office. There was no way she could ever let her
employees see her like this. *Again, that is. Score one for
Brenda. This time.* Violet was none too happy but she
had more important things to think about. Her friend had
bested her, but Violet was nothing if not wily. She was
nothing if not resourceful. She was nothing if . . .

Her receptionist's head jerked upward when Violet's
office door opened. Violet strode toward her, calm and in
control once again. She knew what she had to do and
everyone had to see her do it. She picked up the receiver
and punched out some numbers.

"Tracy? Violet Jackson. So, what is going on over
there?" She laughed a fake laugh that would have been

believable had it not been forced through a grimace instead of the requisite smile. "Has your boss lost his mind? I thought he was going to look at all the bids before making a decision."

Bickman's overworked assistant was a competent, resourceful woman. Violet had known from the first moment she'd tracked Tracy down as she left work and followed her halfway home to accidentally trip over her and introduce herself as a "new designer with a few ideas" that Tracy was a force to be reckoned with.

Tracy, on the other hand, was used to being targeted by eager business people, job hunters, and paparazzi on behalf of Ronald Bickman. Tracy answered warily, "I'm sorry, Violet. I tried to convince him to continue seeing designers but he was really impressed with Odyssey Designs."

"It doesn't take much to impress him, does it? Never mind. You've got to get me in to see him."

"Oh, Violet, he's already made up his mind."

"Has he already signed the contract?"

"Not yet, but it's right here in his in-basket."

"Pull it for me."

"I can't do that, Violet."

"One meeting. I just need one meeting. It's not as if I'm panhandling. We are already scheduled to meet on Monday; just move the appointment a few days early."

"I was going to call you about canceling that."

"Look, this is a courtesy thing, Tracy. I'm not trying to be a pest but the man didn't even give the rest of us a chance. Now, I'm sure somebody is telling him that Brenda is the best out there, but he doesn't realize there's a whole flock of us. And frankly, Brenda is following my lead. Everybody in the business knows that Melting is my technique. He can settle for Brenda or he can work with the original."

"I don't know."

"Ten minutes, that's all I need. From one professional to another he really needs to show some courtesy. Why, if the media knew how he'd blown off some of the best designers in the city, well, there might be bad publicity, don't you think? I mean, I wouldn't say anything to the media, but these things get out, especially with Brenda going around telling everyone about it. It would be in his best interest to reconsider. I know you can convince him of that."

Tracy was quiet for a long spell. "Okay. I'll give you a half hour day after tomorrow in the interest of fair play. I'll work it out with him somehow. But if he says no in the first ten minutes . . ."

"I love you!"

"Then you accept defeat and go away quietly."

"You're a gem!" Violet yelled and hung up to award her assistant, Carol, a smile that the woman didn't return.

"Did you just schedule yourself to see Ronald Bickman when your friend already has the deal?" Carol asked.

Violet waved her hand in annoyance. "Oh, pshaw, she took my technique, anyway. Besides, she would understand. This is a dog-eat-dog world, Carol. You didn't think those tears of hers were real, did you? She screwed me over and then had the nerve to admit the only reason she got the contract was *because* she screwed me over. I can't sit still for that. I love the girl but she needs her behind whipped and I'm the sister to do it. Do me a favor, call the florist and send some flowers to Tracy, a really big arrangement. And send it to her home, will you? We don't want Bickman to get any ideas."

"You mean, like you're bribing his secretary?"

Violet wrinkled her nose at her. "Whose side are you on anyway?" Didn't really matter, though. She knew one thing: she was going to get that Bickman account or die trying. Her stomach rumbled menacingly. First lunch. Then strategy.

Chapter 2

Nothing topped off sweet revenge quite like spicy kraut. Violet spent most of her lunches in her office scarfing down a bag of potato chips while working but today she had to get out of that office. Being located downtown meant she had a decent amount of restaurant choices, but she really loved the hot dog vendors. She still remembered when her father had been alive, still remembered the occasional trip to a game or to the park and the vendor who would load up her hot dog so that a little girl could dream about someone making something special just for her, something just to her specifications. She would look to her father with a smile and he would chuckle at her expression, and then they would share a walk or a talk and all was right with the world. Her taste in toppings had changed but her love of the experience hadn't.

She had just been handed her hot dog covered in mustard, onions, and sauerkraut; and when she turned to walk away her heel caught on something, almost toppling her.

"Darn!" she yelled, checking her heel and relieved that it was still fine and the hot dog had only lost a little kraut in the incident. She looked down to see what had almost done her in and saw a piece of something that reflected light. She squinted and the glare disappeared but she could still see metal. "Hey," she said to the vendor, "can you hold this a minute?" She handed her hot dog to him.

He looked at her like she was insane. "I'm busy, lady."

"I just asked you to hold it for one second."

"I don't want to hold it."

She rolled her eyes and put the hot dog on his cart earning a glare from him with which she was not concerned. It wasn't the vendors she had soft feelings for, only the hotdogs.

She looked down at the metal that appeared to have an edge of lace. Kneeling, while making sure to keep her skirt smooth so she wouldn't award all the lunchers in Bicentennial Park a look at her goodies, she reached down to grasp the metal. She would be highly embarrassed if it turned out to be a bottle cap, but her curiosity had gotten the better of her. She worked it from the dirt with her hands, getting them dirty, but doing it nonetheless. Behind her the vendor was whining about the amount of space her little hot dog was taking on his big cart, but she was busy. Finally, her back-and-forth motion pulled the piece free and it came up. She smiled triumphantly and looked at it.

It was a piece of jewelry. A brooch. A large, gaudy, tacky piece of jewelry. But the metal seemed real and it seemed sturdy. The stone no doubt was a big piece of glue, but perhaps she could use it as an accessory, maybe something to pin to a curtain or on a lampshade. There was something about it, something that stopped her from tossing it onto the ground, where it probably deserved to be.

She dusted it off, thinking, and spoke out loud: "I'm no expert but you look African to me. And I know just the person to tell me for sure." She wrapped the brooch in a napkin, dropped it into her purse, and stood, walking over to retrieve her hot dog. "Thank you," she said to the vendor. He mumbled some not-too-kind words under his breath but she intentionally ignored him as she sauntered away biting down on her delicacy with relish. People didn't know a thing about customer service these days.

That afternoon after work she made a stop at her favorite antique shop on Parsons Avenue. It was a great place to shop for things to accent her designs. She had spent a pretty penny on items she found there to accent her works of art, which was what she considered every completed design. Tables, chairs . . . she had a keen eye for style that spanned the ages.

She entered the shop, approached the counter, and rang the bell. She stood there, tapping her foot on the floor and fingernails on the counter, growing more impatient by the moment before finally leaning over it for support to enable her to toss her voice through the doorway behind the counter and into the little room beyond. "What's a girl got to do to get some service around here?"

Seconds later an old man shuffled out, not surprised in the least. "You young people, no respect. And don't go flashin' that smile at me 'cause I know your mama ain't raised you right."

Violet promptly dropped her cordial smile. "Don't worry about what my mama did, old man. I'm here on business."

"What kind of business? I ain't got nothing new in and you done already bought up the best stuff in here."

"I'm not here to buy, Skeeter. I'm here to sell."

"Sell? What you got to sell?"

She pulled the brooch wrapped in a napkin out of her purse, unwrapped it, and handed it to him. "What do you think of this?"

He looked at it closely, pulled out a magnifying glass from under the counter, and pressed it up against the brooch to look closer. As Violet watched she saw the unmistakable sign of recognition before he made a valiant attempt to disguise it. He cleared his face and looked at her innocently.

"That looks like a fine piece of costume jewelry you got there, darlin'."

Violet narrowed her eyes at him. "Doesn't look costume to me," she bluffed, though she had indeed thought it was costume jewelry until his pitiful poker face had given it away. "That looks like a ruby to me."

He rolled with the game. "They make 'em nowadays so you can't tell the real from the fake."

She tossed back, "But this isn't a new piece, Skeeter. It looks pretty old. Strange pattern. Not European."

He threw on his wise, amused old man expression. "You think they didn't have fakes back in the day? Look, whyn't you hand that over and I'll take it off your hands. I'll even give you a coupla' dollars for it. Bound to be somebody out there want to wear something big and gaudy like that."

Violet watched him a moment longer and her lips pinched with the resolution that the old man was an old liar and not to be trusted. "Thanks, Skeeter. But I think I'll hold on to it. I could use some good costume jewelry."

His eyes darted to the piece. "Okay, I'm being generous 'bout this. But I'll give you two hunnert for it."

She felt a lick of satisfaction. "For a piece of paste? That's awful generous of you, Skeeter. I couldn't take advantage of you that way."

"It's okay. I got somebody in mind who loves to throw money away. I buy it for two hunnert, she'll buy it for double that. So you see, everybody gets something out of it."

Violet smiled and wrapped the brooch back in her napkin. "That's awfully tempting. But you know, I can use a good piece of costume jewelry myself."

"Okay. Three hunnert."

"Thanks, Skeeter." She turned to leave feeling his eyes on her the whole way and knowing he was panting after the piece like a dog in heat. Heck, she thought as she walked out, it might be worth enough to get her out of her crummy apartment and into a place with some real style. She left the store practically skipping.

By the time she reached her apartment she was running through the possibilities. She would have to find a reputable appraiser. Skeeter was a thief to the nth degree. That piece could be worth a fortune and he would steal it from her with a smile and a shake of his old head. Not in this lifetime!

She pulled the jewelry out of her purse and tossed the purse on a table. Unwrapping it, she looked closer at it. It still looked like a big old glob of paste to her. But then again, when was the last time she'd had a good look at a real ruby? Unfortunately, precious gems did not make their way into her possession every day. Perhaps she'd misjudged it.

She went into the kitchen and reached under the sink, rummaging around for a cloth. She had some solution for cleaning silver somewhere. She was going to look for it but stopped herself. She'd seen on TV somewhere that some people had cleaned the value right off an antique. No, she'd leave the cleaning to the professionals. But she did use the cloth to pull some of the remaining soil from the crevices. There, it looked a little better. The stone, itself, was breathtaking, really. She buffed the surface lightly, looking deep into it like Skeeter did, trying to see the worth. She didn't see anything but she did feel the strangest flutter in her abdomen. Apparently her lunch was wearing off. She shrugged. Still looked like paste to her.

"Well," she said to the piece. "Skeeter was willing to scam me to get you so you're not going anywhere until I figure you out." She rolled it in her palms and buffed it a little more. "Oh well, maybe if nothing else you'll be good luck." She put it down onto a table and sighed. She then hummed her way out of the room and into her bedroom, but not before noticing a sparkle in the depth of the glob of "paste."

Maybe it was time for a visit to the optometrist.

Chapter 3

The morning rose and woke Violet with a smile on her face thinking of Bickman. He wouldn't know what hit him. She'd sell her case like she'd never sold anything in her life and then she would tiptoe into Odyssey with a smile on her face and fake tears and ask Brenda to be happy for *her*. She flushed with pleasure just thinking about it.

She proceeded with her morning toilette: showering, brushing, polishing, and shining. Her daily peppermint face mask tingled on her skin and she knew the firm encasement would soon birth moist, supple skin, one of her best features if she did say so herself. She'd remove it after coffee. And last, but not least, she returned to the bedroom and sat cross-legged on her bed as she meditated. One second, two seconds . . . that was enough!

Hopping off the bed, Violet wrapped her fuzzy pink robe tight around herself, put her feet into matching pink fuzzy slippers and proceeded out of the room and across the living room to the kitchen. She poured herself a cup of coffee, placed it on the table, and headed to the door for the morning paper, her body sensing a large mass in the shadows between the kitchen and the door. She tilted her head, and darned if the shadow didn't appear to have a shape, kind of like a large man crouching, forearms resting against spread knees in a warrior stance. But that was silly. She really needed coffee.

She took a step toward the door when, before she could think straight, the shadow moved and stretched and the large mass morphed into an equally large man who stepped forward and now stood before her. He was tall and broad, imposing mostly because of the dark eyes almost hooded by the prominent brow. His mouth was tight in a line and his jaw was square and firm. He stood there, intimidating even though he seemed there by happenstance.

He began to speak, a voice low and deep, rich with the promise of ability to rumble at will. But it was calm as he said, as matter-of-factly as you please, "I am King Taka Olufemi of Jaha. Do not be alarmed; I come in peace. And for goodness' sake, cover yourself, woman; there is a man in the room."

Violet froze, feeling her blood gel in her veins. The skin of her face was itching like crazy under the peppermint mask—an inconvenient allergic reaction to fear. She'd discovered it the first time she stood to give a presentation before a lecture hall in college. Fifteen minutes later she was so relieved to be done she barely noticed that her face burned like crazy after a fifteen-minute unconscious assault by her own hands. No wonder that hall of students looked shell-shocked by the end.

Luckily, the promise of gunk under her manicured nails and even more intense terror at her very first home invasion kept her hands from her face. But Violet was no wimp. Fear wouldn't keep her stupid. She soundlessly moved into the kitchen, opened a drawer, and pulled out a gun to point at him.

"And this is Smith & Wesson of Violet's house. You've got two seconds to get out before I shoot."

The man sighed and spoke, his eyes to the ceiling. "This gets old. Every time the same thing. Since when did a nobleman of Africa become the most dreaded and feared mortal on the earth? As if I would stoop to the behavior of a common criminal simply because I have brown skin. It is an abomination. It is a cruel joke."

Violet cocked her pistol. "Okay, that didn't work, so let's try it again. Turn around, walk out that door, and take your little friends—or whoever the heck you're talking to—with you."

He looked at her, his eyes boring into hers uncomfortably. "If I walk out the door, woman, you will forfeit three wishes. You are free to do so but I warn you, it is unlikely you will ever get the chance again if you decline."

"Oh, I see. You're here to grant me three wishes. Right. A genie."

"I am no genie. My Arabian friends died out long ago. Though my offerings are similar I am not of that species. Alas, there is no category for me. I am in a unique confinement. Surely, the only one of my kind."

"Confinement," she said with a quick twist of her face, which clearly told him what she thought of his explanation.

"You tire me, woman, and I have been aching to get out for a good long time. I think a cup of that juice of the bean would help to revive me."

She had to do a double take when she realized he was looking at her coffee pot. *Coffee?* This joker had a lot of nerve and she was losing patience and itching to do something with her trigger finger.

"One more step and you won't have to worry about revival. I mean it. Who are you and what are you doing here?"

He breathed in exasperation. "Who am I? A fool. What am I doing here? Making a further fool of myself." He walked into the room right past her, seemingly oblivious to her panicked waving of the gun, and sank into the sofa. "I am old, woman. So ancient, if you knew exactly how much so you would put that silly weapon away in respect and deference to my age and wisdom. I am Taka Olufemi, King of Jaha, the jewel in the heart of West Africa. My purpose here is to grant you three wishes. Decline this and I will go away, but it seems a silly thing to do. You have power at your disposal and a once-in-a-lifetime opportunity to better your life, which is more than some of us are awarded. Not to mention the fact that it will earn me a short time of freedom."

Violet's head and body swiveled back and forth in disbelief from where he had been and where he now sat. Had the man really made himself at home on her sofa? And her with a gun trained on him? *He must be mentally ill.* She rubbed her forehead. "Okay, let's take this one step at a time. Look, I don't want to shoot you, so just answer the questions I ask. How did you get in here?"

"You brought me into your home."

"That's a lie." She looked to the door that was still locked, the chain still on the hook, the bolt still on. "I locked the door last night so don't give me that crap."

"You came upon a piece of jewelry, did you not? You are the holder of the piece, are you not?"

The piece. The piece? Ah, the brooch. She looked to the table and it was still there. "And?" she prompted.

"The jewelry is my vessel. It is my home. I am only released when a person such as yourself polishes my stone."

"Okay, enough of the filthy talk, mister."

Taka rolled his eyes. "I do not talk filth, woman. I am a king. I wouldn't lower myself to speak filth."

"Yeah, yeah, King Taja of Kaka."

"You intentionally massacre my name. You are an extremely disagreeable woman."

Violet had had it. "I'm an incredibly disagreeable woman who has lost her patience. Get out!"

"You are relinquishing your right to your wishes?"

"I'm giving you a chance to live, scumbag. Go on, there's the door."

"The only way I can leave is through my stone. You must take the jewelry and dispose of it. It doesn't matter where; it will survive for as long as the Great One deems it necessary."

"Whatever. Look, go!" She waved the gun at him in an effort to be scary.

He merely sighed. "Goodbye, woman. I regret you have pilfered this opportunity."

"Yeah, yeah." She perched, one hip jutted out and her gun up in the air in a Bonnie and Clyde stance, ready to pop it right at him if need be. She hadn't yet had an opportunity to put those shooting lessons to good use.

She backed up to give him room to go by her. She wasn't an idiot. He was big; she wouldn't give him the chance to get too close. The second he left she would call the police; surely some institution would be missing a big guy who called himself King Tacha of Baba.

But as she stood there waiting, he faced her, unmoving, and yet his image wavered, watery like a painting. She blinked; surely her eyes were overtired because his very body seemed to be slimming, and his features seemed to be smearing. His colors were dissipating, his clothing melding. Her mouth went dry as his face blurred and seconds later what stood before her was a plume of smoke. And seconds after that, the top end of the plume pointed, rose into the air, and carried the rest across the room, pointed itself at the brooch which sat on a table, hovered for a moment, and then shot into the stone like a cannon causing the jewelry to buck, jerk, and fall onto the carpet with the impact.

Violet's fingers shook with a sudden onset of palsy. She looked at the jewelry on the floor. It was still and harmless. *And yet* . . . She stepped closer to it, staring.

There had to be an explanation. There had to be a logical explanation. She was still dreaming; that was it! But she wasn't dreaming. The sofa still held the imprint of his behind but he was gone. It didn't make any logical sense.

She looked down at the jewelry, stuck a toe out, and kicked it, jumping back quickly. It didn't move. It was sitting there harmless as you please. And yet the man had disappeared into it. It didn't make any sense! She racked her brain trying to remember all he'd said, something about being a king, something about granting three wishes, three wishes. But if he wasn't a burglar, he might very well be what he said he was. But she didn't believe those kinds of things could happen. But he disappeared right before her! *But, but, but!*

She thought about Skeeter and his eyes when he'd recognized the piece and how he'd tried to cheat her out of it. She thought about the three wishes the big guy had told her not to pilfer. Three wishes. Anything she wanted.

She picked up the brooch, looked at it hard, and then began rubbing the stone furiously. "Come back! Come back. I changed my mind. You have to give me a chance!" She stopped and nothing happened. She put the gun away, and went back to rub the stone again. Nothing happened. Finally she moved to sit on the couch, staring at the piece in despair. "My God, what if it's real? All those stupid fairy tales are true? No wonder he wanted me to sell it to him so bad. The thief!" She put the brooch on the coffee table in disgust and rose to wander into the kitchen, too absorbed in her thoughts to notice the plume of smoke materialize. At the sound of his voice she whirled to see him standing there again.

"Ah, she comes to her senses. It is about time; your stubbornness almost cost you dearly. Usually my friend is not so generous to allow a second chance. For some reason He has taken pity upon you; though if it were up to me your ingratitude would have already sealed your fate."

Violet's eyes widened and she smiled, cracking the mask and getting a waft of peppermint scent. She could tell he was talking because his lips were moving, but darned if she could hear a word he said. Her brain was racing with possibilities. But first, she had to know he was the real McCoy. "Okay." She rubbed her hands together. "Do something. Prove it."

"What?" Taka looked at her, annoyed and insulted.

"Prove it. Prove who you are."

He rolled his eyes upward. "I am here to do good for them and yet I have to prove myself constantly. They are ungrateful creatures." He glared at her. "I suppose we can't move on until you are sufficiently satisfied with parlor tricks?" Her look affirmed his suspicion. He sighed. "Close your eyes."

"Not a chance. I want to watch." Violet was a consummate skeptic, and proud of it. She hadn't gotten as far as she had by being gullible.

"Just one second. A long blink."

Violet frowned. *Okay,* she thought, closing her eyes briefly, about two seconds. "There, I blinked," she started, to be struck dumb when she opened them again. Her eyes grew wide as a different scent reached her nose and filled the air around her. Her lips curved slightly, falling open involuntarily. Her apartment was filled, every corner, every open space, with violets. She turned in a circle to see them all. She shook her head with disbelief. "My God. You've filled my apartment with—"

"Flowers, yes. Women seem to like that best of all. No matter the place or the time, women always like flowers."

"No, you've filled the room with violets. That's my name, you know. Violet."

"Sheer coincidence, I assure you," he said. "He chooses the type. A parlor trick to get mortals to believe."

But Violet did another twirl looking at them. All different shades of violet, like the sky sometimes right before dawn. Like the silk that decorated some of the walls of Shades of Violet. Like . . . He couldn't know, could he? When she was in high school she went through a particularly bad period because she didn't seem to fit in with any group of friends. Her mouth was too smart for most people and she didn't have enough money to be with the "in" crowd. She wasn't smart enough to be a nerd. She was just an outsider, and felt it every day.

One of the most special days of her life, she'd awoken one morning to find her mother had filled her bedroom with pots of violets. They weren't fancy or expensive. Some were African violets, some were other kinds. They weren't all the same color, or even all healthy, but they were all violets. And they were all for her.

When she'd come down to breakfast, her eyes shining with emotion, her mother had been at the stove cooking, with her back to her. Violet had not known what to say since it had seemed their relationship had taken a back burner in recent years since her mother had remarried and had new children to care for. So she'd sat down at the table staring at her mother's back though filled with emotion, willing the right words to come from her trembling lips.

But amazingly, she hadn't had to say a thing. Her mother, feeling her eyes on her, had said, simply, "You're unique; that's why I named you Violet, honey. Don't ever forget that you're special. You're every shade of special."

And now, today, violets filled her room and she felt that same moment of complete acceptance and love. She also felt, without a doubt, the man in her home was not there by coincidence.

She turned to him, her eyes glittering. "You're for real?" He glared at her fiercely and she caught a glimpse of what he must have looked like going into battle.

"Please tell me I will not have to go through my intro-duction again," he growled.

Violet smiled, raising her hands in mock terror at his visage, not at all disturbed by his countenance. Now that she knew he was, perhaps, a genie of some sort, she knew she was safe. Genies couldn't harm people, could they? She decided that they couldn't and straightened her back with her newfound confidence. She began to pace.

"Okay, just tell me the rules." She smiled as a thought came to her. "Brenda is going to throw up with jealousy."

"I think I will take some juice of the b . . . some of that coffee first. I know you merely forgot to offer it."

"I didn't forget anything. I don't care about the stupid coffee. Tell me the rules!"

He crossed the room, opened some cupboards until he found a mug, poured himself a cup, and drank it down cautiously, seeming to relish the taste. Violet took that opportunity to look him over. Big. Tall. His clothes were nondescript, just a pair of gray pants, a moss-colored shirt, and a long, gray overcoat. Nothing special. His face was harsh, too harsh to be handsome. And she could barely see his eyes under his scowl. But his lips, they had potential. They were full and curved and might actually be attractive if he smiled, she thought.

"Ah, so long since I've enjoyed simple pleasures such as this," he said.

Violet pulled her thoughts away from him, tapped her foot, and frowned. "Come on! Stop playing with me!"

He gave her an indulgent look over his coffee cup. "There was a time when the chase was as much fun as the acquisition, but you modern folk have lost the concept of delayed gratification. You cannot wait five seconds for your reward. You're like children reaching for glittery things. Impatient. Impudent. Try waiting hundreds of years." Her expression told him his lecture was lost on her. "Fine, the rules are simple. You have three wishes available to you. They must be concrete wishes, nothing like world peace and that sort. You are allowed to alter your own life, not that of others. Choose your wishes carefully because once they are chosen you cannot change them. I will remain with you until you make your final wish. Once it is granted, I will go back into my stone and you must take me out of your home and deposit me where I can do good for another. You have three days, at best. Do you understand?"

Violet nodded and then moved into the kitchen to give him a bear hug. Taka stiffened in surprise, taken off guard, but he did not move away.

"You came at the most perfect time possible," Violet told him. "I didn't believe things like this could happen. It's a miracle."

"Miracle?" he repeated, seemingly uncomfortable with the notion. "Be careful, little woman. Even miracles can have a price."

"You'll help me though, right? You'll give me some advice? Maybe tell me what wishes have the best success rate?"

"I am not a statistician."

"Okay, okay, let me think. We've got a lot of work to do. What is your advice?"

"My advice is to be careful what you wish for. And loosen me from your grip. It is not proper for a young woman to clutch a man so who is not her betrothed, even if the mud on your face is a strong deterrent of attraction. And for the sake of all that is great, clothe yourself, woman; even now I can feel your female assets through the cloth of that pathetic covering."

Violet released him to give him a wink and a smile. "You come out of that thing cranky *and* horny. Don't worry, genie, I understand."

"My name is—"

"I know, King Taka. But 'genie' is much easier to say. And I'm Violet. Remember that; we're going to spend a lot of time together in the next few days."

"Days? I appreciate your desire to award me some freedom, but it doesn't take long to grant a wish."

"At least not the first one." It had taken her about half a second to decide on what was most important. Security was key; and if she couldn't get the emotional kind, she would settle for the financial kind. "I want money. All I could ever need or want. That's my first wish."

"How original."

"So, now what do I do?"

"About what?"

"Did you get my first wish down? Do you need a pad and pencil or something? Do you have it?"

"Is there something about my demeanor that leads you to believe I am daft? The wish has been granted. Now give me two more and I can get out of here and move on to someone more gracious."

"It's granted? You're sure?" His angry silence was her response. "How do I know? I don't feel richer. Should I call the bank?"

"Do what you like but know that it sometimes takes time for that particular wish. It reveals itself in its own time. Things must be arranged. The stars must realign. The forces must make all sorts of shifts you know nothing about—"

"But it's granted?" she interrupted him and looked at him expectantly. His face hardened with irritation but he gave a curt nod. "Good. I'm going to get dressed. I better see that money soon or you're going to have heck to pay, genie. Now, help yourself to coffee, but we're going to breakfast so you might want to go light."

"We can break our fast right here."

"'Break fast,' how charming. No, I've already made plans to meet my friend Brenda. She's going to freak!"

Violet happily scurried into the bedroom to prepare for a day that had suddenly become ripe with opportunity. She'd start with scrubbing off the mask and then making herself up to look as wonderful as she felt.

Chapter 4

"You did not tell me, Aniweto, how tiring it would be," Taka said to the air around him as he sat on the sofa, broken and tired. The Almighty had gotten rid of the flowers. The woman with the light green mud on her face was still getting dressed and he was still waiting like a manservant. Oh, how he had fallen.

"How many centuries has it been since I walked the earth as a man?" he asked. "How many years before His anger subsides? Often I wonder if it would have not been better had I ended it all those years ago. I was a fool to believe He would ever allow me the prize I sought. My grief and desperation made me vulnerable to His proposition. That stone, created as a gift with such love, has become something I loathe. I look at it and see all I dreamed for and all I have lost."

So many years ago and it felt like yesterday. He'd been willing to take his own life, been angry enough to say things he never would have dreamed. And all these years later he knew he'd been had.

"He will never allow me the one thing I asked. Is He so petty that He must have the last word, must use His might and power to keep me under His thumb? Foolish question considering my current situation. He's even taken you from me, Aniweto. He could not even allow me your comfort. Or perhaps you are of the same cloth; perhaps you choose allegiance to Him over me? No matter. Do what you must; you will never break me, nor shall He. For eternity I will grant wishes if only to spite you both further."

His words were angry and sullen, much like his emotion. Often he spoke in this manner, hoping to provoke his only confidant into conversation. Somehow, that conversation was what he missed most of all, even though with his words he cursed the very friend with whom he so wished to converse. But there was no answer. Instead, the woman came in from the back room. *Wonderful.* He saw the humor in it, really. He'd been so demanding before; now he came across a person even more so. The Great One had a sense of humor.

"Are you ready?" she asked.

Taka looked up, prepared to offer a barbed, sarcastic response when his face went still, his eyes wide. His heart began beating the rhythm of a herd of wild horses as the impossible impossibly stood before him. Only seconds before he'd cursed Ani for not giving him this end. Now, he realized, the agreement had not been in vain after all, for standing before him was his wife. Zahara. After all these years and thousands of miles, he had finally paid penance enough; he had finally satisfied the Almighty enough to release him from pain and bring him his heart once again.

He rose slowly, trembling, his eyes roving her face, searching every corner. In his darkest moments he had wondered if he would remember his love's face if ever he saw it again. He had begun to doubt his memory but, now he knew, he could never forget this beauty. He could never have passed her on the street and not known her. Her face struck a chord in his heart and in his soul that he would know for eternity. He longed to reach out and stroke the velvet skin. He wondered if it would feel the same. He wondered if it would blush with fire under his fingers as it had before.

Almost as if she could feel his thoughts she touched her skin. "What's wrong? You look sick. Why are you staring at me? Do I have something on my face?"

He changed a thousand times in that moment. He felt himself softening toward her, her presence melting his tension, smoothing the rough edges like only Zahara could.

"Forgive me," he spoke slowly, his lips slightly parted with breathlessness as he suddenly felt as shy as a child. "It is just that . . . your beauty, it has stunned me. Being confined in my prison, rarely do I get to see such . . . exquisite loveliness."

Violet's eyes widened. "Well, thank you. That's a very nice thing to say. But you still don't look well. Can I get you something? Water? More coffee?"

His lips curved minutely. He had all he'd ever wanted right before him. "No. I am fine, now."

"Good. Let's go, we're running late." She turned, digging through her purse for keys.

He snapped to attention. "Where are we going?"

"A nice little restaurant, you'll like it. Look, I'm thinking if we spend some time together you can give me better advice about my last two wishes. And I can introduce you to my friends."

Inner calm fled like the wind. How silly of him to forget the terms of his challenge. She didn't remember him. She only knew him as the genie there to grant her wishes and she'd already used one. She didn't remember their story and he wasn't allowed to tell her. His only hope was to somehow slow the clock, give her spirit time to remember how she loved him, her body the closeness to remember how it burned for him. They needed time and privacy for the lovemaking, not interruptions from the world.

And then there was the fact that he had not been out of his stone for—judging by the stiffness in his joints—many years, maybe decades. He didn't know the time or the ways of the people. How he would handle himself in public? He didn't want to make a fool of himself before Zahara, not after she'd known him as her strong and capable king. Embarrassment rushed through his body and he supplied the only excuse that came to mind.

"It is not wise to tell people who I am. They tend to react in unpredictable ways. It complicates things. It would be better that you and I stay here. Together. Alone."

"No, no. I have to tell Brenda. And your timing couldn't have been better. She's been getting on my nerves a lot lately; it's time to show her that she isn't the only one with good luck. And breakfast is a standing appointment. She would think something was wrong if I didn't come."

"Violet . . . that is your name?" He had barely registered it before. "I would not suggest it. We will stay here. Together. Alone."

"Look, genie, don't you have to do what I say? I'm not entirely up on my fairy tales, but I don't recall reading about any genies who argue. Am I right?"

Taka stiffened. Violet persisted. "Am I right?"

"You are correct."

"Then let me decide what is best for my life. I asked you for advice, not for your two cents. Are you coming?"

She didn't bother to wait for his answer but opened the door and walked out fully expecting him to follow. Taka swallowed his surprise and his pride and followed her as she grumbled something about a missing paper and he grumbled something in the way of a prayer.

Chapter 5

The restaurant was small and chic, a perfect place for entrepreneurs and important people to network. Violet and Brenda tried to meet there at least twice a week. Violet spotted her sitting at a table and pointed her out to Taka. She led the way to the small table and Brenda's eyes zeroed in on the newcomer immediately.

"Brenda, I'd like you to meet my cousin Taka," Violet lied easily.

Brenda looked him up and down appreciatively. "Well, hello, Taka."

He tried to turn a grimace into a smile and held Violet's chair for her as she sat.

Brenda took in the action, more interested in the man than his manners. "You didn't tell me you'd be bringing a guest. What's the occasion?"

"Well, you know, it's rare that I get family in for a visit so I thought I'd introduce him around."

Brenda turned to Taka, resting her chin on one hand. "How long will you be here?"

"Three days," Violet and Taka said simultaneously.

"Oh, how nice. So, is Taka an African name?"

"Yes, it is," Taka confirmed, proudly.

"What part of Africa?"

"Jaha," he said.

"I can't say I've ever heard of Jaha. Where is that?"

Violet was getting annoyed. Couldn't Brenda see that the man was special? Sitting there asking stupid questions.

Who gave a crap where he came from? He was a genie! She wanted to scream it to the world but caution stayed her for the moment. She satisfied herself by snapping, "For God's sake, Brenda, can you let up off the man?"

"I'm just asking a question."

Taka addressed Brenda's question. "Jaha is on the west coast of Africa."

"Really? I'll have to look that up."

"Jaha has been the leader in trade and commerce in the region for centuries," he continued, happy to talk about his country. Happy to remember his people and their accomplishments. "People from miles around come to Jaha because they know we trade in quality merchandise. Our government is a model for other countries. Our architecture and art cannot be rivaled."

"That's interesting, considering I've never heard of the place." Brenda smiled at him blindingly, then asked, "So how are you related to Violet?"

Taka blinked at the sudden subject change. She had not been interested in his village at all, he realized. She had been placating him. He felt a streak of hurt and embarrassment and looked to Violet but she had pulled out a plastic thing with a mirror and was checking her image. As if her visage was more important than common courtesy. As if his words on her homeland and kingdom were insignificant.

Violet was looking in her compact mirror to see if she glowed. Pregnant women glowed, she heard. Surely a newly rich woman, recently blessed with three wishes, would glow as well. She noted her eyes were especially attractive and bright this morning. And her lips looked positively wealthy!

Taka said to Brenda, vindictively, "I am not related to Violet by blood; she is lying to you."

Violet caught the last part of the sentence and snapped
her mirror shut. "Hey!" For a moment she was annoyed.
But, she remembered, she'd wanted to tell the truth
all along anyway so the genie had given her the perfect
opening. She had to tell Brenda the truth now. Brenda
would be so jealous she would crap green for a week!

"Okay, okay, I give. Taka is not my cousin." Violet's
expectant smile invited Brenda to probe.

"Well, who is he?"

Violet twisted her neck coyly, enjoying this game.

"Please tell me. You're killing me!" Brenda declared,
dramatically.

"I just don't know if I should," Violet teased.

Taka's eyes furrowed farther under his brow the angrier
he became. The games, the silliness, when there were so
many more important things to talk about!

"By all that is holy," he snapped, "will the two of you stop
this madness? What she is dying to tell you, Brenda . . .
May I call you Brenda?"

Brenda tossed a seductive glance his way. "Absolutely."

"What she is dying to tell you is that—"

"Let me do it! Goodness, you are such a spoil sport."
Violet showed pinched lips to Taka and then turned to
Brenda, smiling. "Taka is a genie."

"What?" Brenda's tone went flat as the suspicion she
was being had ratcheted up.

"If you are going to tell her the story at least be accurate," he said back, his face equally pinched. "I am not a
genie. I am a king."

"Not anymore, you aren't."

"Once a king is a king he is a king for eternity," he said
sternly.

"Whatever. Look, will you let me do this? She doesn't
know from kings. Look at her; do you think she knows
anything about royalty? Brenda, honey," Violet leaned

toward her friend and spoke to her as to a child. "Remember those stories we used to read as kids about the genies in the lamps and such? That's what Taka is, only he wasn't in a lamp. He was in a brooch I found in the dirt at Bicentennial Park."

"I object to that characterization," Taka steamed. "You make it seem as if I were rolling around in the dust like a sow. I'll have you know that brooch is a one-of-a-kind piece made by the master jeweler of mother Africa, an exquisite piece of art."

"He's granting me three wishes, and I've already placed my first one. Can you believe it?" She leaned back in her chair, a satisfied look on her face. A waiter was walking by and she snapped her fingers at him. "Hey, you! Mimosa. Yesterday!" She smoothed her hair and looked at the other two as the waiter scowled at her. "I've only come here twice a week for the last four years. You'd think they'd know what I want by now."

Taka watched the exchange with disgust. A queen did not treat her subjects like that. Zahara had never treated the servants in that fashion.

Violet felt Brenda's eyes scrutinizing her.

"So what you're saying is," Brenda said, "you picked up a piece of jewelry and rubbed it and this man popped out. And he is staying at your place with you for three days. And he is granting you three wishes. Is that what you're saying?"

The waiter handed Violet the mimosa and she snapped it up immediately without a thank-you. He turned and walked away with an attitude, which she caught. She shouted at him, "And lose that attitude when you come back or you can pull your tip out of my rear end!" She took a sip and smiled at Brenda. "That's right. Couldn't you just scratch my eyes out with jealousy? I mean, isn't this incredible?"

Brenda was still for a moment and then her face hardened. "Is this your way of getting back at me for putting you on the spot the other day? Because if you really don't want to be my maid of honor . . ."

"I couldn't care less about your wedding. No offense. I'm telling you the truth."

"That this man here is a genie?"

"Right!"

"So, you're telling me, he is not your distant cousin?"

"I don't have any distant cousins."

Brenda's face hardened further. "I hope you're getting a good laugh out of insulting me, Violet. I don't mind a practical joke, but this is going too far. Does Jerome know you are running around with a strange man?"

Jerome. Funny, Violet hadn't thought about her boyfriend all morning. But it was great she could always count on Brenda to keep track of the men in her life.

"Hey, look, I didn't believe it either, until he filled my place with flowers and disappeared into thin air. I mean, one minute he was standing in my apartment, the next minute he was floating in the air like smoke."

"Good Lord, Violet, don't tell me you and this guy are getting it on. What about Jerome? If he finds out you're cheating on him . . ."

"Listen to me, Brenda, Taka and I aren't sleeping together. He's a genie, I told you!"

"I don't know whether to be pissed or worried. You've really been working too hard lately. Cheating on Jerome won't get him to appreciate you more, you know."

Violet wanted to scream with exasperation. "No, I don't know a whole lot about cheating, Brenda, but since you're the expert, why don't you tell me how it works?"

"When are you going to stop throwing that up in my face?"

"Throwing it in *your* face? You're the one who announced to the whole party that not only did you take my man, but you were marrying him and asking me to stand up for you at the wedding. Now, that takes nerve."

"Are you upset about that, Violet? Why didn't you say something? You are my best friend, but I can't let you treat Jerome this way. I love him like a brother."

Violet mumbled under her breath, "You would love him like a two dollar ho if I left you alone with him for five seconds."

Taka's head had gone back and forth between the two but now he couldn't stop himself from interjecting. "What kind of madness is this? What games do the two of you play? I thought you were friends but you speak like enemies."

"Who asked you?" Violet snapped.

Brenda leaned toward her. "Violet, if you're still bothered by what happened I will understand if you decline. But don't ruin a perfectly good relationship with Jerome because you're mad at me. Look, just explain to him that Taka was there when he wasn't and maybe he'll understand how lonely you've been feeling."

Violet felt herself growing hot with anger. "Yes, that is exactly the line Gary used on me."

"And get rid of this man; he'll only cause you problems."

"Oh no, he isn't going anywhere. And you're not going to say a word to Jerome. As far as he's concerned, Taka is my cousin. I'm really disappointed I couldn't share this with you, Brenda. I was hoping you'd be happy for my good luck. I guess it's too much to believe you'd be happy for my good news."

"I guess so."

Taka had grown an appetite after being out of his stone for several hours but in the short time between sitting and now, it was almost gone.

"I have no patience for this," he declared. "If I do not leave right now my brain will surely explode into a thousand pieces. I will be outside when the two of you are finished with your feminine games."

"Oh, no, he didn't," Brenda started. The two women watched as he got up and left the restaurant, cutting an impressive image despite his annoying demeanor.

Brenda leaned to Violet. "Okay, what gives? Who is that man? And don't give me that cousin crap."

"I told you. He's a genie. He showed up in my apartment this morning."

"Is that right?"

"Yes, that's right. I wouldn't have believed it either but I saw him appear and disappear right in front of my eyes."

"Amazing."

"You don't believe me. You always were close-minded. It doesn't matter though because he is granting me three wishes and you bet your butt I'm taking advantage of them."

Brenda picked up her cup of coffee and sipped it stiffly. "I had no idea," she said.

"No idea what?"

"That you were still so bitter over the fact that Gary and I are a couple. This little effort to snatch the limelight is not going to work."

"This is not a ploy, Brenda."

"Whatever. Look, if you don't want to be straight with me, that's fine. I just hope you have a better story for Jerome."

"Keep your mouth shut to Jerome or I'll filet you like sushi."

"Don't worry, I'll play along with your game. I just hope for your sake it doesn't all blow up in your face. So where did you really find him?"

Outside, Taka took a deep breath. He looked around
and marveled as he always did how life had gone on without him. The world was so different from the one he had
grown up in. Technology and conveniences had changed.
He'd grown as well, in fits and starts, learning of the new
worlds only in the brief moments he was released. He had
long since stopped being surprised by the new things. But
now, more than ever, they left him feeling sad.

He felt energy pop in his ears; awareness opened the
air around him, and his attention sharpened. Could it be?
His friend suddenly sitting on the bench next to him told
him it was so.

Aniweto. Despite the centuries passed Ani still looked
the same he had the day of the massacre. The same
he had when Taka was twelve, five, and at his earliest
memory. Taka had never cared that he was the only
one who could see Ani. Before long, the legend of young
Prince Taka, blessed of all the Jaha kings for his ability to
speak to the Almighty through the angels, was weaving
its way through the countryside. Ani, always humble, had
told Taka countless times he was merely a messenger.
Taka had not cared what he called himself; all he knew
was that Ani held him in his arms as a babe, held his hand
as a child with a man's burden, held his dreams as a man
when he'd married the love of his life. Ani had been good
to him then. Things were different now.

"It appears the unlikely has finally happened," his
friend said with his gentle voice.

"So you speak to me now, do you?" Taka groused, still
hurt at 400 years of abandonment from his only friend.
"You are no longer stewing in angry silence, then, Ani?"

"Watch yourself, son. I love you, always, but you did
a great wrong to our Father. You disappointed me. You
behaved not like the man I know you to be, but like the
child so certain he is favored that he has fear of nothing

and respect for no one. I raised you better, as did your parents. We are waiting, still, for your repentance."

Taka laughed. "Repentance? For what? For daring to stand up to Him?"

"You have no legs to stand to Him, Taka. Have you not learned that yet or does your pride still fool you into thinking you are on equal ground as those on high? Even the Almighty, Himself?"

It was a trap and he knew it! The Almighty was surely waiting for him to compare himself in order to zap him into Hades with a bolt of lightning. He might end up there but it wouldn't be due to Ani's word games.

"My friend, if my pride is inflated it is because you made it so. I didn't get to be this way myself. Now, all of a sudden I am too proud? What do you expect? I was but a child when you came to me and spoke to me. You were aware of what the village would think when they discovered I had your ear. They would feel I was blessed. You treated me thus and it is no fault of mine. It is only natural I be a proud man. I am a king and a warrior and the best in all the land. The best our Father ever put on this earth. You did that. You made me who I am."

Ani smiled slightly and Taka knew his argument was a good one. But his friend didn't fall into the trap, either.

"Our Father put only one 'best' on this earth and that was His blessed Son. Maybe a distant second best. And while I take credit in the gifts you have learned from me, the inflated pride is yours alone. Its misuse does you a disservice."

Taka frowned. "Alas, it seems disservices abound for me. The agreement is no good. That woman is not my Zahara."

"Violet does, indeed, possess the spirit that was once contained in the woman you knew as Zahara."

"She is not the same."

"You were told she would have no memory."

"That woman is a greedy, shallow, whining shell of my wife. She is a bottom-feeder. She is petty and simple. She is not my wife!"

"Are you preparing another tantrum, Taka? Did not spend quite enough time in your stone, you need a few more centuries to figure out how to speak without sounding like a horse's backside?"

"What, precisely, have you come to me for, Ani?" Taka twisted in his seat to glare at the man who, as always, seemed unmoved by his emotion. "Are you here to gloat? Are you here to laugh at the foolish king? Well, I have not heard your voice in centuries; maybe I do not wish to hear it now. How about that? Maybe you tire me with your lectures and sermons and recriminations. Maybe you should tell Him that. What more punishment can He mete out? He's already done His worst."

"Oh, not quite. He can leave you here for centuries more. Or He can throw you into limbo or hang you in oblivion. Or He can let the evil one spend the rest of eternity pulling you apart limb by limb, putting you back together only to do it over again. You do not want to experience that. Unpleasant, very unpleasant."

"I don't care. When will you realize I mean what I said? I am weary, Ani, but my weariness is nothing compared to my love for Zahara. If I cannot have my wife an eternity of torture would be blessing enough."

Ani blew out a breath of exasperation, as if Taka were the one being obtuse. "You infuriate me with this single-mindedness. I suppose I should be impressed by your allegiance to your idea of love but as with everything, you go too far and misconstrue."

"My idea of love is the only idea worth speaking of; for if a man is not willing to do whatever he needs to be with his love than he is not truly in love, nor is he truly a man. Which brings me back to the subject at hand: I do not know that woman. She has the face of my heart's blood, but she is not the same."

Ani was quiet a moment, putting his thoughts into words. "Zahara had a beautiful face but it was not her face you fell in love with, was it?"

"What are you saying, Ani?"

"I am saying He gave her Zahara's face only so you could find her. Her spirit, that is the true gift. She has the same spirit; you just have to reach it. Reach her."

"Hmm, and if I don't want to muddle through the muck to get to it, what, then? I will burn for eternity?"

"Well, yes, there is that. But there would also be another tragedy. You would miss getting to know this kind and gentle person called Violet."

"Kind? Gentle? Are you speaking of the woman in that restaurant?"

"And you would miss your one chance to say good-bye to the wife you claim to love. You would sacrifice all these years of confinement for fear of a little work. Don't do it again, Taka. Don't give up when you have a possible future looming before you."

Taka looked at the doorway of the restaurant. 400 years and that was what waited for him. 400 years and this woman was all he had to show for it.

His shoulders sagged in defeat. "Is this life ever to be fair to me, Ani? Will I ever smile with joy again? Will Zahara ever look at me and remember the love I held for her? Will I ever be able to love my wife on earth again?"

But as was all too common, when he looked to Ani for answers his friend was gone.

Chapter 6

Violet was glad when Brenda finally left but smiled sardonically when the server brought the bill. Apparently her friend had helped herself to a bottle of the most expensive champagne before Violet and Taka even got there. And despite the fact it was the rich girl's turn to pick up the tab, Brenda had conveniently forgotten that, as well.

Violet frowned at the amount but pulled out her credit card anyway. When she finally left with a bag in her hand, she spotted her genie across the street on a bench looking bereft. *Must be hard for him,* she thought. She'd pranced him out like a show horse when he'd already admitted it had been awhile since he'd been out of his stone. *Hah!* That sounded crazy, even to her.

She wondered if she'd made a mistake telling Brenda the truth, but excitement had gotten the better of her. It was so rare for good luck to come her way. And good luck by way of a large, grouchy man, well, who could have seen that coming?

"Thought you might be hungry," she said, handing him the bag.

He looked up at her, surprise on his features. He reached inside to pull out the container, looking at it speculatively. "You brought me food?"

"It's no big deal, okay, just food. I don't want you dropping dead of hunger before you can get me my wishes. And it's just . . . I'm sorry we got so abusive. Normally there's no one around to see Brenda and me go at each other. People usually don't understand our love-hate relationship." She sat down next to him and smiled. "She's so jealous she could spit."

"Is that right? She is jealous of you and me together?"

"She's jealous that I have a genie. You thought she was jealous of me with you?" Violet wrinkled her nose at the silly notion.

"It is not an illogical assumption. I am a handsome man, you are a beautiful woman; we obviously make a striking pair. And in the short time I have known her she seems an incredibly insecure and shallow sort. Much like yourself."

Violet's face scrunched in confusion at that last statement but she went on to set him straight about Brenda. "She's engaged to be married."

"And that is supposed to mean something? You believe she cannot be jealous of you and me together simply because she is betrothed?"

"Boy, I thought I had conceit cornered, but you take the cake. No, Brenda is happily engaged to Gary, my ex. She's not interested in you or what we look like together."

"Ex what?"

"My ex-boyfriend. The man I used to be with. She stole him from me. Now they're getting married. Ain't that a crock?"

"I don't understand, she stole . . ."

"She stole him."

"Stole him from . . ."

"Me."

"Stole him from you?" Taka grew confused. "Why would any man want her over you? I admit, your personality leaves much to be desired but it is comparable to hers at least. Physically you are much more attractive. A curvaceous body, beautiful skin, hair shining with health, the smile of an angel; there is no contest. All things considered you would be a much better mate. It's preposterous that a man should leave you for her."

Violet ignored the insult and accepted the compliment with a flurry of pleasure. She had to take them where she could get them.

"That's my feeling exactly. God only knows what I was thinking with Gary. But amazingly, they seem to be happy together. Go figure."

Taka was silent for a moment, then: "How does one handle such a betrayal in these times?"

Violet shrugged. "You just have to go on, you know? You have to move forward. I was mad as spit for a while, but Brenda and I are joined at the hip. And it's not like I wanted him. I was holding out for a man worthy of me".

"Spoken like the words of a queen."

"Ooh, I like that. Spoken like a queen. Maybe I'll use that in advertisements. Hey, you better eat that before it gets cold. Their Eggs Benedict is incredible."

"I do not have money to pay for this."

"Did I ask you for money? Hey, it's the least I can do for the man granting me three wishes. Heck, I just bought Brenda a bottle of champagne for giving me indigestion."

He softened with gratitude, opening the container to flip one half onto the other and ate the meal as a sandwich, nodding in appreciation. Violet seemed to remember the cup in her hand and handed that over as well. "Doesn't work without the coffee."

He set the box on his lap and pulled the coffee lid off, taking a big swig. He then looked at Violet with a mischievous glance of appreciation that made her laugh out loud.

"I should probably go to work today, but it kind of feels like a holiday."

"I would say you should definitely take some time from work so we can talk." He finished his food and brushed the crumbs from his lap.

"Talk about what? I thought you wanted me to get my wishes in as soon as possible so you could get back into your rock."

Taka frowned remembering his rudeness before he knew he was in the presence of his queen. "I was hasty earlier."

"I don't see that it'll take three days. I could probably knock them out in an hour or two."

"No, no. I . . . You . . . It is not good to rush your wishes. Give it at least a day."

"Mhmm." Violet looked at Taka suspiciously. His face was undergoing all sorts of strange contortions. There was certainly a story with this man. Shame he most likely wouldn't be around long enough to share it, but at least he'd leave her plenty to remember him by. "Okay, I just need to make a stop in to work to check my messages."

"Your leader will allow you to leave?"

"Leader," she smiled. "You're funny, genie. We call them bosses these days and yes, my leader will allow me to do whatever the heck I darn well please."

He looked at her blankly.

"My leader is me, genie. I work for myself."

"And how does one work for oneself?"

"I own a company. A business."

His eyebrows went up. "You are a vendor?"

"I suppose you can call me that, but my product is a service. I'm an interior decorator. I decorate homes and offices."

"They pay you to do that?"

"Oh, they pay me top dollar, mister," she sputtered resolutely, using a finger to make her point. Not that he should care, but as far as reputations went, she had no problem spreading her good one among the genie crowd. "I can do any home, any business, anytime. I make palaces out of dumps. Homes out of pits. There is no one better than me, so if you ever decide to retire or . . . oh, oh! If one of your wishees should happen to wish for a beautiful home, you tell them they don't need to burn a wish. Just give them my name. Violet Jackson. J-a-c-k-s-o-n."

He looked at her for a moment, stunned by her pitch, she was sure, before moving on.

"So, people pay you and you pay yourself?" he clarified.

"Exactly. And I pay my assistant. The others just work there for free."

"Free? Apprentices?"

"You got it."

"Hmm, free labor. Very clever."

He didn't know the half of it, which was why Violet felt compelled to show him her shop. Okay, maybe she wanted to show off a little. Sue her.

"Here it is. Shades of Violet. What do you think?"

Taka looked around the showroom at the array of fabrics and upholstery, the color charts and swatches, the rooms into which he could glimpse stacked chairs, vases, small tables, linens, rugs, and every manner of accessory. On the wall were panels of silk fabric in every shade of the rainbow and he was struck by how much just the colors alone reminded him of the central meeting venue of Jaha. Could it be that a part of her remembered their Great Hall? Could it be that Zahara truly was just waiting to be released?

His heart revved at the thought but he knew he could not let her feel his excitement. He could not make her nervous or uncomfortable. He needed three days and he would never get them if he rushed her.

"Your business is impressive. I like how you've used the accents. I like the beads."

"Sort of retro, I know, but they kind of grabbed me, you know? Carol. I'd like you to meet my cousin."

Her assistant looked up lackadaisically from her phone conversation and then did a double take on seeing Taka. She put her hand over the mouthpiece and tossed a seductive glance his way. "Good morning, stranger."

Taka continued to look at the interior. "This is very attractive. And you run this place completely? No man involved?"

"Well, there are men involved. There's Eric and Ralph. They're involved in making sure we have coffee and doughnuts."

Taka swallowed a smile. He knew women had come a long way in earning rights over the years, but he had to admit it was still a shock, albeit a pleasant one. His society would never have allowed a woman to be a leader over men, even if she ran a business for herself. Why, Zahara had been just as intelligent and courageous as his men, more so than most. But in their time, despite honor of their women, they did not look kindly upon a woman taking a role traditionally held by men. He wondered if, perhaps, Zahara would have wanted to be more than just his wife. If, perhaps, someday she would have grown tired of his constant inattention, and decided to focus her energy elsewhere. She could surely have run a business. She could have done anything she wanted.

She has.

Taka stilled as Ani's voice encroached upon his thoughts. He looked at the happy face of Violet as she saw her business through his eyes.

He had been selfish with Zahara. So much life, so much enthusiasm. He would have smothered it with his own desires. She would have had to bend, as his queen. He would have had to make her bend or lose the respect of his men. He was glad that had not come to pass before the end. And he was glad to see her enjoying her own, now.

"I admire your use of color and space. I like it a great deal."

"Why thank you. I've been mocked for my taste and style but I think it reflects me, don't you?"

"Who makes fun of you? Give me their names," he said, dryly.

Violet laughed at his perfectly timed comedic delivery, complete with deadpan expression. "You are so funny." She turned to her assistant. "Listen, Carol, I'm just going to take care of a few things in my office and then I'm leaving. I'll be showing my cousin around town today."

Carol muttered under her breath, "Must be nice."

"What was that?"

Carol did not respond but Taka said, "Your assistant is insolent. In my day that would be rewarded with a missing digit on the hand or foot."

Carol looked at him with eyes no longer clouded by lust. "What are you, some kind of freak?"

"Time out, you two," Violet said. "Taka, please, in my office. Carol, no calls." She closed the door behind them. "You're supposed to blend in, genie. No more remarks like that."

"I've been watching her," he said in a low voice, peering out through the blinds at Carol under hooded eyes, nearly invisible in a squint. "She slips little pads of paper into her purse. She took two doughnuts from that plate when everyone else takes one. She switches behind you and mocks your conversation when you are turned."

Violet smiled. Darned if the genie wasn't showing a decent amount of concern for her. No one ever stuck up for her or watched her back; she'd had to watch her own for most of her life. She almost didn't know what to do about the warm flush of affection she suddenly felt for the big man.

"It's okay, genie, I know she filches office supplies. Everyone does. And I know she makes fun of me behind my back," Violet said, cutting off eye contact as a flash of hurt from her experience walking in on her own staff doing an overblown impression of her reemerged. They had her right down to her fast walk and hair flip. But they also caught her nervous facial itch, her shrill tone, her paranoia over being outplayed by Brenda, and a mini hyperventilating jag she'd thought she had in the privacy of her office with the door closed after Gary told her if she called again he would file a restraining order. She laughed it off at the time but it hurt more than she cared to admit. "It's no big deal, really."

"No big deal?" The big man looked offended as he began to pace, alternately looking at the floor and back out the glass window to Carol, his source of ire. "Treachery is a big deal. Betrayal, disrespect, those are all big deals. If a person betrays you once they will betray you again."

"Not always."

"Always and a day. A snake is a snake is a snake. And if ever I've seen a snake it is that woman out there." He finally stopped pacing to face Violet again, arms folded obstinately and his face fierce with his conviction.

Violet envied his certainty. She wished things were so cut and dried but she knew the truth; love hurt and loyalty faltered. She looked down to shuffle some papers on her desk into a neat pile.

"Not always," she said again. "And if it happens, so what? No one cares anyway. In the large scheme of things you should know better than to rely on anyone or anything other than yourself. It's your own fault if you forget that."

Taka barely heard her mumble, but felt her pain from across the room. She'd been hurt, somehow, by something or someone. He would bet it was Carol, the snake. "She does not like you. Not only does she not like you, she would like to do you harm."

"What, are you a psychic, now?"

"It doesn't take a psychic to feel the negative vibrations she puts off. You are a perceptive person; you must feel it."

"So what? She's a secretary. It's hard to find one who's not disgruntled these days."

"A secretary, an assistant, a right-hand man: they all have the power to do serious damage, from the inside out."

"And what should I do? Get rid of her? The next one won't be any better. I know; Carol's my fifth in four years."

"Try a sixth."

"My, my, so protective. How very warrior-like of you. Primitive and all that."

"I am not primitive. My people were cultured. We were educated and educators. Far from primitive."

"So that whole comment about missing a digit?"

"An exaggeration, of course. We only extricate limbs and digits from men."

"I see. Look, can you hang out while I make a few more calls?"

"Do I have a choice?"

"Nope."

Taka moved to sit in the chair opposite her and she stared at him until he got the message.

"I see. I am to wait in the main room with the snake and her lizards. Fine." He opened the door and out tossed a smug, "It'll give me a chance to gently persuade your assistant of the error of her ways. And there is a young

man I saw looking at your backside. I will have a word
with him as well."

Violet fumbled the handset and as the voice on the other
end said, "Hello? Hello?" she contemplated hanging up to
deal with Taka. But she saw him leaning casually over the
desk, no apparent physical intimidation happening, and
finished her call.

"I do not know you or this place or your ways but I say
once and no more, if you do not respect Violet Jackson
I will return. Every day I will watch you and every day I
will report to her the type of person you reveal yourself to
be. Perhaps you feel you would pass this type of scrutiny
but if not, I strongly suggest you curb your negative
tendencies and become the professional assistant she
pays you to be. And you!" His voice caused a cessation
of movement behind him and he didn't bother to turn to
speak to the passer. "A gentleman does not visually ogle
a queen."

"Queen?" the crackly, young male voice said, uncer-
tainly. "I was just ogling Violet."

Taka pinched his lips to hold in his temper and turned
to look at the young man who froze under his glare,
dropping a sheet of paper but too petrified to move. Taka
had that effect on lesser men.

"Ogle her again and it will be the last ogle you ever
enjoy."

"Yes. Yes, sir!"

The youngster shuffled off into another room and Carol
was sufficiently subdued when Violet emerged, looking
around dubiously as though she expected he'd torn the
place to pieces. He read the relief on her beautiful face
and took in the sigh that moved her beguiling chest under
her blouse.

Yes, he was ogling. But a king was within his rights to ogle his queen.

"Okay," she said on a smile, briskly heading to the door. "Let's go."

"Yes, ma'am." He followed.

Chapter 7

Violet squinted up at the sky. It was a beautiful day, but the calls she'd made had robbed her of some of her previous joy. They had more customers now than ever, but sometimes it was getting the new ones that cost the money. Advertising and entertaining, just plain having the materials to show potential customers: it was all expensive. She always ended the year in the black, but throughout the year it seemed the money went out faster than it came in. That meant she wouldn't be able to hire a new manager like she'd wanted. *Maybe Carol?* She snorted to herself. *Maybe not.*

She looked at the large man beside her who was similarly enjoying the beauty of the sun despite the fact that she wasn't rich yet like she was supposed to be. He was a genie. She'd made the wish, right? What was going on?

"I called the bank. Where's my money?" she fairly snapped at him and was rewarded with a squint of annoyance from him. She had to use her hand as a visor to see his shadowed face.

"How should I know?"

"Look, you're supposed to have the inside scoop. If the wishes aren't happening you need to follow up."

"Do not tell me what I need to do. My job is to set the ground rules. It is up to my friend to decide how the wishes are to be fulfilled."

"Typical."

"What do you mean by that?"

"I mean, this is just the type of red tape crap that is typical for people these days. No one wants responsibility. No one wants to say, 'this is my job, I'll make sure it gets done.'"

"Are you implying that I am one of those types of people?"

"I'm not implying it; I'm saying it outright."

"I have no power, woman. I am a king without a kingdom. My friend decides when, if, or how I emerge from my stone."

"And that's it? That's all?"

"What do you suggest?"

"How about you stand up for yourself, make something happen? How 'bout you go to your friend, or whatever, and ask him when my wish will come true? How about that?"

"And you will accept the answer and stop haranguing me?"

"Certainly."

"Fine."

"Good."

Violet was appeased. She looked up and down the street. It was relatively busy this time of day, but it was such a lovely day. And it'd been awhile since she'd had some time off. "Hey, you want to go do something?"

Taka looked at her dubiously. Was this a trick? She seemed to run hot and cold so he had no clue. "This is your time to use making your decisions."

She heard a slight note of petulance in his voice. Obviously kings didn't get a dressing down from commoners where he came from, but she didn't want to fight with him. She didn't want him mad at her. She had no idea why.

"I'll make my wishes in plenty of time; don't you worry about that. I was just thinking, it's such a pretty day and it must be awful cramped where you are. Is it like the bottle in *I Dream of Jeannie?*"

"I told you I am not—"

"I know, I know. Not a genie. But do you get cramped, tired? Do you have a bed? How's it work?"

Taka looked at Violet and wondered if she had some mental sickness that could swing her from anger to polite conversation so quickly. She looked normal enough. Better than normal. He scrutinized her face to see if she was planning to mock him, then grudgingly admitted, "It is not a physical discomfort I feel while I am inside. My body is different when I am changed. When I am in my stone I merely feel I am hanging in a place with no sound, no light, no smell, or taste. It is almost as if I do not exist."

Violet wrinkled her nose. "That must suck."

"If that means it is bad, yes, it can be."

She thought, what could she plan for him that he might enjoy doing? Was there anything an old-timer might like to do in modern times? An idea came to her and she nodded her head with satisfaction. "We're going to have to make sure you have as much fun while you're out as possible. It's my civic duty. When you go back into that rock you're going to go happy, genie."

Taka felt a lightening of his soul. She was offering an unexpected kindness. The second that day. It surprised him, but pleased him nonetheless.

He followed her back to the car and when they got in, he looked at her while she drove like a maniac, taking a road that was high and busy with a multitude of cars, but she was passing all of them.

He held on to his arm rest and was glad that he had attached himself to the seat with the belt as she'd instructed, but his curiosity got the better of him.

"Where are we going? I do not remember taking this route to go to your office."

"We're not going home," Violet said. "I had a brilliant idea. I'm thinking, you stuck in that stone all the time can't be fun. And you men like to be in control a lot, right? That probably hasn't changed since you were around before?"

"No, you are right. We liked control in my day as well," he admitted.

"Good. I'm taking you to a little spot where my stepdad took me when I was sixteen and he taught me to drive. And I'm going to give you the same speech he gave me." She cleared her voice and dropped it an octave. "'Violet, this is not some party mobile for you to drive your little boyfriends to wild parties so you can drink and do whatever you want to.'"

Taka backtracked, surely he couldn't have heard her right. "Are you saying you are going to teach me to drive?"

Violet dropped her stepfather's voice and went back to her own. "That's what I'm saying, genie."

"Drive what?"

"This. My car."

He paused. He couldn't deny the streak of pleasure that went through him at the thought. The last thing he'd driven was alive; and his horse had not been driven so much as guided and persuaded into doing what he'd wanted. The last time he'd been out cars had only just been invented and were more like buggies slugging along. Now was a different deal entirely.

"I do not know the first thing about a machine such as this," he admitted, in a questioning tone.

"It's easy." Violet waved her hand. She pulled off a highway exit on the south side of Columbus and took a long road into an area of trees, bushes, and various patches of bare dirt. She found the biggest patch of dirt and pulled in.

Taka's eyes sparkled, but caution made him wary. "I am not certain I should do something like this."

Violet looked over at him. She saw the look in his eyes and interpreted, "You may not be certain you should do it, but you certainly want to do it, don't you?"

Suddenly, every fiber in his being was hyped. Yes, he wanted to do it! He didn't understand the machine, but he did want to try it. "And you can teach me?" he asked.

"Of course. Now, get out and let's switch places." She turned off the motor, unlatched her seat belt, opened the door, and hopped out of the driver's seat, seemingly in one movement. Taka paused only a moment, then did the same, passing her around the back of the car and earning a wink and a slap on the behind.

"Get a move on, genie!" she called.

He blinked in surprise. He'd never in all his years been slapped on the behind by a woman. It wasn't that bad a feeling. Shrugging, he moved on to climb into the driver's seat and belted up again, shutting the door. His hands stroked the wheel anxiously. "I do not know that this is a good idea," he said.

"You said that," Violet said, noting his caressing of the wheel was directly contradictory to his words.

"But you did not hear me."

"No, I heard you, genie. I'm just not listening to you because you're being contrary. Just like the drivel that comes out of the mouths of most men is wrong and contradictory. You say one thing and do another. You can pretend, but I only have to look at you to see you want to drive this car. Look at you. Why don't you kiss the wheel, already?"

That snapped him out of his reverie and he glared at her. "I do not lie."

"Well, maybe you're lying to yourself," she said. "What, are you scared or something?"

Taka glared at her. How could he have forgotten how Zahara liked to taunt? It was why they'd gotten into that fight as children in the first place. "There is not a task on this earth that would frighten me."

"Then man up and stop whining. Okay, listen, quick lesson. There's really only a few things you need to know." She pointed down. "Gearshift. The D is for drive, the R is for reverse, the P is for park, and the N is for neutral in case you ever have to push it somewhere without the motor being on. Those other numbers: don't know, don't care." She pointed to his feet. "The gas pedal makes it go and the brake pedal makes it stop." She pointed to the ignition and handed him the key, allowing the others to dangle. "And this is your key to a little excitement. This will start all this." She moved her hands in a circle, denoting the car. "Any questions?"

Taka's mind was in a whirl but she could almost see him mentally calculating all she'd told him. "That is all I need to know?"

"Well, for right now, anyway. I mean, there are rules for the road and all that, but that's why we came out here in the middle of nowhere, so you can't run anybody down. Now, ready?"

Taka didn't know where the excitement came from, but his nerve endings tingled much like the first time he'd ridden into battle. He slipped the key in the ignition as he'd seen her do, and turned. As before, the car burst into life, idling.

"What now?" he asked, his hands stroking the wheel and his body slightly forward in preparation.

Violet had a moment of hesitation, wondering if this had been a good idea after all. The temperature in the car had gone up, almost as if the big guy next to her had gone into idle as well, waiting for the precise moment to strike. But since she'd pretty much called him a wuss for not doing it, she couldn't very well admit she was wrong now. No, she would see what happened to a giant genie with a pint of adrenalin running through his veins.

"Foot on the brake, always start on the brake so that you can ease into speed after you shift into drive. Now, hold that button with your thumb and shift into drive."

He did that and then waited in suspense. "Now, what?"

Violet shrugged. "Now, slowly let off the brake."

He did that.

"And sloowwlllyyy step on the gas."

Taka put his foot down gently and the car revved like a giant beast. He added a little more pressure and the car lurched into a halting drive. Then, Violet watched as his eyes widened with excitement, and his mouth opened. He yelled, "Woo hoo!" and stepped firmly onto the gas sending the car moving forward with a screech of her tires and a whirl of dust.

"Take it easy, genie," Violet said, belatedly wondering if this was a good idea. It didn't matter though because they were knee-deep now with Taka moving the wheel this way and that, kicking up dust, testing the speed and the brakes, and hollering with glee with each turn and stop.

Taka felt alive for the first time in years. The machine under him was as powerful as his horse had been, only he had complete control. It was an amazing feeling. It made his heart race and his breath short, yet he embraced it for all it was worth. It would probably be the only time he would ever get the opportunity, so he took the car through its paces, testing every aspect of its speed and maneuverability.

Hmmm, Violet thought. *I've created a monster.* She watched the way he moved, the flush of happiness on his face, the body rigid with excitement. Good to know the stereotype about men and toys was true, but perhaps she should have started him off on a Big Wheel.

They went in doughnuts over the hard grass, Taka laughing every second and Violet having to fight to keep the smile from her face as well. They must have been twenty minutes in, having done figure eights until Violet was almost dizzy until, finally, he straightened and stepped on the gas, headed for the tree line.

"Hey," Violet said nervously as they careened over bumpy grass. "Hit the brakes. Hit the brakes." She looked over at him as he ate up more grass. "I said hit the brakes." She looked at the forest coming up too fast. She licked her lips which suddenly were dry. "Hit the brakes. I said, hit the brakes! Hit the brakes!" She threw her arms over her face as a tree came barreling their way, sure that she'd seen her last of life, when suddenly he did just what she'd said. The car came to a sudden, loud stop about two feet from a large trunk, spitting up dirt from behind and throwing her into the comforting restraint of her seat belt. She felt the stillness, peeked at the tree which, amazingly, was not in her lap, and peeked at him through her arms, shaking. He put the car in park and turned off the ignition, smiling at her.

"I heard you the first time," he said, cockiness oozing out of him like toothpaste from a squeezed tube.

Violet felt rage bubble in her and lowered her arms to yell at him. He had a sick, reckless sense of humor, scaring her that way. What kind of freak was he, anyway? To try a stunt like that. The same stunt she'd pulled on her stepfather at sixteen. Admiration made its way to the surface. This genie wasn't so bad after all.

"Okay. You got me, genie. Had me scared for a minute there, but you're a fast learner."

"You don't get to be king by being slow," he said.

"I thought you got to be king by being born. No guarantees of speed or intelligence there."

But he wasn't listening. He unstrapped and opened the door, climbing out of the car with pep in his step. Violet was the one who hesitated this time.

She got out and passed him on the backside, stunned when she felt a telltale palm whip smartly against her backside. She grabbed her behind and whirled, but the man was whistling and climbing into the passenger seat. *The nerve of that genie!* She smiled and got back in the car.

"Don't think just because you can drive you're big stuff. There are a whole lot of rules to follow. They don't just let anybody drive you know." She belted and started the car. "You have to have a license to drive one of these babies."

"Yes, and what are these rules then?" Taka asked.

She pulled onto the road to take them to the highway. "Well, when you're driving, you have to be on the right side of the road, in this country. And there are traffic lights to tell you when you can drive and when you have to stop. And you can't just do any old speed, mister. You have to abide by the law." They were on the highway and flew past a sign with sixty-five in bold.

"Was that a sign for speed?" he asked.

"Hmm?"

"That sign you just passed." He leaned over and looked at her speedometer. "Is that to correspond? That cannot be. You are driving much faster than sixty-five so that must have been for some other rule."

"What? Who's going over sixty-five?"

"You are. From that device it looks as if you are doing seventy."

"Anyway, as I was saying. If you were of this earth and all, driving would be an honor and a privilege but since you're only a guest, well, you don't need to worry your pretty little head about these things. I've been doing this for years. I'm an expert."

She whipped in front of a car on her left, gained speed and did the same to a car on the right, then gained more speed and shot off to the right on an exit. "See, you can't do that if you don't know what you're doing," she said. Sure, she'd been showing off a little. But somebody had to show genie just because he knew his way around a gearshift he wasn't all that.

"Well then," Taka said, amusement coloring his words. "I'm honored to have learned by the master." He settled comfortably in his seat. "By the way, master, that sign would imply the speed on this road is thirty-fi—"

"Look, here we are!" Violet said, parking at her next destination.

"And where would here be?"

"Eastland Mall. It's like a giant building with stores and restaurants and stuff. I was thinking we could go get some lunch and maybe shop a little." Okay, she was taking advantage of the fact that he had no idea how much normal men hated to shop with women, but this was her one day off and it never hurt to have a male perspective.

Taka grimaced as he remembered how much he hated to wait around when Zahara was being fitted for the thousand pieces of jewelry, clothing, and accessories to make up a single outfit, not to mention the endless conversations on whether to braid her hair to the left or to the right. He always loved the outcome but the process was worse than reeds under the fingernails.

"You cannot make me go inside," he declared, adopting his most fierce expression to her apparent delight. She smiled at him as if he were a child and it infuriated him more. "Woman, I did not leave my stone to be tortured by you. I may have to grant your wishes but I will not do this. I. Will. Not."

Chapter 8

Taka grumbled as he tried to wedge his massive body in a delicate chair outside the fitting room in the ladies' clothing store, the newspaper in his hands his only relief. At least he could see the date and read a little bit of what was going on in the world while Violet tried on clothes. He was so absorbed he only felt an occasional bump as people passed.

For her part, after the hundredth time of peeking out of the fitting room to see women intentionally stray too close to her genie, and other women sauntering into the communal area to "accidentally" award him a glimpse of scandalous lingerie, Violet lost her pleasant mood.

By the time one woman made her third trip out of her little private cubby area in her thong underwear, Violet could no longer contain herself and poked her head over the top.

"Sweetie, if I had a body like yours I wouldn't be prancing in front of anybody. You need to keep your narrow little behind in your room before I have to come out there. He's with me."

The woman looked highly insulted, but dragged her butt into her cubby like Violet suggested, rightly interpreting the violence in Violet's tone. Violet had honed her skills of intimidation to an art form and they came in handy for times such as this. After all, she had to protect her genie. Sure, he was big and all, but he was an innocent to this time; he had no idea how aggressive women of today could be. And he was not spending her precious three days knocking boots with some skinny-behind hoochie. Not if she had anything to say about it.

Taka was too busy reading the disturbing stories in the newspaper to notice Violet's protection. Some things never changed. All the murders and crime; people were still betraying each other. And if it wasn't a violent crime, it was a financial one. He thought back to his loss of Jaha. On his first jaunt from his stone after the massacre of his people the legend of Jaha was still alive. He'd learned that many countries in Africa had fallen to tribal warfare and transatlantic slavery, the likes of which no one had ever seen. It upset him to think that even Africans participated in this trade against their own.

He even felt some regret that he hadn't remained to rebuild his kingdom. By his next appearance, this time in Asia, he'd discovered Jaha was no longer spoken of. Only mystics and time travelers remembered Jaha; any living evidence had died out. By the next jaunt, history books never even mentioned the ancient kingdom of Jaha. It was as if his country and people had never existed.

"Ready to go?" Violet stood before him, clothing draped over her arm.

"Thank the heavens," he could not contain. A short while later they were back at Violet's apartment and Taka was looking forward to finally spending quality time with her. "Thanks for carrying the bags for me," Violet said, leading the way in. "Oh, and don't forget yours for being such a good sport!" She took all the bags but one. "That will look great on you!"

"I do not know why you bought clothing for me. I cannot take it with me. I told you, I have no control over my dress. That is determined by the same power that keeps me from feeling hunger or fatigue while I am inside. I am clothed in the dress of the time when I emerge from my stone."

"I know, I know. But while you're out here you might as well have something nice. Besides, you'll need it tonight."

"Why?" he asked, on guard. "What do you mean?"

"Oh, did I forget to mention? Dinner. With Jerome and Brenda and Gary."

"Absolutely not. No. Absolutely no."

"Why? How long's it been since you had a good meal? You scarfed down breakfast and lunch was just a quick bite. And you look like neither meal could sustain you, anyway."

"You push your luck, woman. It is bad enough you are lying about who I am."

"But you'll get to meet everybody. Wouldn't you like to meet Jerome? I'm sure you two will hit it off right away."

"Who is this Jerome person?"

"You know, my boyfriend."

Taka fell quiet. The "boy" friend. An odd development in the relations between men and women over the centuries: "friends" who held no requirement of commitment yet functioned as if they deserved the rights that should only come with such commitment. Not every relationship between men and women in his time had been a marital one, but at least they'd never been so cavalier.

He'd conveniently forgotten talk of the man at breakfast as the "boy" friend was rightly insignificant in the larger scheme of things. Perhaps this morning news of her being with a man had not bothered him because he disliked Violet so. After spending the day in gentle companionship with her, he had no desire to see her with another man. He was just coming to know her himself.

He'd never had to see Zahara being wooed by another man. As king, once he'd expressed interest in her no one else had dared approach her. Fortunately, she had been

as happy with the match as he. He'd never had to worry
about wanting a woman who did not want him back.
In other kingdoms, the desires of the woman meant
little one way or another, but he had wanted Zahara to
be as excited to be with him as he was with her. He'd
plied her and her parents with gifts and, finally, one day
summoned her to ask her if she would consider becoming
his wife. It had caused a minor scandal and he'd taken
plenty of ribbing for it from neighboring kings. But it had
won Zahara's love and respect, which was worth the loss
of face.

He spent the next hour stewing over his predicament
while Violet dressed. He would have to get rid of this
Jerome man, somehow. Certainly he was no worthy
suitor or he would have made himself known sometime
during the day. No flowers, no gifts, no jewels, gifted farm
animals, or communication; she might as well be alone as
attentive as this man was. Attentive or not, Zahara was
his. He'd traveled hundreds of years and thousands of
miles to find her again and no living man would keep her
from him.

When Violet emerged from the bedroom in a dress
of emerald that stopped at her knees and showed very
nearly every curve of her splendid body, Taka tightened
with tension. Her skin practically gleamed against the
brilliant color. The dress not only made her skin glow,
it cupped her bosom enticingly and held it up and out
like an offering of sweet fruits on a platter to an honored
guest; they were smooth and round, moist with the
scent of . . . was that shea butter? Shea butter was only
for him! Imagining this "boy" friend sampling his shea
butter–coated breasts made his stomach turn with bile.

"Genie, what's wrong? I can feel that cold draft from
here." Violet breezed through the room, noting his
stiffness as she passed him to pour herself a glass of

water. *What does he have to be tense about?* she thought. Another free meal. And more time out of his rock. You would think he'd be thanking her.

"This time and the ways of your world are foreign to me," he grumbled. "I will stay in tonight."

Violet turned to look at him, arms crossed. Boy, he really did look uncomfortable. She could barely see his eyes his face was so stiff in its frown. She almost gave in and allowed him to stay home. But, frankly, she kind of liked his company. He exuded a strength and confidence that were very attractive. He was like a male version of herself. His presence was akin to having her very own bodyguard. And she was mildly amused at the way his eyes seemed to be drawn to her body and then would look away quickly as if trying to avoid her.

Oh yeah, she caught that look in his eyes when he spotted her in this dress. It was cute. It reminded her of a boy back in high school who was so entranced by the sight of her little beebees he'd spilled soda all over himself trying to get a look. And they'd grown much more since then. They were darned near perfect, now. She could hardly blame the big guy for staring.

Violet walked to him and reached out to take his hand, looking up and speaking as soothingly as she would with a child. "It'll be okay. Don't be scared. I'll be right there with you."

Taka bristled and glared at her from under his brow. "I am not afraid. I'll thank you to watch your tone with me, woman. I am no child to be placated."

"Okay, okay." Violet raised her hands in submission. "I didn't mean anything."

"What would I be frightened of? Do you think you and your friends and your world are so impressive that a man like me cannot figure them out? It is dinner. We will eat and drink and have conversation. I will sit with you and

your friend who is a boy and we will speak civilly. I am
a king, I have spoken to dignitaries and politicians the
world over; your little friendly boy does not intimidate
me."

"Okay, I'm sorry," Violet said, recognizing the dulcet
tones of wounded pride. She really shouldn't tease him so
much but men were so easy to rile. "Oh, I almost forgot!"
She did a little hop and scurried from the room only to
return a second later with the bag she'd brought home
earlier. "For you. Perfect for this evening."

"Why do I need to change?" Taka asked. "I am already
clothed."

"Yes, you are. But those clothes leave a little to be
desired."

"You are being shallow. Clothing is of no consequence;
it is the person who is important."

Violet sighed and stuck one hand on her hip with annoyance. "So I suppose that means when you were a king
you weren't dressed in the finest clothes and jewels in the
land, huh?" She stood there for a moment inspecting her
nails until he conceded and snatched the bag from her.

"Fine. I will change into your modern clothes to impress
your friends, as I know that is important to you. I will be
out shortly."

Violet hid a smile as he walked into the bathroom
stiffly and closed the door behind him. She made herself
at home on the sofa for the wait, crossing one leg over a
knee to allow it to swing. Her shoes were shiny and new;
she thought of the way his eyes got dark when he saw her
legs in these shoes.

"Whoa, get a grip, Violet." There had to be some sort of
law against trying to seduce a genie, right?

An hour later Taka and Jerome sat across from one
another, eyeing each other like adversaries.

"So," Gary said, watching the other two men. "Taka, what'd you say you do?"

Violet answered, "He's a foreign dignitary, aren't you, Taka?"

"What the heck is that?" Gary asked.

Jerome gave Taka a dirty look. "Means kisses behinds of people from other countries."

Taka said softly but with steel, "I would imagine you know a great deal about that 'kissing of the behind' you speak of; your manner of speech would suggest so. Frankly, I prefer the lips of a beautiful woman to a behind any day."

"Too bad you ain't got one," Jerome countered, leaning over to kiss Violet. Taka's jaw flexed, as did his fists under the table.

"Ah." Brenda smiled. "That's sweet."

Taka frowned even harder. "Is it supposed to be romantic to grope a woman in public? Where I come from you would have your legs tied to a mule and be dragged through a hill of horse dung for such a disrespectful display with a woman who is not your betrothed."

"Darn, man," Gary declared. "Where you come from?"

"Why don't you go back?" Jerome followed.

Violet saw the food coming and interrupted, gratefully. "Oh look, food's here. Thank God, I'm starving." The sight of the ribs and fries on the platter made her mouth water. "Where's my soda?" she asked the waiter. She frowned when it was obvious he'd forgotten it. "If I wanted my drink after my dinner I would have ordered it as dessert," she snapped.

"She gets cranky when she's hungry," Jerome said.

"I'm paying for service," she insisted. "I'm not paying for him to walk around with his head up his behind." She said the last part loud enough for half the restaurant to hear and then turned back to her plate, smoothing her napkin over her lap.

Jerome looked at her platter and gave her a sideways glance. "Dang, baby, you gonna eat all that! Your girl over there doesn't eat like you do."

"I'm. Hungry," Violet said.

Brenda prodded her lettuce leaves with a fork. "So am I, but this salad is going to be fine for me. It absolutely fills me up every time I get it and it is so delicious." The four of them watched Brenda take a bite of lettuce and squint her eyes in ecstasy. Violet flushed as her stomach growled in protest.

Taka looked at Violet. "Nonsense. Animals were made to be killed and eaten. The body cannot function without protein; it will starve itself into unattractive emaciation, as your tiny friend's body clearly displays. Eat your fill, woman. But, in the name of all that is holy, you must be kinder to the help. It is unladylike and unbecoming for a woman of your standing to berate them so. You are too decent a person to allow that representation to be all they know of you."

All heads looked to him in shock and then everyone at the table burst into laughter; everyone but Violet who looked at him, intently.

Who did he think he was to call her out like that? She never intended to be rude to the wait staff but she always felt, somehow, that if she didn't whip them into shape first they would take advantage. She had to show them, and everyone, that she was in control of the situation, didn't she? She had to show the world she was a force to be reckoned with, right? Then why did she feel the flush of shame? And why was she suddenly offended that everyone else at the table found the prospect of her being a woman of "great standing" so hilarious?

Taka had stiffened under the laughter assault but he still held Violet's gaze long enough for Jerome to notice and go on the assault, himself.

"Listen to him. Who does he think he is?" Jerome asked. Violet kept Taka's gaze, also, until the genie dropped his to his plate, picking up his utensils to eat, a flex in his jaw his only sign of tension. She felt strangely disappointed with the loss.

"You should try the salad, Violet," Brenda said, after Violet had firmly and resolutely inserted a pork rib in her mouth. Violet looked over at her friend and, not for the first time, wondered at her suspect timing. "Especially since you'll be my maid of honor. You have to look nice in the dress. As a matter of fact, I brought it."

Violet's eyebrows went up and she noticed the plastic rustling behind Brenda and asked, rib in mouth, "Dwess?"

"It's right here. I'll wait 'til you're finished to give it to you. It goes perfect with the flowers I ordered."

Violet swallowed rib meat and said, "Isn't it customary to be fitted for one of those things?"

"Yes, but it's okay. I know what size you are. A ten, right?"

All eyes looked at her and Violet wanted to cross the table and pimp slap Brenda. Sure, a ten when she was prepubescent. Brenda obviously wanted Violet to admit to the whole table that she was actually a fourteen. Witch. She looked at the dress and did a double take. "Cripes, Brenda, is that orange?"

"It's melon. It's the in color this year."

"Good God, did we or did we not take the same fashion class that taught us that what is in fashion is not always what is most flattering? And is that . . . Gosh darn it, Brenda, are those sleeves or balloons?"

"Sleeves, silly. Chiffon. And the top is satin and the skirt blouses out."

"Like a dang on Southern belle on crack." Violet tried to hold in her horror, truly, but this humiliation was too complete to keep her quiet, even in front of her genie. "I am going to kill you. I'm going to put your head down in your fiancé's soup and hold it there until the life drains out of you."

"I knew you'd like it! I told you she'd like it, Gary."

She supposed there was some value in the fact that Brenda never took any of her threats seriously. It would be one of those cases where, when her lifeless body showed up floating in a bathtub, with a bridesmaid dress–colored melon slice shoved in her mouth, people would say Violet just snapped; nobody ever saw it coming.

Jerome looked across at Taka under hooded lids. "When you getting married, man?"

"I have been married. I am a widower."

Brenda gasped loudly, concern on her face. "I am so sorry. That's terrible." She then stopped and seemed to remind herself that she couldn't trust a thing he said. "You almost got me there. I almost believed you."

"I do not lie," he said sternly.

"Violet, is he lying?" Brenda asked her.

Violet rewarded her with a hiss. "He is not a liar. If he says he is a widower than he is. For pity's sake, can you please leave the man alone?"

Jerome asked Taka, "What'd she die of?"

"Jerome!" Violet yelled.

"It is fine, Violet." Taka raised a calming hand to her and turned to Jerome. "She was murdered. But she fought all the way. She fought like the wife of a warrior with the spirit of a queen, spirit that can surpass any misfortune. She lived a short life on this earth but that life was as grand as the highest mountain and as precious as the most delicate of flowers. I yearn and long for her every single day with every fiber of my being." The table fell quiet for a moment and then Gary interrupted the peace.

"So how was she murdered? Knife? Gun? Bomb?"

"Good God, Gary," Brenda said, scandalized by her fiancé's lack of tact.

Violet agreed. "How tacky can you be? You are all embarrassing me to death. I am embarrassed right now to know you all."

Jerome said wryly, "And yet, here you sit." He laughed.

Gary joined in, remarking, "She couldn't be too embarrassed. She dated both of us; she must like something."

"You got that right!" Jerome declared.

"Oh, for heaven's sake." Brenda blushed. "Cut it out you guys. That's just as tasteless."

Taka took it all in as Violet ate, seeming to avoid eye contact with him. He'd caught her eyes before and he knew she felt something. Knew it. Now, he could feel a barrier around her. She was shutting him out. She was blinding herself to what she knew was madness. These people, this situation; it wasn't just her treatment of the help that was beneath her. He felt hurt and let down. He felt further betrayed and lonelier than he ever had.

For a moment, almost as if she felt his sadness she looked at him, but he was no longer in the mood to look at her.

Violet felt a stroke of hurt when Taka looked away, again. She wondered at the disappointment she saw in his eyes. She wondered why suddenly the eyes that had lit a fire earlier were now so cold. She looked at her messy plate of ribs and over to Brenda's neat little salad and lost her appetite. It wasn't until she heard Jerome that she realized he had taken in the whole transaction.

"Hey, man. You sitting over there glaring at folks, you need to lighten up," Jerome said.

Gary agreed wholeheartedly. "He's right, man. You way too uptight."

Taka grimaced with the effort to withhold his temper. How dare the man intrude when he was having a "staring-avoiding-staring" match with his wife?

"Now, see, here's what you need to do to release some of that tension." Jerome leaned across the table to Taka in a conspiratorial manner. "You see that honey over there at the bar? What you need to do is go over there, tell that honey what you're all about, and go hit that."

Gary laughed.

Violet had lost any amusement she might have had and watched as the two men in her life goaded the genie. Bringing him had not been a good idea.

Taka looked at Jerome. "Hit that? What does that mean?"

Gary snickered as Jerome leaned closer to whisper the explanation in detail. Violet's eyes widened as Taka finally understood and . . .

A half hour later Violet helped Jerome through the door of her apartment as he leaned against her, still groaning over his newly blackened eye.

"That dude is crazy," he whined while Violet tried to soothe his bruised ego. Taka came in behind them, ignoring them both to sit on the sofa.

Violet glared at him. "You didn't have to hit him. We'll never be able to eat there again."

"A man who speaks such filth deserves to be hit. And you, how could you enjoy the company of such a cretin?"

Jerome straightened. "What'd you call me, man?"

"Oh, shut up, Jerome. You know he'd crush you like a bug," she told her beloved. He smartly backed down, looking indignant.

"I must relieve myself," Taka said heading to the bathroom without looking back. "I expect him to be gone when I return."

Violet's eyebrows rose. Wasn't that some crap? The man was stalking around giving orders like he lived there or something. Bad enough he'd tried to ruin her night, now he was giving orders? She would have to set him straight sooner rather than later, but right now she had to take care of Jerome, the big baby. She helped him to the sofa and went into the kitchen, filled a plastic bag with ice, and returned to put it on his eye. Her ministrations and small kisses on his wounded eye caused him to turn to her with kisses of his own. She pulled away and he groaned.

"Come on, baby. It's been a week."

"I have a guest."

"That crazy mother? He shouldn't even be here. Why can't he stay at a hotel?"

"He's family."

"Then you come home with me. Come on, what's going to happen in one night? He can't watch himself, he gotta have you around all the time?"

Violet looked at the door. She didn't know if she should lose more time but she needed a break from the genie and his eyes. The man was always watching her. "I don't know."

Jerome kissed her again and she felt a small flutter in her belly. It had been a week and she had needs. It didn't help that Taka was a good-looking son of a gun. She was only human; she wasn't blind. After spending the day with him she'd noticed more and more, like the size of his hands, the firmness of his jaw. When she'd picked out the outfit he now wore she'd pictured his body in the clothes, never dreaming he would fill them out the way he had. Who could have guessed beneath his nondescript clothes was a body sculpted to near perfection. Shoulders so wide she could hang curtains on them, a chest so broad and well formed it would put bodybuilders to shame.

Abdomen tight so that the sweater swung free just where she longed to slide her hands underneath.

Was it wrong to get hot over a genie? She looked at Jerome. "Maybe an hour or two, then bring me home."

"Yeah, yeah." He gave her a long, promising kiss.

"I mean it. An hour, two at the most; that's it." She had to get back to wishing.

"Yeah, yeah, let's go."

"Wait, I want to say good night."

"Come on, Violet."

"Go wait in the car! I'll meet you there in two seconds. Go!"

He groaned, but got up and left. Violet waited for Taka to return, his ferocious expression relaxing when he noticed Jerome was gone.

"That was fun," she said. "If I had known you would punch my boyfriend I would have had you two meet sooner."

Taka pulled his shirt off and stretched. Violet sucked in a breath and felt a moment of dizziness at the sudden sight of his bare chest. Just as she'd imagined: covered in bittersweet dark chocolate skin, begging to be warmed by her mouth, his arms veritable logs of corded muscle, and his back . . . *Breathe, Violet, breathe!*

"It is good he is gone," Taka said, sitting on the sofa to pull off his shoes. "He is a pain and a distraction. He has ruined my evening."

Violet came to her senses, shaking herself out of her lust fog before he could notice. She sounded almost like herself when she spoke again. "Cut it out with the complaining. You sound like Jerome."

"Bite your tongue woman. That worm and I have nothing in common."

"Bite *your* tongue. That worm is going to be my husband."

He looked at her, confusion on his face. "Why would you bind yourself to such a creature?"

Violet laughed. "He's not a bad guy. You made him jealous, is all."

"Then where is he? Where I come from a man does not allow another man to reside in his woman's hut if he is indeed in love with her."

"Not that way; he thinks you're my cousin."

"Then there is little reason for him to be jealous."

"He's not jealous of you and me. He's jealous of you as a man. And who would blame him? You question his manhood and stalk around like you own everything."

"He should be man enough to withstand the presence of another man without feeling threatened."

"Like you? Look, genie, I've had three cosmos so I really don't want to do any serious thinking tonight. Let's just agree to disagree. We can continue in the morning."

"You should not drink so. It gives you a headache."

"Yes, mommy," Violet snapped. She couldn't imagine how he knew about her cosmo headaches.

"What do you mean, calling me 'mommy'? I am not your mommy."

"Then stop acting like you are."

"Ah, I'm exhausted. I'd forgotten how tiring a mortal life can be, and all I did all day was eat and entertain. My friends would chide me for being soft. My men would wait for me to sleep and then roll me in clay and feathers for my weakness," he said, somewhat fondly. He yawned while stretching on the sofa, pulling a throw onto his bare chest and then looked at her expectantly over the back of the sofa.

"Why are you standing there? Will you not change for bed?"

"I'm going out for a little while."

"Out? Where? For what?"

"It will just be for a little while. Jerome and I need to talk. He needs a little push in the right direction."

"I do not even want to know what that means," Taka said, anger finally taking its release. He'd done what she'd asked. He'd put up with nonsense. He'd worn her clothes. He'd gone shopping. And now she was off to play some games with some worthless man.

He reached over, fumbled a couple of times, and finally managed to click off the lamp. "Do not wake me when you return."

Violet tapped her foot impatiently, hands on her hips. If this wasn't a full-blown tantrum she didn't know what was. She thought genies were supposed to be wise. "Boy, it didn't take you long to become a modern man."

"What do you mean? What are you saying?"

"Nothing. Go to sleep." Violet threw him one last look in the dark and gave up, slamming the door soundly on her way out.

Taka stood, clicked on the light, and began pacing. Then he walked to the door, opened it, and slammed it himself, just for the sake of it.

A surge of energy and a popping in his ears and he didn't have to wait to know he was about to get a scolding. Before Aniweto arrived he was already on the offensive.

"I do not want to hear it! I do not need you tonight with your lectures and recriminations. I am not in the mood to chat, friend."

"Yet you pace like a caged cat. Why?"

"Why? Why? Were you there this evening? That charade of a meal; we might as well have been dining with the traitorous murderers who did us in four hundred years ago! She cheapens herself with fools and surrounds herself with people who would do her harm as quickly as look at her. Her friends are as good as her enemies and the exasperating woman will not listen. Why?" Taka put a hand to his forehead feeling the unmistakable sign of a very real headache. He'd forgotten how wonderful those were.

"It's lunacy," he continued, pacing again and trying to rub the pain from his forehead. "Insanity. Does a mouse need its tail snapped a thousand times before it realizes the cheese is rigged?"

"Humph. May I make a correction?"

"Correct all you want; you will not make me understand the point in her actions."

"Aghh." Ani threw up his arms, dramatically, in disgust, and began a pacing to match Taka's own, rubbing his forehead like a mimic. "Lunacy, I tell you. Four hundred years locked in a brooch and he still doesn't realize he's not the one who died all those years ago. You were never 'done in,' Taka, she was. Along with all the rest of your people. She doesn't have the luxury of centuries of hindsight. She doesn't have the memory to put this into perspective. Perhaps she wants to never remember again. Can you blame her?"

Taka stopped as the memory came upon him so quickly and vividly he gasped. And with the memory, almost immediately, the pain.

Chapter 9

1600 AD: Jaha, West Africa

The Great Hall was lit by candlelight and the brilliant violet, rose, and orange of the sunset. There was no sunset in the world like a sunset in the kingdom of Jaha. It was said his land was blessed and loved best by the Almighty, evidence written in the sky. Tonight the colors of the sunset lit the inside of the hall, the table of food, and the faces of their guests like fire; a fitting image for this important gathering of leaders.

Taka gazed across to the other end of the table where his queen, Zahara, sat. She was even more beautiful than the sunset. Her warm brown skin, her syrup brown eyes that could raise his spirits, bolster his strength, and caress him with love all in one glance. She was his favorite thing to look at. The brooch pinned to her shoulder sparkled in the light and set the beauty of her skin aflame. A gentle smile from her, subtle and discreet, promised that later, when they were alone, she would be neither of those things. A lick of desire stirred deep within him.

But it wasn't just his desire for her that made him anxious to be alone with her. Their conversations were always interesting. Her character studies, almost always accurate. Even tonight he sensed reticence in her upon entering the hall in her tight smile and cautious manner, but she was as charming and intelligent as any noble. He hadn't had time to speak to her before but he would be interested to hear what caused her caution. But that conversation would have to wait a little longer.

Pulling his attention away from his favorite subject he turned instead to the man beside him. He and this particular leader of a neighboring village had never been friends but they were here for a purpose. The second the man stopped speaking he took over.

"Then we are in agreement?" Taka encapsulated the conversation, anxious to be done. "We cannot allow invaders to pick us off one by one. We have a common purpose. Our villages fight as one, our goal one goal. More wine to toast!"

He held out the carafe and his eyes found Zahara again. Her eyes were warm in his when they shifted slightly, breaking contact. Taka felt the coldness of the loss of attention but suddenly, the expression on her face made him take notice. Her eyes widened and her mouth opened in a soundless scream.

Taka threw the wine carafe aside quickly to reach for his sword an instant before cold steel entered his side from the man closest him, as easily and ruthlessly as if he'd been a goat to slaughter. He clutched his side and watched as his hands were sliced upon the retreat of the steel, spilling hot blood from the wound of his torso into the deep gashes in his palms.

"Taka!" Zahara's scream pierced the previous solitude and at once a flurry of activity took over the hall. His guests were pulling swords quicker than his eyes could track. His men were struggling to fight the sudden attack, stunned by the sight of him, their leader, struck down before their very eyes. And as in a nightmare, Taka's brain calculated as man after man stormed the hall. Countless men, pouring in like a thousand ants overrunning a feast at a picnic. But these men came in slicing with swords, swinging with hatchets and machetes.

"Zahara," he breathed on a thin breath as pain had stolen his breath. For a moment his wife simply held his eyes in her own, stunned. As the moment stretched, so did his arm toward her even though the long table made it impossible to touch her and his wound made it impossible to stand. She reached toward him as well in a matching gesture, which ended abruptly when a rough arm came around her waist, pulling her struggling body away with force.

"No!" Taka cried at the sight. He would gut any man who touched his wife in disrespect. He would make the bastard pay with his head!

He grunted with effort to pull himself to his feet in order to protect her but the Great Hall swam around him and darkness claimed his sight; much like the strangers who came to his table that day his body, as well, had betrayed him.

Taka blinked his way into the present. He was back in the apartment, back in the United States, a different place and different time, but the feelings from centuries before were still just there on the surface, ready to pop open his heart.

"That was unnecessary," he ground out. "You imagine I've forgotten that day?"

"Yes, I believe you have," Ani said. "You ask if a mouse needs its tail snapped a thousand times before it realizes the cheese is rigged? Mice are one thing. The spirit that is Zahara is another. Maybe she prefers the devil she knows."

"What does that mean? What kind of riddle do you toss at me now?"

"I'm afraid I may have protected you too much as a child. My proximity gave the impression you were

owed special treatment in life, that you wouldn't have
to suffer the pains common to every man. I have ease of
communication with you and that's always been a gift to
me, as well, but you are human and some things can't be
explained in words. Humans need to feel to learn. I'll tell
you this: there is a flow to life. A natural current. Life will
follow that current and only a disruption can change it.
Only our Father has the power to disrupt it and He did
that for you. He stretched your whirlpool into a long,
winding stream. But you need to understand, He didn't
bring you all this way just to let you cause more pain for
the woman with the spirit you knew as Zahara."

"You say this as though I am the problem. I am only
reporting what I see."

"Yes, she is wounded. Her spirit, almost fatally. She
is so wounded that He allowed this interruption in your
cycle. He allowed you to do this because Violet needs you.
You are working for the Almighty, Taka Olufemi. You will
bring His child back to us."

Taka's hands went to his hips as he stared at Ani.
All these years he'd suffered because that was what the
Almighty wanted? "You both lied to me. You tricked me."

"Watch your mouth, son; we did no such thing. You
were given a choice. No, our Father didn't change life's
rules just so you could hold your wife in your arms. We
have different goals, but the same route nonetheless."

"The same route?" Taka thought of the dinner, the
conversation. He thought of Violet's behavior and choice
of men. He thought of how silent she'd been when they'd
laughed at his wife's murder. "Violet Jackson is not a
route I wish to take."

"Is that right?"

"Yes, that is so," Taka admitted, looking away from the
sudden recrimination in his Ani's eyes.

"Let me see if I understand. You believe her so pathetically inadequate that she no longer deserves your love? She fed you, clothed you, took time out of her day to make sure you enjoyed yourself, and you are a stranger."

"That was kind of her, but it doesn't change who she is."

"You don't know who she is!"

The uncharacteristic boom in the angel's voice reverberated through Taka's body and for a moment he faltered, silenced, finally. "I meant no disrespect," he said with bowed head, his alternative to groveling.

"Taka," Ani went on. Taka raised his eyes to find Ani's eyes filled to the brim with love. "The journey was for you, also. You judge too quickly, son, as if afraid if you waver you'll show weakness. Violet deserves more than a quick judgment and determination she isn't worthy. At one time she had complete faith in you, Taka; the least you owe her is the benefit of the doubt."

With that, his friend faded from view leaving Taka even more frustrated than when he'd arrived. Didn't he realize how much Taka wanted this to work? Didn't he see how much just one day had taken from him? Didn't he feel how much it tore him apart to see his wife in harm's way again?

He lay stretched out on the sofa again, pulling the mini blanket over himself. He braced his head on a bent arm as his eyes adjusted to the darkness. He only had two days. Two days to bring Zahara back or he was going to the everlasting inferno on a fool's errand.

Chapter 10

After light petting, a few kisses, and some murmurs of sympathy over his newly blackened eye, Jerome slammed the door shut behind him and came at Violet like a released convict, just like she liked, normally.

She screeched with surprise when he tossed her over his shoulder, short-lived when he buckled slightly and staggered his way into the bedroom to toss her onto the bed. He'd never tried that before. Certainly trying to make up for the loss of face after the dinnertime pummeling, but he failed miserably. It was the rubbing of his lower back with his hand and the pained expression on his face that ruined it.

"Darn, baby, you might have broke my back," he complained, going through contortions to prove his point.

Violet propped herself up on her elbows on the bed and frowned as she watched him make way too much fuss. She knew she wasn't light as a feather, but she was only a size fourteen! Maybe if he wasn't so puny with his pot belly and weak little boy arms, he could have lifted her just fine. Maybe if he had an ounce of class he would have avoided making noise about it. Maybe if he cared about her even a little he would have put on a happy face and bluffed his way through.

"It's okay, though," he said, a smarmy smile making its way over his face as he came toward her. "I'll let you make it up to me."

Make it up to him? Violet, Violet, why do you put up with it? her little voice inside said. She'd been ignoring the little voice for years. The little voice only told her what she didn't want to hear. It may have been absolutely correct, but she so didn't want to hear it. Her little voice made her vulnerable. It told her things like, "Just be yourself and people will like you." "Hard work will make you a success." And the oldie but goodie, "Open your heart to love." Well, she'd done those things before and been rewarded with rejection, exhaustion, and a broken heart. She and the little voice were enemies. So she did the opposite, as usual, and watched as Jerome came toward her. That's when her stomach flipped the first time.

"Stop," Violet said, pushing him away. Funny, her arms were shaky like noodles. She couldn't recall that ever happening before.

"What?"

Violet looked up at Jerome and therein lay the first problem. She normally tried not to look at Jerome when they got together. He wasn't an ugly man but there was no physical attraction from her end. At this moment in particular, she had as much desire for him as she had for a bikini wax, and unlike previous times, she couldn't force her stomach to quiet down and take it. It rumbled so loudly in protest that she threw a hand over her mouth to keep from losing the plate of ribs all over Jerome and his blackened eye. Then she ran to the bathroom.

To his credit, when she got back to the bedroom he made sympathetic noises. He even stroked her hair gently and said, "It's okay, baby. The food must've been bad. Get it out of your system?"

She nodded and ran a hand over her clammy, moist forehead. Goodness, she couldn't remember ever having a reaction this strong. Maybe it was the ribs and not him. Her agitated stomach gave credence to his theory.

"I'm going to sue those . . . incompetents," she sputtered. "I'm going to make sure they never poison anybody else. I'm going to make them sorry they ever . . ." But there was no need in finishing her whine because he was already at her again, kissing her feverish neck with gusto. This time when her stomach rolled she knew it had nothing to do with the ribs. Fact was, the more Jerome touched her the sicker she got. She pushed at him again and he finally pulled away, annoyed.

"You said you were okay," he barked.

"How about a half a second to make sure, Romeo? I know I'm irresistible but do you think you can wait to make sure I'm not dying before you try to get your groove on?" she snapped back, finally annoyed. She straightened her bodice pointedly, making every effort not to look in his face and using the time to figure out what the heck was going on.

From the very start she'd only been mildly attracted to Jerome. But she hadn't chosen him for his looks; she'd chosen him because he was moderately intelligent, had a decent job, and was somewhat malleable. Violet's strength was that nine times out of ten she knew how to manipulate his stubbornness to her favor. Reverse psychology was always a handy tool. And last but not least, she was a woman and a woman always had the power of sexual persuasion. At least, usually she did.

There had been plenty times in their relationship when they'd had sex to their consensual agreement. A couple times when they'd had it so that she could make up for a wrong she'd done. Lots of times when they'd had it simply to prevent his eye from wandering another way. She could count on one hand the number of times she'd actually enjoyed it.

Sex was overrated, she decided. There simply were not the fireworks that television and that *Sex and the City* show would have women believe. Sometimes she faked it. Okay, lots of times. But this time, she couldn't fake it. Not even for her own much-needed release. Not even superimposing Morris Chestnut's image onto her clueless Jerome could get her to let him touch her tonight.

But wait a minute. She closed her eyes and swallowed hard picturing six feet seven inches of bittersweet chocolate with shoulders as wide as a building and a chest built for a monument; strong brow, firm jaw, hawkish nose, eyes dark with intensity, and lips full and sensual, eager for tasting. Instantly the first twinge of lust returned to her libido.

"What's up, Violet? You okay or what?"

He came at her again, his head turned sideways, eyes closed and mouth open in order to insert his tongue into her mouth and for a brief, horrifying moment he looked like a bass her father caught when she was ten. She suppressed the gag, but he must have sensed something because his eyes flew open; her eyes must have betrayed the horror and disgust she was feeling because his widened even farther.

"What the—"

"I'm sorry, Jerome, I can't. Not tonight. I'm really not feeling well."

"But you said—"

"I know what I said; I changed my mind, okay? I'm sorry."

The normally unperceptive Jerome's squinted eyes told her he thought something else was up. He backed away and looked at her. "You saying you don't want to?"

"That's right. I'm sorry, not tonight."

Then he tossed a cloud of frustrated anger her way as he climbed off the bed to pull off his clothes.

"Did you hear me? I said—"

"I know what you said," he said without looking at her. "Whatever, Violet. Look, ain't nobody gonna be begging after your stuff so if you want to keep it to yourself, go ahead."

What? Huh? Of course somebody was gonna be begging after her stuff. Usually it was him! Now the little punk was trying to play her.

"Fine." She climbed off the bed too, to stand on her heels, smoothing her skirt. "Take me home then."

"I'm tired," he said. He had stripped to his underwear and was now pulling back the blankets and climbing under. "I'm going to bed."

Violet put her hands on her hips. "You can't go to bed; you have to take me home," she said to his shoulder and the side of his cheek.

"I ain't got to do nothing, Violet. Now climb your chunky behind in bed and shut up."

"Excuse me?"

"You heard me. I ain't going nowhere. I put up with a lot of crap tonight, Violet. The least you could do is break me off a little somethin' somethin'. But if you ain't gonna do that I ain't got to put out no special effort. So why don't you climb in and get some sleep like I'm about to do."

She shook her head in disbelief. "Let me get this straight: a few minutes ago you were as sweet as sugar to me and now you're being a jerk? How is that right?"

"A few minutes ago you were being sweet to me too. And then you became a witch. How is that right?"

Violet picked up the pillow closest to her and threw it at him. "Come on, Jerome, take me home. I want to go home now."

He moved, shrugging his shoulders under his sheet. "You know how to call a cab."

Violet stood there for a while until she realized he was really not going to drive her home. He was having some kind of snit and unfortunately she was stuck there. That was, unless she was willing to wait outside a dark apartment building in the middle of the night in a not-so-great neighborhood for a cab.

Ah, what the heck. She kicked off her shoes and unzipped her dress, climbing into the other side. She reached over and retrieved her pillow from where it had landed over him, and settled down.

Sleep didn't come but thoughts of the genie who was supposed to be granting her wishes did. The genie's presence was overwhelming. She couldn't think clearly when he was around. And there was something teasing her, constantly, like she'd forgotten her keys or left the oven on, or something. She snorted; that was ridiculous because she hardly ever used the oven and her keys were safely in her purse.

But still, it was something important enough that she couldn't shake it. Like her thoughts of the genie; getting those wishes was important, but thinking about him as if he were a man? That was just plain silly.

After a few hours of drifting in and out of sleep and hearing Jerome snore beside her, the black sky turned dark blue through the window and the day had risen enough that she felt okay getting a cab.

Once home, she walked gently on the carpet outside her apartment hoping to make as little noise as possible. Little noise was good; it increased her chances of being able to sneak into her bedroom without waking the genie sleeping on her sofa. Though there was no logical reason why she should care, but she really didn't want to have to answer any questions this morning. There was no way she would admit how poorly the evening had gone, and contrary to popular belief, she really did not like to lie unless absolutely necessary.

Chapter 11

Taka had not fared much better over the long night. Being in a state of limbo meant that usually he did not have the luxury of sleep or the respite of dreams to break his monotony. But finding himself in the apartment alone, not knowing how long he would be that way, provoked him to try his hand at the most basic of human needs. He had curled up on the sofa and blessedly, almost immediately he felt the first watery flutters of sleep teasing his consciousness. Several times his eyes opened quickly and he wondered how long they had been closed that time, since he had lost track. Even this was pleasurable to him.

When he was a little boy his thirst for information was insatiable. To appease it, his father, the king, would teach him things all the time. He allowed Taka to sit in the kitchen to watch womenfolk create sumptuous meals from seemingly little. He allowed Taka to watch the man who would file the hoofs of the horses, and keep them bathed and healthy. He allowed Taka to watch the warriors train in the field, tossing their spears and fighting each other by hand to increase their strength. He even allowed Taka to watch a child being born, and Taka held the hand of the young mother, barely out of childhood herself, as she grimaced, screamed, and squeezed life into the world from within the safety of her gentle thighs. He'd seen a lot as a child. But what remained with him the most were the lessons he learned from his father's tongue. It was one such lesson that came to him with clarity while he slept.

His father squatted on the ground beside him as Taka struggled to remove a tuber from the ground. It was in a little garden that was Taka's very own piece of land. His parents had felt the future king should know what it felt like to farm, especially since so many of the villagers survived by farming. So instead of having him watch, they'd set aside a little square of land just for him to tend. Nothing too big, but big enough for a child. No one else was allowed to so much as add a drop of water even if the land was parched. It was Taka's lesson, and because he was such an ambitious child, he took it seriously.

He'd chosen to grow potatoes. Both the white kind and the more familiar sweet potatoes. Now they were ready to come up, and his father sat beside him while Taka dug and pulled and grunted against the plant that seemed to refuse to be pulled. Finally he fell back on his behind, his eyes round with frustration, his tender palms red and burning from the effort.

"I cannot do it, Papa," he said plaintively to the man who watched him with knowing eyes.

"But you can, my son. You cannot give up."

Taka grew angry and stubborn. "I cannot. The roots are stuck in the ground so deeply they cannot be moved."

"Everything can be moved, Taka. Nothing in life is immoveable."

But Taka had grown so tired and dejected, and so annoyed by his father's insistence that he do what was obviously impossible, he crossed his arms with indignation. "It is a worthless plant. The whole garden is worthless. I do not care if it rots."

The look on his father's face told him that he was being ridiculous, but Taka refused to budge. His father gestured toward the plant for him to start again. Taka looked away, fully expecting to receive the wrath of his father's anger in return. Instead the king spoke to him gently.

"My son, you will learn that in life few things will come easily. As the son of the king you have privileges that normal people do not, but that does not mean it will always be so. In order to become a man, a good man, you must learn to fight for what you want. And fight for what is yours." He reached down and pulled the plant, testing its dedication to the ground and feeling it give a little. "I will not always be here to ease your way, Taka."

Taka's arms fell and he looked at the large, strong man beside him. "Where will you go, Papa? Why will you leave me?"

The king released the plant to smile at his son who, he knew, thought he would live forever. He reached out and smoothed his son's wooly hair. "We are men, son, and must go the way of all things that live. Just like the animals we raise, so will we too someday pass on. And when I go you will be responsible for many. For that reason, more than most, you must learn how to hold on to what is yours." He gestured toward the plant again. "You do not give up because it is too hard. You must fight even harder."

But Taka's thoughts were still stuck on the idea that his father might someday leave him. He looked upon him with stricken eyes. "I will ask Ani to keep you with me always. You and Mama. He will do it for me."

The king frowned. "Taka, you are truly gifted to speak as you do with the Great One. But it is right that someday we will be gone. That is the way of life, son. You must accept that."

Taka did not want to accept that. No, it wasn't right, and he would never say it was. He would fight it, just as his father said. Just as he would fight the resistance of the plant in the ground.

The king smiled as Taka pitched forward to grab the plant and wrestle with it, straining his round face. He thought Taka's renewed energy surely meant his son now understood the importance of working hard. But Taka's energy came from his anger and determination. Anger that he should be told that something he loved could be taken from him, and determination that it would not be taken easily.

Taka woke, sitting up on the sofa, bathed in sweat, heart pounding. *Ah, this is what it is like to dream.* He remembered now. Far from peaceful, beautiful images it could also bring this pounding fear, this awareness.

His father had died in battle when he was fifteen years old and he had learned that despite his relationship with Ani he was, indeed, not immune to loss. And he had become more determined than ever to keep what was his. Now he realized what had driven him to make the agreement. It was not only his great love, but also his great desire for vengeance against the Almighty for daring to take something from him again.

Taka spent the rest of the night and the early morning fumbling around the apartment checking out the surroundings and modern conveniences. He found several bags of little disks wrapped in foil, labeled with variations of chocolate. Ah, he remembered chocolate: a treat for the gods. He tore open the light covering of the bag and unwrapped a disk, sniffing it before tossing it in his mouth whole. He stopped when something burst between his teeth. He looked at the wrapping again. Crisped rice within chocolate! He chewed slower and then increased his speed as his tongue oriented itself to the new, delightful taste. It seemed there was one decent thing about modern times, at least.

He fumbled with the machine that had held coffee the day before and looked it over a few good times, figuring out where the water went and what to do with the little papers in the box beside that said COFFEE FILTERS. While he worked the machine, he called out to Ani to continue the conversation they'd begun the night before. Perhaps to pick an argument about the Almighty's clever use of dreams to whip him into shape, but Ani wasn't in a conversational mood, and Taka yelled out in frustration.

At that moment Violet walked in the door looking guilty, her shoes in her hand. Taka was caught a moment by her beauty, fighting the urge to immediately go to her and pull her into his arms. His one piece of heaven on earth. His one selfish desire.

"I heard you speaking to someone," she said, dropping her purse and keys on the table, the shoes on the floor, and walking into the kitchen to look at him suspiciously.

It was the look that woke him up. It was not the look her face should bestow upon him. Zahara's face had always looked at him with admiration and unrestrained love. But this face, Violet's face, looked at him with suspicion. Guarded caution. Doubt. Mistrust. He felt his heart seize with the impact and looked away from her, she hurt his eyes so.

He fumbled with the machine and she still stood there with her arms crossed and her hip jutted out, apparently having eyed her bag of treats on the counter.

"Well, just help yourself to my stuff, why don't you?" she said.

He took an extra-long time chewing, made a point of swallowing loudly, and stopped destroying her machine long enough to pull another candy bar out of the bag to, pointedly, begin chewing again.

Zahara had never been selfish. Zahara would have given the last morsel of food to a stranger, even though she was queen. And he would have given everything he had to her. Gladly, without being asked, he had showered her with gifts and tokens of his love. It had been a joy to share with her. And yet this woman now looked at him as if he were a thief for having eaten some candy.

"You have no food in this house," he said gruffly. "I am supposed to starve because you are too self-involved to remember you have a guest?"

"I fed you yesterday, didn't I?" she snapped back. "And who were you talking to before I walked in?"

"That is my affair."

"It's my apartment; it is my affair."

"If you had been here you would have no need to ask me to whom I was speaking. The next time, if you are so concerned, perhaps you should stay home and watch me."

"Mhmm. Move over, I need a cup. Coffee. I need coffee."

He moved and watched her lean awkwardly in front of him to reach for a mug off a high shelf. The green dress was only slightly mussed from the night before, but her skin was as perfect as ever. It glowed with life, like if one were to mine it they would fine gold living just beneath the surface. The brown was so warm and inviting, so comforting and soft even though it could flare with fire at his slightest touch. Even now, he was so near he could touch her, so close it would be easy to lean down and sniff the perfume of her hair. The braids were gone and the black strands were straightened somehow, but he still recognized it. He still recognized her scent, her essence. His lungs longed to fill with her perfume.

"Excuse me, genie, are you blocking me from the coffee as payback for what I said about the chocolate? Because that's mine too," she said, cruelly interrupting his fantasy.

It was only when he stepped back farther that he realized how close he'd come to taking her in his arms. Fortunately, she seemed none the wiser as she poured herself a cup of coffee and sipped it desperately, plopping into a chair at the little kitchen table, stretching and wriggling life into her feet, all the while unaware that he couldn't keep his eyes off her.

"Where have you been?" His voice was too hoarse and he put a touch of anger in it to mask her effect. "I have been waiting for you all night. Three days and you have already squandered one." His statement generated nothing but a blank look and as she took another sip of coffee with a deadpan expression on her face, he analyzed the look more completely. It was a look he remembered vaguely from a time long ago. A look some of his warriors would wear while they gathered to practice or to battle. A look that would usually come with a ribald story of their intimate activities with their women the evening before. A look of success and acquisition. He glared at her, his face contorted with disgust.

"By all that is sacred and holy, please do not tell me you allowed that imbecile license to your secret garden? Woman, how could you let that pathetic insect of a man defile your body? Your temple? It is like . . . like. . . a dog taking a piss upon the altar."

"In all fairness, the defiling went both ways."

"I do not want to hear this; the absurdity cuts my ears like a thousand blades. You allowed that piece of nothing to take you without the blessing of the Father. You allowed him to use you for your precious gifts while he offered nothing in return. He is not worthy of your charms."

"Says who? We are engaged to be married, sort of. If he's not worthy yet, I don't know when he ever will be."

"I have met the cretin; he is not marriage material. Oh, he would marry you, of that I have no doubt. With pomp and circumstance he would put on a show for the world but you have only to look into his beady eyes to see what he lacks. How can a woman of your intelligence and insight become so close to a man and not see that beneath the shell there is nothing of substance? You have so much to offer; why would you give it all to the likes of him?"

"You have no right to judge him. You don't know him," Violet said, her face pinching with annoyance.

"It is not him I judge; it is you. This man selfishly takes the most sacred and honored from you as if it is his right because you allow it. It is wrong and it I will not pretend otherwise."

"Good Lord, who asked you to pretend anything? Who even asked you? Now I remember why I never had a roommate. I was in a good mood until I walked in here."

"Rubbish. You will not convince me in a million years that that toad of a man you call a fiancé could possibly satisfy you properly, any more than you can convince me that in the aftermath you could feel anything other than revulsion."

"Genie—"

"Perhaps I misjudged you. I suppose I assumed that because you have a business and speak with a sharp tongue that you are more intelligent than you actually are." He poured himself a cup of coffee as well, taking a big sip. He couldn't sit opposite her not knowing where she had been and whom she had been with. If it weren't for his strong stomach . . .

He turned away and stalked to a window, preferring the freedom to speak to her without having to visualize another man's hands on her or see her big brown eyes smirk with amusement at his pain.

"I am in this time and place to grant you three wishes, an opportunity that will never come again in your lifetime, a gift written about in books and relayed in childhood stories as a fantasy because adults are too jaded and hardened to even entertain the idea that there is a Higher Power and that He has the ability to grant miracles. I am a miracle standing in your home, woman. I have traveled a thousand miles and lived hundreds of years to fulfill a destiny. There is no more personal a relationship than that and if any living being has more of a right to judge you and this situation I would like to see them. I would dare anyone to argue that I do not—"

The slam of a door stopped his string of conversation. Only a half-empty coffee cup sat at the table.

Chapter 12

Violet pulled off her unzipped dress and flung it across the room. It was bad enough she'd had a bad night with Jerome and discovered she had unseemly desires for a genie, but to return to find him wide awake and stuffing himself with her period chocolate, well, enough was enough.

The thigh-highs came off easily; she shot them into the hamper like basketballs, missing both times, when she heard the indignant bellow of her soon-to-be homeless new roommate as he banged on the door. Apparently he'd paused the love affair with his own voice long enough to realize she'd left the room.

"I am a king!"

Humph, she thought with an eye roll.

"You will not treat me like that vagabond you allowed to pillage your womanly treasures!"

Good Lord, what would the neighbors think? Probably the same thing they already thought, that she was a scandalous floozy. At least that was what she hoped they thought. A bad reputation was a boon for a woman such as herself. It was the good girls who got all the grief. But for the sake of argument, he needed to be set straight.

"Keep your voice down!" she yelled back. "It's none of your business who pillages my treasures! Now get away from my door or I swear I'm going to take that little rock of yours and throw it into the Scioto!" A lie, of course. Now that she knew its value she was never going to part with the thing. Who knew; if this whole thing worked out, maybe she could rub it again in a couple of years, maybe wear a disguise and trick him into three quickies.

"I am trying to help you see the error of your ways, woman. You would do well to listen to me. And show a little gratitude for the gift I am."

"Gift? Ha!" she laughed, losing the bra. "I knew a genie was too good to be true. I can't just get three wishes like in the books? No, apparently Violet's miracle comes with a price. I don't know if the three wishes are worth listening to your mouth, genie." Bluff, of course. If this thing was legit, three wishes would be more than worth the sound of his voice. She'd listen to him gripe until down under froze over if it would get her what she wanted.

"I can sit in silence for the remaining two days waiting only for your wishes to come. Is that what you would prefer?"

Violet couldn't help but smile at that ridiculousness. She dropped her underwear and wrapped herself in her robe. "Don't even tease me like that; we both know you don't have the self-control to keep your mouth shut. You've been whining and complaining since you came out of that stone. Releasing you was like releasing my worst cases of PMS all wrapped up in six feet of overgrown baby." *Way, way overgrown baby. Overgrown baby with shoulders like balls of granite under a layer of dark brown velvet and abs firm enough to tap dance on.* "Why don't you make yourself useful and find my newspaper. My neighbor seems to think he is entitled to it the way he helps himself to it every day. Just like a man."

"I do not know what PMS is and I am closer to seven feet tall, and the true problem is that you cannot tolerate someone asking you the questions you know you should be asking."

Violet opened the door and stopped suddenly at the solid wall of his chest before climbing her gaze upward into his dark eyes. His look was fierce, but not fierce in the usual way; fierce in a way that made her suddenly hot under the terry robe. Smoky and intimate. Her hands clenched the robe closed in response to the sudden perverse desire to let go and let it all hang out.

Now, that couldn't happen. She could not get busy with a genie. She might be a bad girl, but she tried not to mess with the cosmos. That begged the question, why would the cosmos put a tasty morsel of a man like this in front of her? Surely the cosmos knew what she was missing in the bedroom department. What good could come of putting man candy in her path? Surely the cosmos knew she was almost engaged!

The slight tic in his jaw found an answer somewhere in her nether regions as she picked up the earthy scent of him, the heat of his closeness, the beguiling way his neck bent ever so gently, as though awaiting the feel of her hand on the back of it, pulling the ultimate prize closer.

She longed to run her hand in a long swipe from his arm all the way up in a smooth stroke ending in the short, short, textured hair. She could almost feel it in her hands, could imagine her fingertips in it so clearly it was unseemly. As if his body could see her private thoughts, his full lips parted slightly as though ready to kiss her silly. And she was ready to be kissed silly.

Get a grip, Violet. The man is a genie! He's not even real. He's like a cartoon character or something! At least that's what she had to tell herself to get her body functioning like normal again. She swallowed her desire and planted one hand on her hip, riling the ire that worked so well for her on a daily basis.

"Are you going to block me at every turn, genie? My period chocolate, the coffee, and now the bathroom; you're

really starting to be more trouble than you're worth." She
waited for his response, anything to take her mind off the
assault she had almost committed on his person, and was
surprised when only a strange, choked sound emerged
from his voice. Then he stepped out of her way and she
breathed a sigh of relief. Skirting him, Violet stomped
into the bathroom, slammed the door behind her, and
immediately sagged against the other side.

That was close. Too close! As honest as she was to
herself about her lack of physical attraction to Jerome,
she didn't want to be a cheater and one second more
standing that close to genie and there would have been
some crazy, unreal, cartoon cheatin' going on.

One minute she was threatening to throw his home into
a place he'd never heard called "Scioto," the next minute
she was standing before him clutching a covering in a
way that made it clear she was bare underneath. He'd lost
all sense seeing her standing before him, close enough
to stroke and be stroked. He could almost feel her hand
on the back of his neck pulling his head and lips toward
hers. Sometimes Zahara would use a slim middle finger
to tease the back of his neck, stroking back and forth
leisurely until the fire of his desire could take no more
teasing and he would groan a kiss into the sweet skin of
her neck to stop the exquisite torture. A gentle, soft laugh
from her, so low in her throat to be almost silent, would
signify her conquer of his will. It was a sweet, sensual
sound of pleasure she always made when he capitulated
to her. He always capitulated.

Though his body had waited for her touch, the lack of
it reminded him of who he was and what he was almost
about to do. He had only been capable of choking out a
pathetic husky sound in apology and allowed her to pass,

watching her backside in pale pink fuzzy cloth switch by him to enter the bathroom. After she slammed the door on him, yet again, Taka had looked down at the telltale sign of his own sudden distress and covered his shame with both hands, gently pounding his forehead against the nearest doorframe.

Taka took a shaky breath through shakier lips and looked to the ceiling to speak to his tormentors. "This is no use. She is not my wife and you will not allow me to help her become my wife. I have condemned myself to a lifetime of torture for this woman whose only likelihood to my wife is her face, and body," he gurgled, taking a deep breath on that note. "And you will not allow me to remind her of who she truly is."

Silence.

A frown sprung up between his eyes and he fidgeted. He had to do something with this pent-up frustration. He was feeling angry and helpless and knew himself well enough to know those feelings would only gain in intensity if he did not alleviate them.

Something popped into his head. Violet had said something before that he'd only barely heard but now rang like a beacon in his head. The man next door stole her paper every morning? Stole from her? A common thief. Right next door. Like a cool glass of water to a man starving of thirst, he sighed with relief that he'd found a proper outlet for his anger. If he could not speak his mind to the spirit of his dead wife, he would most certainly make due with a neighbor who took liberties with Violet's property. Happily he stood and walked to the door to make a short visit with the neighbor.

Chapter 13

Violet made sure the coast was clear before making her way back into her bedroom for morning meditation. Her quiet time quickly dissolved into further thoughts of the genie and comparisons to her almost-betrothed.

So what if she didn't have the hots for Jerome? At least he didn't criticize her every move. So what if Jerome was not the best man in the world? At least they understood each other. Sure, maybe he used her more than he loved her. But she knew that going in. Had she known the second she'd laid eyes on him that he would never love her? She couldn't answer that, even now. But she could answer the question of why. Jerome was easy and safe. And there was nothing wrong with that.

Still, it was a little annoying. If she was headed for disaster, wouldn't it be a genie-like thing to do to smooth her path a little? Would it kill him to use a little genie sense to steer her in the right direction? She always sensed that there was more he wanted to say, more she needed to hear; more, besides criticisms or put-downs. Something about his deep, hooded eyes told her he knew much more than he revealed.

She finished dressing and left her bedroom just as he was stomping in from the hallway, muttering under his breath. She raised an eyebrow.

"Who were you talking to this time?"

He tossed her newspaper onto the table. "You shall have no more trouble receiving your daily paper. The man next door folded like a Chinese fan the second I looked at him. Men today are mealy, pathetic little cowards, are they not? In my day, if a man was not prepared to fight to the death for what he felt was his right then he, himself, would not deign to assert himself. Today, you have thieves who are more frightened than their victims and men who talk filth to women out loud and then are surprised when they are smacked down." His eyes darted to her like a spear. "And, by all that is holy, why does it take so much time for women to prepare themselves for the day?"

"By all that is holy, why do men always complain when they know they like the results?" Violet breezed past his shrewd stare. She dumped her old coffee for a fresh cup and then unwrapped some chocolate. Breakfast. "Besides," she explained, "I took a little time to meditate. I was feeling a little un-centered. There's a little more tension in my home these days than usual." She intentionally punctuated that point with a direct look and a loud sip of coffee.

"Is that a fact?" His eyes narrowed slightly. "Perhaps if you discard a little dead weight there would be no tension at all." He sat on the edge of her sofa and returned her steady look.

"I'm sure you would like nothing better than to take care of that for me, genie."

"You are correct. But my friend tells me I am not allowed to discard the trash in your life. Even if it is rotten and putrid and the stink of it fills every corner and crevice of your life, it is not my place to solve that particular housecleaning issue. So I will not meddle."

"Were you this clever when you were a king? I don't know what sin I committed to piss God off so much that He sent you down here to be a pain in my rear end but I suspect I know what you did. You mouthed off at Him, didn't you? You did that same thing to Him that you're doing here and He didn't tolerate it and put you in that rock, right?"

"I'm not discussing my stone with the likes of you," he said, petulantly.

"The likes of me?"

"That's right. A woman who would throw herself away on trash and then have the audacity to approach me as if I am less than nothing. I am a king. You would do well to remember that."

"Oh yes, King Taja."

"You know my name. Do not toy with me."

"My, my. The king has a temper. Well guess what?" She bent forward at the waist to lean toward him. "So do I! I don't care whether you're a king or knight or jester; you're not *my* king and you will not be giving orders around here. I'm the one in charge of this palace."

"You are in charge of nothing. In my day power was in strength and in battle, and rightly so. Today, it seems the only respected power is in the ability to control one another, no matter to what end. You are a puppet on a string. The female friend, Brenda, she seems to spur you into action very easily. She makes you anxious. Like too much of this juice of the bean. And yet where she leads, you follow."

"I'm not following anything. Brenda and I have been friends for years. We've always been competitive, but that's the reason I am where I am today. She helps me to try harder."

"At what?"

"Everything. Work, love, everything."

Taka looked at her. "Is life so much of a competition for you, then?"

"Life is a journey. And no, I may never win, but I'll die trying. I'll rest when I'm six feet under, not a moment before. I'm a fighter, genie. You don't know me, so naturally, you don't understand my approach. But someday I will have everything I want, you mark my words."

"I see. Then perhaps the problem is in what you want. That man of yours . . ." His face soured on the topic. "He takes your power as well. He takes your pride and your dignity. He takes your smile away and brings hardness to your face. He makes you nervous, encourages your meanness. He enjoys seeing you wound others, enjoys seeing you wound yourself. They will all cause you pain. I see it, clearly."

"Yeah, well." She snorted without much mirth. "I know what to expect from them. They've already hurt me as much as they can, so there's nothing else they can do to me. I'm more worried about strangers like you." *Whoa, whoa, whoa, Violet. Danger, Violet Jackson, danger!* her instincts screamed. "I know you think Jerome is a mistake—"

"Your mistake is that you are negligent toward yourself," he said, his face going serious. "I recognize negligence because I was negligent toward my wife. Perhaps because I knew her heart was mine I did not worry over it. Not until it was all gone did I realize what I had lost. I would hate to see you deny yourself and follow my path."

Violet felt heartstrings tug at the despair in his voice. *Poor genie.* If he would only follow her way of thinking he would never, ever have to feel such pain. She and Jerome may not have been in love, but they would never leave each other as lost as the genie sounded.

"I'm sorry for you," she said.

"I am sorry for my wife. She never knew how deeply she held my heart, and how much I regret that the trust she placed in me was misplaced. You asked if I am being punished. My punishment is of my own making; I am finally old and tired enough to admit it. But my task was never meant to be a punishment. I am on a mission. It is a different thing," he said unconvincingly.

Violet wasn't the religious sort, but she was curious. "So, when I hear you talking, do you talk to God? That's who sent you here?"

"That is who sent me here, all right," he grumbled. "But that is not to whom I speak. I only speak to friends."

Hmm, trapped in a stone and sent to do missions he hates by God, who isn't his friend? She didn't speak her thoughts but he must have read it on her face.

"No, you come to the wrong conclusion," he said.

"Hey, I'm just saying. I pray but nothing ever happens. Then you show up and you're cranky and uptight and not friends with God? Should I be worried, here?"

"The underworld is most certainly in my future but the evil one is not my master yet," he grumbled. "You say you pray? What do you pray for, Violet?"

Violet looked at him, a flush of embarrassment making her face hot. "When I was young I prayed for my father not to die, but he did. And then I prayed for my mother not to remarry, but she did. And then I prayed that my stepfather would come to love me like he loved his own children so I could have my mother back, but he didn't. And then I prayed that I was making the right decision allowing myself to love someone and we both know how that turned out. And a lifetime of little things I've prayed for that never turned out. So then I stopped praying. And I stopped being disappointed."

"No, I do not believe that is true. I believe you live in disappointment. You have obviously given up on hope."

"Hope and twenty-five cents won't buy you a cup of coffee, genie." She shrugged. "I make my own opportunities. Everything I have is because I've worked hard for it. You're the first thing that's ever been given to me, and frankly, this experience isn't turning out to be a screaming success. And look at you, you're always so sad. You believe in something, whatever it is, and look where it's gotten you."

He grimaced. "It is because I know how good things can be that I am so unhappy now. I have tasted euphoria and I have tasted the dregs of despair. Presently I am so close to the mouth of the underworld I can feel the flames licking my face," he said cracking another wry smile. "Perhaps that is my destiny. It doesn't have to be yours."

Violet didn't know how to respond to that. Sincerity was not something she came across often and her emotion took to it like a thirsty man to water or a lonely woman to a confidante. She liked his honesty. She liked his face. She liked the intensity in his eyes and the way his followed hers steadily. She liked that he didn't back down or cower to her aggression. She liked the way she felt when he was near. She liked too much about him.

"Listen, about this, us, and our constant butting heads; I know in your own way you're trying to help me but you don't understand. You were a king, once, and this" —she gestured around her—"this is all just silly nothing to you, that's obvious. The only logical conclusion is that we're both being punished and this is like some sort of existen-tialist afterlife on earth or you're the ghost of Violet's lost conscience or some such nonsense. Regardless, why don't we just agree to not tear each other apart until I figure out what to do with the last two wishes? I'll try not to be too much of a pain, even if you do take up a lot of space in my tiny apartment. I'll try not to harass you if you do the same. Deal?"

The expression in his eyes was indecipherable, his voice without its customary accusation. "Your life is not silly. I never said your life was silly."

"Genie, I'm not clueless. I can tell how you feel about me. I can feel your disgust and I can see it in your eyes.

Last night you looked at me like . . ." She sighed as the wave of hurt from the night before swept over her again. She didn't understand why she should feel anything. But she did. "It doesn't matter. Heck, if I were looking in on my own life, maybe I'd think it was pointless too; but I've worked hard for it, put a lot of blood, sweat, and tears into it. It's the only life I have and it's important to me whether or not it is to you. My decisions may be wrong to you, but they're mine. My mistakes to make, even if for half a second I may wish someone else was making them. I don't always know what to do, King, but I'm doing my best. Isn't that what you did when you were human? The best you knew how?" She looked at him hard for a moment and, when he didn't answer, went on, too committed to stop now.

"And, I'm sorry about last night. You didn't want to come to dinner and I was being selfish. I just . . ." *Tell him, Violet! Oh, what the heck.* "I just thought it'd be nice to have a friend; you know, a new person at the table who isn't personally invested in making my life miserable." She laughed slightly at the revelation she only just discovered at this moment. It was true. The people in her life weren't very nice. And neither was she. "My bad. Don't worry about tonight; I won't make you go through that again."

Violet trailed off awkwardly, already sorry for her honesty. He was looking at her like she'd sprouted three heads and she felt like she might as well have. She felt terrible. This self-reflection crap was a crock. She much preferred the ignorant bliss of yesterday.

"I've got to get going." She stood up and smoothed her skirt, heading for the front table and her purse. "I've got an appointment. I'll be late."

She jerked open the front door and was two steps out when she slammed it behind her and leaned against it.

The moisture in her eyes was unwelcome and unbidden. *Get a grip, Violet!* It didn't matter what he thought of her. He'd be gone in a day. Gone with his judgments and complaints and scowl. For some reason, that didn't make her feel any better.

She wiped her eyes, took a deep breath, and headed off to start her day.

Chapter 14

Taka sat at the table, still stunned, looking at the closed front door. His body quaked with the need to follow Violet out, chase her down, and pull her into his arms. He knew with visceral certainty that he had finally been touched by his wife's spirit. But it was as he had been told: Violet Jackson had been hurt and now preferred the devil she knew. But with Violet there was hope within her hopelessness; fearlessness within her fear; happiness just waiting for unhappiness to step aside.

He knew this behavior and recognized it well because he was exactly the same. He was a prime example of a man who wanted one thing and courted the opposite outcome.

He was a walking conflict and she was his mate.

Taka felt shame for the first time in a long time. What a disservice he had done to them both by refusing to scratch the surface. He'd been so disappointed that Violet didn't hold his wife's memories or life experiences, he hadn't taken a moment to discover hers. He hadn't spent a second trying to get to know her until just a few minutes ago.

But he was learning, even if he was slow to it. His self-righteousness would be the ticket to the destruction of them both. Somehow he would have to temper his natural arrogance if he could hope to make this work. And he had less than two days to get it right.

He finished off the coffee and was rinsing the pot when a knock on the door jarred him from his thoughts. Opening it, he had to drop his eyes to see the surprised face of a girl who appeared to be pre-woman and a shorter young boy with a backward cap over braided hair beside her. The girl-woman held a white bag with a scent that wafted up to his nose. His stomach grumbled in recognition of sustenance.

"Who are you?" the woman child asked. "Where's Violet?"

"Violet is not here. May I help—"

"You a lie," the little boy declared.

Taka looked down at the child, amused by the audacity of such a small little thing to challenge a grown man's word so openly. In his day a child dared not speak to an adult in such a manner lest he be cuffed across the head. Taka's hand itched to correct the slight but he restrained himself.

"I do not lie, imp."

"Violet ordered this food," the boy said. "I heard her voice through the phone myself, she was talking loud enough."

The girl scrutinized the white paper attached to the bag. "She said, 'deliver it to my apartment.' That's what it says right here." She looked at Taka suspiciously. "Who are you? I ain't never seen you here before."

Taka brightened. Yet again Violet had surprised him; he would have more than chocolate treats to coat his belly. He grabbed the bag from the girl-woman's hands.

"Violet ordered this?"

The girl nodded.

"Then who I am is of no concern to you. Thank you." He went to shut the door and the girl stopped the action with her body, moving unsurely into the doorway, seemingly to follow him. Taka headed to the kitchen. He wondered at the boy and girl still loitering anxiously in the doorway, but his stomach growled like a dog chained near to a roasted piece of meat. Being in his stone all these years did not atrophy the body. In fact, he was in the same condition he had been in the night he almost died, short of the stab wound in the side. Fully conditioned and ready for battle. Easily able to consume massive amounts of food to keep his strength and muscles strong and firm. And right now his muscles needed protein and two strange children were not going to keep him from it.

He pulled the white container out onto the counter and opened it, pleased when it contained an overwhelming amount of food. Eggs; two brown, cylindrical items that smelled like meat; two strips of something else that smelled heavenly; round, flaky pastries of some sort; and a smaller container filled with something off-white in color. He looked to the girl in question. She looked back.

"I . . . It's gravy. Sausage gravy."

He pointed at the links.

"Sausage," she said in a tone that suggested he was crazy.

But he continued, pointing at the strips.

"Bacon."

"And what animal makes this sausage and bacon?"

"Darn, mister." The boy came in farther, a look of such irritation on his smooth baby face Taka wondered how someone so young could even form such an expression. "Where you come from you don't know what bacon is?"

Taka was growing weary of the child's rudeness. He looked to the girl who appeared shell-shocked as he grabbed a fork and prodded the eggs. There was something underneath.

"It's an omelet!" she said quickly.

"Yeah, just an omelet," the boy repeated.

Taka didn't care; he dug his fork in and shoved a big bite into his mouth and it wasn't until he was chewing that he noticed the two of them backing slowly toward the door, eyes wide. That was when the heat hit him.

First his tongue began a slow, seething fire that spread to the back up on the roof, opening up on his gums. *The little vagabonds!*

"It was supposed to be for her!" the boy declared, as if the explanation was sufficient. "Run, Tasha!"

Taka vaguely heard their escape as he fumbled around for a glass and, when one wasn't readily available, went to the sink and fumbled with the gadgets until water ran into his cupped hands. As he drank he managed to curse them through gulps. *Hooligans!* If his lips weren't burning he would chase them down.

"You are lucky I don't turn you both upside down by your ankles and shake the mischief out of you!" he yelled. He could only hope they were still close enough to hear his rasp.

Finally after a few minutes the burn had dimmed to a simmer and he went back to the offending food, poking around with his fork. There, under the layer of cheese and over the top of the eggs he found the hidden layer of dried red pepper flakes, about a quarter of an inch thick, topped with small strips of glistening fresh pepper. He recognized the offender from his travels. Small but deadly. Habanero.

"Ragamuffins," he groused. But then he picked up the box and used his fork to scrape away most of the spicy blend, knowing that some heat would remain. A little pepper he could take, and the food was good. He only hoped pepper was the only offending ingredient in this meal. After the minor surgery, it was surprisingly tasty. He put on more coffee to wash it down and sat back down at the little table, sipping and thinking.

The food had obviously been meant for Violet. Sabotage even from babes; what a complete circle of betrayal she had woven for herself. If he didn't find a way to unlock the part of her she hid behind her shell, it wouldn't matter. If she was going to spend all her time romping with the cretin of a man she called her fiancé, the whole subject was moot anyway. He might as well curl up in his stone and prepare for the Almighty to slingshot him straight to the devil.

A knock at the door made him look at it for a long moment, wondering what other torture awaited on the other side. Should he answer it or should he leave it? A second, forceful knock followed and he stood, walking to the door and pulling it open with gusto. One of the men from the night before: the one named Gary. The ex. Taka frowned.

"Violet is not here," he said gruffly, and began to close the door only to have the other man put his hand up to stop it.

"Hey, I didn't come to see Violet. I came to see you," he said.

Taka's frown deepened. "And why would you want to see me?" he barked, looking down at him.

"Can I come in?" Gary asked. "Look, brother, I won't be long but I don't want to be standing out here in the hall spreading my business."

Taka gritted his teeth and opened the door to allow the man entrance. Gary sauntered to the kitchen where he immediately went to the coffee pot and poured himself a cup. A cup of Taka's hard-made coffee! It was enough to make him want to pummel the man into the ground.

"You said you have something to speak of. You cannot speak and drink at the same time."

Gary, who'd gotten his cup halfway to his lips, put it down and shook his head. "You are one unfriendly S.O.B."

Taka didn't know what S.O.B. meant, but if it was an extension of the "unfriendly" adjective, he was satisfied that he was coming across with the desired effect. He nodded and said, "Yes, I am an unfriendly S.O.B. So now that that is established perhaps you will get on with what you have to say and be on your way."

"Okay, look, man, you ain't got to be getting all uptight with me, okay? I'm just here for one thing. You know me and Brenda will be getting married soon."

"I gathered that."

"Well, gather this. Keep your cousin on a leash."

"I do not understand." Taka tightened. He suspected he did understand. He suspected it was an expression he was not going to like, especially since it involved his "cousin" and "leash" in the same sentence.

"Just what I said, man. Look, me and Violet had something awhile back, but it wasn't nothing. We was just kickin' it, you know?"

"No, I don't know." Taka leaned against the counter, his blood starting to thump in anger. "Why don't you explain it to me? I am unfamiliar with the ways of this . . . place. Enlighten me."

The maggot had the grace to blush either from embarrassment or sudden discomfort. "Look, man, all I'm saying is, I don't think Violet really understands it's gonna happen. I mean, I *will* marry Brenda. And I don't want no drama. I don't want her to be making trouble for my girl and getting her all upset. Maybe you should tell her that."

"You're concerned for the emaciated woman? That's why you're here?"

"Emac . . . ? Yeah, man, Brenda. Violet can be one mean b . . ." He stopped at the warning on Taka's face. "One mean woman when she wants to be. And I don't think she really believes that me and Brenda are tight. But it's gonna happen. I'm marrying Brenda. And since you're here and all, I thought you could help Violet get through this with her head on straight. I ain't gonna be tolerating no crap from her. What we had is over. Period. It don't matter how good she looks. It's over. Tell her that."

Taka put his hands in his pockets and kept a rein on his temper as he thought that over. When he spoke he chose his words carefully, his voice coming out firm and tight.

"So, let me understand you correctly. You were 'kickin' it' with Violet, but broke her heart to be with her best friend. And now that you and her friend are getting married, you want me to help Violet to accept the fact gracefully, keep her mouth shut, and participate in the wedding to make Brenda happy. Despite the fact that the both of you betrayed her and hurt her. Despite the fact that the two of you have the morals of two dogs in heat; and even less class and dignity. Violet is the one who should keep quiet. Is that what you're saying?"

Gary blushed and shrugged. "Yeah, man. That's what I'm saying." At Taka's look he went on, "Hey, life goes on, brother. Violet and me never would have worked. She's got a big mouth and she's mean as a barnyard dog."

"And you want my help to this end?"

"Hey, you can help or not." Gary raised his hands. "I really don't care, it ain't no skin off my nose. Just so you know, I will call the police on that woman if she pulls some crazy stuff up at the wedding. Violet is like that. After Brenda and me told her about us, she come to my place cryin' 'bout how could I do that to her when she opened her heart to me and all that. Asked me how's come I could just forget about her, just leave her like that. She wanted me, man. I probably coulda had both of 'em but I'm too much of a gentleman for that. Had to cut her loose."

How could he just forget about her, just leave her like that? Is that what she feels? All these years, did she think Taka just left her? Did she think he could possibly have forgotten her? The image of her being dragged away from him flashed in his head and through his heart like a flash of fire. He'd been too weak to even stand and she was alone at the end. All his promises of love and devotion, and when she needed him most he'd been unconscious. His body had failed him, but a true man would have fought until his dying breath. Hadn't that been what he'd claimed to Ani? And where had he been? When his wife, his queen, was murdered, where had he been? Weak as a baby and too overcome with his own pain to protect her. He hadn't been there.

His stomach turned with every word from this man's mouth but it was like a fierce battle, impossible to look away. The man's lips were moving but he only caught the words here and there, too lost in his past to be fully there.

"I told her it wasn't like I killed her or nothing, I just broke up with her. I mean, don't get me wrong, I loved that wom . . . I mean, I liked her a lot. But the closer me and Violet got the more she kept looking at me like she was expecting something I ain't never planned to give to no woman, and then got all upset when I wanted something easier. She got some fantasy about how a man's supposed to love her. Always saying crazy stuff 'bout if I make promises I got to keep them. I ain't make no promises to that woman that any normal woman would expect me to keep. I mean, you say things to get some, right? You don't mean all that. It's like she was setting me up to screw up. It was just a matter of time before I let her down, so I just did it on my terms. Ain't gonna have her running around telling folks I wasn't man enough for her. She wants some man who loves her unconditionally; I cut her loose so she can find him. Let her see how unreasonable she was and how happy Brenda is just to be with me. Someday, she'll look back and realize I was the best she could hope for. Women today. They too demanding, man."

Taka almost snorted at that. The truth was, though he was trash, Gary had been fighting an uphill battle. Violet expected more because she'd had more. She had been his everything. Yes, he'd neglected her to run a kingdom but he'd never done so just because he didn't want to put the time in. He had never forgotten she was his queen and neither had she. Until the very end, she'd known that he would give anything to make her happy. Hadn't she?

"She's liable to try something funny," Gary continued. "She's liable to pull that gun of hers or something and I ain't having all that drama up at my wedding. I know she wants me bad but she's got to let go and accept the fact that I don't want her."

Taka was drained of emotion. Sure, Ani had been talking, but it took this man, this maggot, to make him see. To make him feel. His wife wasn't buried so deeply after all. The heat of indignation for Violet washed over him.

Taka straightened. "You do not have to worry about Violet. She has moved on, and I suggest you do the same."

Gary laughed while he responded, "Hey, I have moved on. That's what I'm telling you."

"I think perhaps you haven't quite moved on yet," Taka said. "You hope that she will make a scene because then it would show you that she still cares. It won't happen."

"So you say. I know this; Violet's one of those women."

"Those women?"

"Yeah, man. One of those women who think she's supposed to be treated special. Crazy, since she ain't come from nothing. She's one of those you gotta pull off her high horse. Cut her down to size. She's fine so I had to treat her like she wasn't. Some women you gotta break so they can be happy with a normal man."

"And you're one of those men, a man who uses women to bolster his own ego. One of those men who only feels like a man when he is manipulating the emotions of women. One of those men who needs the constant turmoil, needs the women to make you feel like a man, always on the hunt for something better because you only shine in the reflection of a beautiful woman's adoration. But when she actually expects something of you, you run like a coward. Or hurt her by trying to make her feel there was anything she could have done to keep a relationship you didn't have the courage to hold on to. A word of advice: there is no woman on this earth who can turn a weakling into a man. I feel sorry for this Brenda person, for the next attractive woman to look your way will surely put her relationship with you on shaky ground. What will your excuse be then? Be sure to think up a good one. Remember you must be able to continue fooling yourself into believing it is all about the women in your life and what *they* lack."

Taka was satisfied to see the man blanch, his face a mask as his words settled in. He then stood aside. "I assure you Violet will not provide entertainment at your special event. Now, it is time for you to take your leave." He had no intention of listening to any more nonsense from this bug of a man.

Gary glanced up at Taka, gave him an expression rife with embarrassment and walked by, stopping just outside the door.

"Hey, man, I could snap my fingers and have her back in a second." He looked Taka up and down.

"Get out before I hurt you," Taka said. His voice had changed with his fury, deep and torn from his depths. Gary wisely turned and walked away, the slam of the door following him.

Taka flexed his fists in anger and frustration. He cared about Violet and the wedding-to-come was another betrayal waiting to happen. Even in the short time he'd known her he could tell she was used to glossing over pain and betrayal. She had made light of this act by her former boyfriend and best friend but she would have to deal with the truth soon, and he had no idea if he would be around to help her through the process. Just as he hadn't been around to help Zahara through the betrayal that had taken her life.

He sat down at the table, his head in his hands. He was useless. What was his purpose here if he could not help his beloved?

"Help yourself, Taka," Ani said in his ear. Himself? He needed no help. He was perfect the way he was. Taka clamped his hands over his ears pointlessly as the sound of his friend's laughter filled his head.

"Fine," he ground out loud. "So I am not perfect. I am as close to perfect as you'll ever get, angel man. You should be more appreciative."

No response to that. Taka settled into his seat, grumpily. Maybe he was not perfect. What had he been accused of, again? Oh yes, arrogance, pride, unwillingness to accept change; those qualities had always been his weaknesses. And, of course, if past experience was anything to go by, the Almighty was still trying to teach him to overcome these qualities. Could anything he do have a positive effect on Zahara's spirit? Could he, in any way, change the outcome of her routine by changing his own? He didn't see how. In two days, how could he do anything that would make an impact on Violet that would free Zahara? He thought about the worm Violet had shared a bed with the night before and though his face twisted with disgust, he stayed focused long enough to think about what that Jerome-person had that he did not.

A job.

He put his cup down. If Jerome could do it, he could. He stood and took his coat from the hook, prepared to leave, when the telephone rang. He was torn about whether to attempt to communicate with the person on the other end when there was a click, then the sound of Violet's voice in greeting, and another beep, followed by a man's voice. Ah, it was a recorder of some sort, then?

"Look, Violet, if you're there, pick up. It's Skeeter. You know, from Skeeter's Antiques: your favorite place to get good new old stuff? Okay, okay, you got me. I'll give you five hunnert for the brooch. That's half of a thousand, Violet; you're not going to get a better deal than that! Look, call me."

Then there was a click and a beep and Taka thought about the message. Someone asking about Zahara's brooch? He didn't know what the man was offering: 500 cowries, yen, pesos, drachma, dirham. Surely he wasn't offering $500 American. That would be an insult. That brooch had cost a hundred times that amount 400 years ago. The ruby alone was the largest found in the world, at the time. The brooch was priceless.

He turned to leave and the phone rang again. This time after Violet's greeting he heard Violet's voice tinged with amusement. The sound of it was like a cold drink of water to a thirsty man.

"Listen, King, if you're there, don't worry about trying to figure out how to talk to me. I just thought you'd like to know I got a call from Harold down at Harold's Hometown Eatery. Apparently you threatened to turn his kids upside down and shake the mischief out of them?" She broke up in pretty laughter and he could not help the upturn of his lips at the sound. "Devious munchkins, those two. The last time they delivered my food they lollygagged around for about an hour and a half. Of course my food was stone cold by the time I got it and you bet your behind I gave their daddy an earful that day. If the food came cold again save it for me and I'll take it back to that raggedy restaurant and teach that whole family what a hot meal should be."

Taka belched a habanero bubble; he was pretty sure they already knew.

"Don't worry, King, I got your back. But you may want to hold off on the threats of bodily harm. In this day and age they'll throw you in jail for that. And the clink ain't no fun; don't ask me how I know. Take care, King. I'll see you later."

Taka smiled at the talking machine, filled with unexpected warmth. Then, he left the apartment on foot and walked down the streets of the neighborhood, peering in storefronts as he passed. He walked until the terrain changed. The small shops gave way to larger strip malls and businesses. He was midstride when he caught a glimpse of the lobby of a company. Next to the front desk, behind which sat a guard, was a concrete lion. He had no particular affinity for the animal—it had killed plenty of his family's pets and food in his childhood—but it was the first signpost he'd come across that reminded him of home. He squinted into the glass of the advertising agency, and then strode to the door opening it wide. The eyes of the security guard widened upon seeing him.

"Can I help you, sir?"

"Yes," Taka said definitively. "I would like a job in this place. What is the manner of business in this establishment? I have a great deal of experience in leadership. I would like a job where I can lead."

The security guard looked confused for a moment, and then hesitantly moved a clipboard toward Taka. "Sign in please, sir. Now, who did you want to see?"

Taka frowned and the guard moved back a little. Ah, the man was intimidated and Taka had not even done anything. People today were easily spooked. "Did you not hear me? Do you have some difficulty with the English language? I would like to find out what jobs you have in leadership. To whom may I speak?"

"Sir, I . . . I can't help you. I'm just the security guard. You have to know who you want to talk to or call the job line in human resources."

"I have to use a telephone to find the information that is already in this building? Even though I am here, now?"

"That's right, sir. That or the Internet. Here, I'll write down the number."

Taka suspected the writing of the number served two purposes: to satisfy his request and to get Taka out of the building. Taka could sense discomfort in lesser men as easily as he could breathe. The guard was scribbling furiously when another man stepped up to the desk. Taka looked at this new man, sizing up the white skin and balding scalp. He looked too young to lose hair, but Taka had seen younger man lose an entire head of hair after a particularly traumatic battle. He wondered what battle this man had lost his hair to.

"May I help you?" He was a smaller man but he had a firm voice and his eyes did not dip, even though Taka towered over him by about a foot. Taka liked this man. Perhaps he was one of the special people.

"Yes. I would like a job."

"A job?"

"Yes. I am a natural leader and organizer. And I am a hard worker."

The man seemed to weigh his words carefully. "Well, normally people apply for particular positions, but . . ." He crossed his arms and looked at Taka carefully. "What kind of experience do you have?"

"I have years of managing. I am very good at putting ideas into action."

"Thinking outside the box?"

"Outside the box?" Taka thought of his home and the many years he'd been forced to live with only his imagination able to escape, sustaining himself on the promise of a future with the wife he loved. "Peculiar term, but accurate. Yes. That's it."

"Well, I have to say, your approach is refreshing. You seem like a go-getter. Do you have a resume?"

"What is a . . . resume?"

A frown sprung up between the man's eyes but then nodded as an idea came to him. "I hear an accent in your voice. Where are you from?"

"Africa."

"So you're bilingual?"

"I know seven languages."

"An educated man, then?"

"I have put philosophers to silence."

"Hard worker?"

"Is there any other kind?"

"Team player?"

"I am more familiar with being the team leader."

"Any marketing experience?"

"I do not understand the term."

"Can you get people to buy things from you they didn't think they wanted?"

"In my experience they called that persuasion. If a king—I mean, man—cannot persuade others to follow his lead he will soon lose all himself. Persuasion is a skill I have well mastered."

"That's impressive," the man said. He seemed a very friendly man. In this time Taka had not run across many. "Well, Mr. . . . ."

"Olufemi. Taka Olufemi."

"Mr. Olufemi, if you'd like to fill out an application we might have a position for you. We'll just need to check your references and look at your prior experience. And, of course, a work visa if you are not a citizen."

Taka stiffened. References he could get the gist of, but how would he fill out an application? He had no valid work experience. And he had not even thought of citizenship. He'd come to this country through a precious gem; no papers came with that. His dilemma must have showed on his face because the man blushed.

"Look," he went behind the desk and pulled out a sheet of paper to hand to Taka. "Here's an application. Go home and think about it. When, if, you become able to work in the U.S. come back. Or, maybe if we can verify your references from home we can sponsor you to work here. You'd have to go through proper immigration channels, but it can be done."

"And what type of job might I qualify for, Mr. . . . ."

"Bellows. Jimmy Bellows. It depends on your experience." Again, Taka's expression tipped him off. He went on hurriedly. "But certainly we can find something. Customer service, maybe. We have some jobs in shipping. A large man like you wouldn't have a problem loading a box or two."

Taka fought the tremor in his hand. He was a king, an educated leader. This was an insult. And yet, looking at Mr. Bellows it was obvious the man was trying to do good. Then why did he feel so bad?

"Thank you, Mr. Bellows," Taka said, raising his chin and holding out his hand to shake the other man's. "Thank you for your time."

"Mr. Olufemi, whatever you need to do, do it. You carry yourself with a demeanor that is just not common these days. You have a forceful and determined personality, a born executive. You could go far with us."

"In shipping?" Taka asked, with distaste.

"It's a start. It's a great way to learn the company from the ground up. Mr. Olufemi, I wish we could give you something more from the beginning but something also tells me there are some things you need to tie up. I was in the lobby and watched you walk in. Call it providence or coincidence, but something told me to give you a chance. I tend to try to listen to that little voice in my head, Mr. Olufemi. It rarely steers me wrong. Today, that voice told me to give you an application."

Taka knew it was his Father showing him that there was a way and if he chose, it would be possible. If he wanted to try this new life with Violet, it would be hard, but it would be possible. "Thank you."

Jimmy Bellows nodded and then headed back his way while Taka left. As he stalked down the street he became angrier and angrier. How was it that a king should have to beg for a job like a common man? How was it that he should be penniless when he and his warriors had procured countless bounties for the good of their people and their village? How was it that the Almighty could allow such a travesty? The treasures of his nation had not simply vanished from the earth; someone had plundered them just as surely as that man who lived next to Violet plundered her newspaper every morning. Theft, pure and simple. It had to stop!

He was striding down the street when he saw the familiar yellow of a book sitting on a metal shelf in the midst of a glass box. He remembered such a book in Violet's apartment; it held phone numbers and addresses of business establishments. Only just this morning a man had called from a shop wanting to buy Zahara's brooch, which meant he knew its value, despite the fact that he was attempting to cheat Violet out of it. The thought of the man trying to steal the brooch—her very own

brooch—from Zahara was enough to make him want
to pound the man into the concrete. He was merely a
modern-day thief, a thief who might have other pieces of
Jahanian jewelry and art.

He went to the glass box and fiddled with the handle
until the door opened, and then stepped inside to open
the book. It was a shop. What category of shop was it?
Some sort of art shop? But he knew art from the past
was no longer called art. Artifacts and antiquities. He
looked up "artifacts" and came up empty but stopped
at "antiques." He browsed the page. They were listed by
names. And what was the name again. Skittle? Screcter?
Oh yes. He spied a name three-quarters down. Skeeter. It
said to look at the ad on the next page and he turned it.
Skeeter's Antiques: The best new old stuff around.

Thief.

He tore out the page and stepped out of the box. A
young woman gave him directions to Skeeter's shop.
He did as she suggested and hopped on a bus, was told
he needed to pay or else the police would be called, and
hopped back off. He took off on foot. By the time he got
to the store he was winded, but refreshed. His anger
had dulled, which was a good thing. Anger only dulled
deductive reasoning skills and he needed to be sharp.

The bell tinkled signaling his arrival and he stepped
inside the small, quiet space. He looked around, immediately realizing most of the articles in this place were junk.
Counterfeit pieces, some not even good replicas, some
made of inferior materials and shoddy workmanship. But
here and there was a decent piece or two. A scarf made
of real Chinese silk. A lamp that was indeed Victorian, as
it claimed. He was surveying the items with a sharp eye
when a man shuffled from the back.

The old man squinting at him stepped back, reflexively.
Taka groaned inside; yet another mouse disguising him-

self as a man. He stepped forward, not at all concerned about being intimidating. He looked him over, found him lacking, and then went back to perusing the items while he spoke, clasping one hand behind his back to keep from prematurely strangling the wrong man.

"Can I help you, sir?"

"Are you Skeeter, the owner of this place?"

"Why, yes, yes, I am. Can I help you with something?"

"Just looking at your treasures. You have quite a collection."

"The best new, old stuff around," Skeeter said weakly. "Can I help you find anything?"

How about helping me find my people? he wanted to say. *How about helping me find my dignity and self-respect, maybe coughing up my village's legacy?* He wanted to say those things, but settled on, "I was looking for something a woman might enjoy."

"Woman?"

"Yes. You've heard of them? Female persuasion, opposite of male, shapely, sweet-smelling creatures who are God's gift to men? This woman is one of noble bearing. A woman of grace and intelligence. A woman above all women." He was curious to see if the old man would pull out another of his murdered wife's stolen precious jewels, the swine. Perhaps he would whip out the earrings Taka had given her pounded from gold as a gift for their first anniversary, or perhaps the striking sapphire wrist bauble he'd given her as a thank-you for all the things she did tirelessly on behalf of the townspeople. Perhaps the silks that had draped her cold, dead body. He had to force himself not to pounce.

He heard the old man swallow before croaking, "You mean like a necklace or something?"

Taka whirled and glared at him, anger making him tense. He was about to tell the man, "No, not like a necklace, like a brooch!" when something caught his eye. He turned quickly and spied a bowl. It was hand-carved wood, an intricate design that simulated lace, a design as familiar to him as his own name. Some of the women in Jaha had taken to carving special bowls such as this for celebration and libation. It was a sacred bowl. It was an honored tool. It was on sale for $1.99.

Taka's blood took fire again and the heat threatened to consume him, but he fought to keep his fury to himself. Taka had always been unaware of his effect on others but he knew of the legend. When King Taka went to battle, men dropped dead first from the fury of his presence before a sword or knife ever lanced their bodies. It had been said that armies could feel him coming before he was ever seen by their eyes. Young warriors would often run in fear of him, willing to face their villages as cowards rather than look upon the angry face of King Taka.

Of course, Taka never understood what the fuss was about. He did not actively seek to take advantage of this natural ability, but he could no more suppress his exceptional maleness than he could expect other men to stand up to it. Some things were just impossible. And apparently he still held his power even centuries later if the way the old man began to shake in his feeble bones was any indication.

Alas, this old man did have a stroke of rebellious courage and seemed to gather it at that moment. "Look, whatchu want? We don't want no trouble in here!"

"Who said anything about trouble?" Taka returned, annoyed. "Silence your senseless babbling and tell me, where did you get this bowl?"

"You want it, take it! Just take what you want and leave."

Taka's eyes narrowed as the implication struck him. Who did he think he was talking to?

Taka was a king. His reputation was beyond reproach. How dare he suggest otherwise?

"I am no thief, old man. Not like some people," he ground out, picking up the bowl to run his fingers along the pattern. "No, I would not defile the purpose of such an item by stealing it, even from a thief."

"Why you call me a thief, mister?" Skeeter said, indignant. "I ain't steal nothing."

"How is it you can sell such an item for such a price? It is ludicrous. This is a sacred piece of art."

"What you know about that?" Skeeter asked, his greed outdistancing his fear. "Guy who sold it to me was certain it was one of those they mass produce over in India for tourists and such."

"This is not Indian and most certainly not mass produced."

"I didn't think . . ." Skeeter trailed off, his eyes now glued to the art. "I thought maybe it come from someplace else, but he told me he knew for sure and I couldn't place it, myself."

Taka turned and placed the bowl on the counter in front of the man. "Ah, another thief. What a surprise. I will take it."

"Well, okay. It's . . ." he hesitated and Taka watched greed war with his cataracts. "It's $199."

"It says $1.99," Taka growled. He didn't know why he was asking. He hadn't a cent to his name. Perhaps he could bargain. Surely the buttons of his coat were worth something? Maybe the coat itself, certainly worth at least $2.50? He began to shrug it off.

"That's a mistake," Skeeter said, licking his lips like the mangy cur he was. "The decimal point's in the wrong place, is all."

Taka stiffened and shrugged the coat back on. "You are a thief and a pathetic excuse for a man. Men like you should be wiped from the earth. You should have your entrails torn out and fed to dogs and lowly swine. You should—"

"Fine, fine! Take it!" Skeeter said, pushing the bowl his way. "It's only a bowl. Take it and leave 'fore I call the po po!"

Taka was taken aback by surprise. "I cannot accept it without paying."

"Yes, you can. It's a gift from me to you. Just promise me you won't come back. Ever."

Taka thought about it. It was a fair deal. And he wanted the bowl. "Wrap it, please."

Once outside, Taka held his package lovingly. It took him ten minutes to find a yellow book. And then he couldn't find Violet in it. But there was another book with white pages and he found her listed, last name first. He found her address and spent another forty-five minutes making his way back, asking directions all the way. He'd left the door unlocked and thought to himself how dangerous it was for her to live in an unlocked residence with so many strangers around. Good thing for her he was there to protect her.

Chapter 15

Violet left her car for the valet in front of the Sheraton on Capital Square and made a beeline to Ronald Bickman's suite. Her briefcase was filled with swatches, testimonies, magazine articles, and reviews; it would take all that to turn this disaster around.

When she walked in the door, Tracy's sad face was the first thing she saw. Tracy was one of those people who couldn't keep a secret to save her life. If Bickman was on the warpath, her face reflected the internal terror the visiting offender should be feeling. Today, her sadness did not bode well for Violet. In fact, she didn't even respond to Violet's greeting, simply pointed to her boss's door with eerie solemnity, her eyebrows raised in warning Violet could read: she'd better not waste his time after Tracy had pulled strings getting her in there.

Violet made a note to self to invite Tracy over for poker after this was all over.

Violet walked in to face Bickman's scowl, but she didn't let that deter her. "Mr. Bickman, so nice to see you. Thank you for taking time out of your busy day—"

"Ms. Jackson, I have to be honest with you. I've already chosen the company I feel comfortable with. I appreciate you coming out, but I don't want to waste your time."

"And I don't want to see yours wasted, Mr. Bickman, which it will be if you go with any company other than Shades of Violet." She propped her briefcase on the guest chair and popped it open, pulling out papers to slide across his desk as she spoke. "These are statistics on the average job times for most companies in town. You'll notice Shades of Violet has the shortest duration. These statistics are the average costs of these other companies. And these are the consumer reviews on those companies. Now I'd like you to look at these." She pulled out a local magazine already flipped to the information she wanted to impress him with. "This is a home designed by Shades of Violet. And this one, and this one. And here is a cost breakdown of my services. My rate is comparable, but my work is beyond anything my competitors can provide. And most importantly, my team can get it done in a fraction of the time of my competitors. Shades of Violet understands the inconvenience of renovation so we hire the best contractors in the city and the best supplies worldwide to make sure you get the high-quality design you want in record time. Because we know your time is important, Mr. Bickman. This last magazine here, this will tell you all about the fact that Shades of Violet is on the cutting edge of all the most progressive design techniques. You see, I invented the Melting technique. As a matter of fact, I own the patent on the process."

Violet stopped talking then and stepped back to allow him to absorb the information she'd thrown at him. She clasped her hands serenely before her as her heart pounded out her anxiety. This was it for her. If she could get this account her life would change. If she could get this account it would validate all the hard work she'd put in all her life. Working her way through college, giving up trips and cars and a nice home to put every cent into her business. No, Violet wasn't a nice person, maybe she didn't deserve a break on that front. But she was good at what she did. Her talent to design was the one thing that was pure in her life. Her business was the one thing, the one place, that made

her feel worthy. Her talent was the only thing that kept her
hoping. This deal would mean everything. She struggled to
keep it from showing on her face.

"You invented the technique? But what about Miss
Daniels? She led me to believe—"

"Brenda is a very good friend of mine. So good that
I showed her my technique. And I give her props; she
executes the process almost as well as I do. But I feel
a man of your recognition must have the real product.
With a deal this size, people and media from all over the
world are going to scrutinize this job. It is important that
any work in your home hold up to the highest degree
of scrutiny. Brenda can do the technique, but she can't
explain how it works. Nor is she familiar enough with it to
be able to experiment with different textures and colors.
Please don't misunderstand me, Brenda is very talented.
But Brenda is only copying what she's seen me do time
and again. As the creator, I am still the only one who can
do it properly and I am invested in making sure it stands
up to my reputation."

He was looking through the papers and she could see he
was thinking now, paying attention. The minutes ticked
off as he flipped through her work. Her body wanted to
pounce on this opportunity, but her head told her to back
off. She'd given him the evidence and documentation she
wanted; now was time for her to make her escape.

"Mr. Bickman, as I know you have a very busy day I
will take my leave now. I just want to leave you with one
last word. If you ask around Columbus you'll find that
my reputation extends beyond my clients. Many of my
competitors will tell you that Shades of Violet is their
primary competition. And I will tell you without a doubt
that Shades of Violet is the last word in interior design in
Columbus. My name and my talent speak for themselves.
Please be brave enough to choose the best for your home

renovation. That is my challenge to you, Mr. Bickman."
She shut her briefcase with a click and pulled it off the
chair. "Thank you and have a good day."

Turn, walk, do not let him see your fingers tremble!

Violet left Bickman's office with him staring after her,
sashaying out with a tremulous smile on her face that
he couldn't see. She glanced at the clock on the wall and
noted she'd done it in nineteen minutes. She walked
calmly past Tracy who was staring after her in question,
then shot her friend a thumbs-up and a toothpaste com-
mercial smile and left as quietly as she'd arrived, despite
the internal screaming.

She didn't have a doubt that she'd made an impression
on Bickman. And now, no matter what happened, at least
she could say she tried. She didn't just roll over and take
it; she fought back.

She couldn't wait to tell Taka all about it. Even though
he'd tried his best to rain on her parade this morning
and was always looking at her like he was expecting
something other than what she was saying to be coming
from her mouth, she still wanted to share this with him.
For some unknown reason she wanted his respect. The
irate call she got from her local restaurant owner, father
and employer of the two juvenile delinquents who made
faces behind her back and smart-mouthed her every
chance they got, well, that put the seal on their friendship
as far as she was concerned.

Glancing in her rearview, a forgotten piece of orange
caught her eye and snagged her brain with sudden epiphany. She knew exactly what her next wish should be. It was
right in front of her nose!

Violet got back to the apartment, put down her briefcase, and looked at the large lump on the sofa. She felt a
nudge of affection for the giant who looked so peaceful in
sleep. She really should let him enjoy his dream, but . . .

Walking over to him she slapped him hard on his arm, waking him as effectively as if she'd doused him with a pail of cold water. "Wake up, King! I've decided on my second wish."

As Taka blinked the sleep from his eyes she tossed the offending orange dress still wrapped in plastic on top of him. "This is a problem," she declared.

Taka shook himself to, pulling the dress away by two fingers as if it were a cobweb. "What problem?"

"It came to me on my way home. The witch intentionally ordered this two sizes too small. And do you know why? She wants to put me through the humiliation of having it altered. And I won't even mention the color again, you get the point."

"It is only a dress. Have it altered; you will still outshine her with your beauty and the glow of your spirit."

Violet stopped short and cocked her head. "That is the sweetest thing any man has ever said to me, King. If I weren't already taken you might have a shot. But back to the dress. I was thinking about it and I've decided on a second wish. I want to be able to eat whatever I want and not be larger than a size eight. There."

Taka rolled his eyes. "By all that is holy, Father, not another one."

"Have you seen Brenda? She's a size negative two. I'm going to look like a horse standing next to her."

"Your body is perfect. You do not need to be thinner. Why do you want to be like these women I see walking around, skeletons with hair? A woman should have meat on her bones. Something to hold. The padding is necessary if good lovemaking is to be had by all. It is, how do they say, a shock absorber."

Violet had to stop and think about that a moment before moving on. "Things have changed since your time, King."

"Must you change with them?"

"Unlike you, I can't just hop along to another time and place. Look, I'm sure there was a time when big was beautiful, but that's not today. I need all the ammunition I can get."

"You speak like you are at war when it is only you on both sides of the battle line. Why do you fight yourself, Violet? Don't you know you can never win?"

Violet thought about that for a moment, then smiled, making her point with a finger gesture. "Or, I can also never lose. Depends on how you look at it, King. Listen, your concern is much appreciated. You obviously have a lot of time to spend pondering the meaning of life but I really just want you to grant my wish."

"To make you like a stick?"

"Size eight, no larger."

"You are already larger, are you not?"

"I can afford to lose a pound or two."

"I do not want to grant this wish. Can you not believe me when I tell you you are beautiful as you are?"

"Once again, very sweet, but let me explain this in terms you can understand. You"—she pointed at his chest—"will be gone tomorrow and I'll be stuck in a time where size fourteen is way too fat. I need to be smaller. It's simple."

"Why? So that bug of a man can wear you on his arm like a bauble?"

"So I should want to be what you consider attractive? What's any better about that than wanting to change for Jerome?"

The question stunned him for only a second. "I will not even begin to discuss how wrong it is to compare me to that slime in the first place; but, since you ask, the reptile does not care about you or your health or your well-being. I care about more than just your appearance, even though

I am highly appreciative of it. I am a person who thinks of you as more than just a plaything. I believe you would be happy as you are if you would simply accept yourself and love yourself. Why can't you see what I see?"

Taka's voice rose with his desperation as thoughts of her wasting away to nothing invaded his brain. She had a beautiful body. He could spend days on end simply staring at it. The thought that it would be ravaged and twisted just to be smaller left him feeling sick and panicked. He hadn't come all this way, all these centuries to make love to a starving woman!

"It is idiocy at its worst!" he continued. "You cannot truly want to defile your body on the word of that bug, that maggot, that—"

"I'm not listening to you," Violet said, putting her fingers in her ears and humming.

He simply spoke louder to drown her out. "And you say you are powerful? Your power is in turning yourself inside out to appeal to others! That is not power; that is conformity and cowardice!"

Violet unplugged her ears and responded, "Then call me a cowardly size eight and take a chill pill. Look, do I have to go to your boss?"

"You are being foolish."

"This coming from a man who lives under a rock?"

"I live inside a precious gemstone!"

"Whatever. My mind's made up. No more arguing. Do it, King. Snap, snap. Snap, snap, I said!"

They glared at each other for a long, angry moment. A muscle jerked in his clenched jaw. "Fine." Taka took one last, longing look at her form before turning away, his head shaking with futility and his spirit lower than ever. "It is done."

His sudden defeat stunned Violet for just a moment and then: "Woo hoo!" She clapped her hands while hopping with glee. Ten years of yo-yo dieting over! Though to be honest, the yo-yo only ever went in one direction. She was always on a diet in her head but the only part of "diet" that ever translated itself to her actions was the breaking of it.

"You have no idea what a relief this is. I'm going to celebrate tonight with three pints of ice cream."

"That's what you think," Taka mumbled under his breath.

"I'll order a pizza for dinner, maybe two."

"Live it up. Fill yourself with unhealthy food and treats, makes no difference to me," he groused. He could not believe she would betray them both this way. All for the rat of a man she threw herself away on. He was angry enough to break something.

"What are you over there mumbling about?" Violet asked. His face was as moody as a thundercloud but he wasn't ruining her high. This wish was a stroke of genius! "I'll share the pizza with you if you're nice to me. Look, I had a great morning and I think we should do something special. It's a beautiful spring day. I'll change and we can go to the park. Would you like that, King?"

His glare only sent her into peals of laughter as she left the room.

What was the matter with women? Were they so unhappy with themselves they went looking for problems?

"I hate this wish above all others," Taka spoke to the ceiling through clenched teeth. "To alter oneself is an abomination."

"That is an abomination? What do you call giving up your mortality?" The words came so quickly and Ani appeared so suddenly Taka did not even have warning of his arrival, his face earnest. "How do you think we feel?"

The phone rang and they both looked at it, content to allow the machine to pick up.

The recording of Violet's voice was followed by a familiar voice.

"Look, Violet, if you're there, pick up. Okay, okay, you got me. I'll give you seven hunnert for the brooch. That's more than half of a thousand dollars. Violet, you're not going to get a better deal than that! Look, call me."

Taka's jaw flexed. Apparently the old thief wasn't scared enough not to try to take advantage of a woman. He was tempted to go back down and pay Skeeter another visit, but thought better of it. He didn't want to end up in the jail place Violet had warned him about. Instead, he turned an even fiercer glare to his friend the second Skeeter stopped talking.

"You should be ashamed of yourself. I am a king and the both of you have set me down here penniless. Where is my property? It is mine and I want it. Give me back my gold, my jewelry, my art, my literature; give me back what is mine. You will not sit me down like a pauper when you know I have untold wealth. You will give me what is due me."

"Your property? Every breath you take, every tool you use, every decoration you wear is our Father's. He loaned it to you for a little while, but it never belonged to you."

Taka stiffened in anger. "And you call Him kind and fair? How can you do so and take everything from me? I am no pauper. The thieves who scoured the remains of my village should burn for taking what my people worked for."

"If you had chosen to stay and protect those things you claim are so dear to you, then Jaha wouldn't be a distant memory and your sacred artifacts would not be strewn all over the world with no one to claim them. You were to be the keeper of the artifacts. Yours was to be the voice to tell the tale of the kingdom called Jaha. You were to record the history in books instead of the story becoming just a phantom tale. You chose to open the coffers so that your enemies could plunder your cabinets; it was not His choice for you or for your people. Instead the legend lives on in the descendants of your murderers. Even today you met one, a man who recognizes the story of Jaha as told to him by his ancestors. Needless to say the truth has been twisted to serve them well."

Taka took a deep breath and swallowed some anger and pride as the implications reached him. He knew Skeeter was a foul cretin, something about the snake-like bone structure!

"No use hating Skeeter, he only believes the lies he has been told. That's the thing about a lie, Taka: when it gets passed around it is as potent as any truth when there is no voice to contradict it."

"Do you know what it felt like to see that bowl on sale as if it were a piece of nothing? Our women carved those bowls, spent hours blistering their hands, so that they could be used to worship the Almighty. Forget about me and my stubbornness and pride. What of them and their work and sweat? What of their legacy?"

"What of the legacy of your entire kingdom? Hear me, Taka. We had plans for you. You would have gone on."

Taka grimaced and turned away. He didn't want to hear this. "Gone on to what? I was good for nothing after what happened."

"Gone on with the memory of an epic love with an exceptional woman. Memory of that love would have been the foundation for the new Jaha; a new society with women having rights unheard of in that time and place because Zahara taught you that women were underestimated and undervalued. Had you not loved so deeply you would never have learned that. Zahara would never have been forgotten. But with your choice . . ."

"You will tell me now how badly I messed things up?" Taka winced with his words, knowing pain was coming his way.

"Her murder was due to evil men. Your choice, not made maliciously. But yes, your decision has ramifications. You see, had you gone on and rebuilt your life the woman you loved first may not have felt so tethered to your restless soul. Violet has no memory of you but her soul senses you. You are not at peace and so she is not at peace. She will always be unavailable to another man as long as she is waiting for you. Maybe she could tolerate temporary relationships with the Garys and Jeromes of the world because they are disposable and she is waiting. Maybe she could even have loved someone else, but in comparison to what she had, would always be wanting. Centuries of looking and not finding have caused a lot of damage. She can't even recognize that you are the one she has been waiting for. She has forgotten what love looks like. Her heart's protection is keeping from her the very one she so wants to open her heart to. And perhaps rightly so."

"Rightly so?" Taka sank to the sofa as the enormity of the situation sank into his consciousness. "Nonsense, I am the cure for what ails her if she would only listen."

"Okay, then, continue on your way. Pressure her. Harass her and nag her until she bends to your iron will. That is your way, Taka. A winning strategy?"

"You enjoy reminding me of my weaknesses. Fine. I have learned, as well."

"And what have you learned?"

"Are you enjoying this immensely, making me recite my findings like a schoolchild?"

"Yes, very much. Thank you for asking."

Taka's brow furrowed as emotions invaded his consciousness. He looked at the kind-faced man who waited expectantly, and finally admitted, "I do want to get to know this woman. I did not think I would find anything in common with her but I like her. She is stubborn and determined. Stubborn and determined to do things the wrong way, but I can't fault her dedication toward her goal. And I can't force her to see things my way, but I have to try to reach her somehow."

"But she's flawed. And, as she said, you will be gone in a day. What could you possibly do for her?"

"So anxious to see me burn for my insolence, Ani?"

"Never, Taka. But only a day ago you begged to be rid of her. What was it you called her, 'a mere shadow of Zahara'?"

"My tongue is sometimes premature in its findings."

"If that is your way of asking His forgiveness for maligning one of His children, you will have to do better than that, but it's a start. As for saving her, she has only one Savior and her prayer should never be to you. Her prayer should only ever and always be to our Lord and Savior, for only through Him can she hear our Father's voice. She is His child to guide, Taka, not yours. Do not look at this situation as one you can rule, Taka. See it for what it is: an opportunity to love the spirit once known as Zahara, again. As for your riches, I've given you something to help you along. It is in your coat pocket. Take it and use it wisely."

"But . . ." Taka said, only to realize Ani had left. He cursed under his breath. When he didn't want him around he could not get rid of him. Now when he needed to talk, his friend had disappeared.

Chapter 16

Taka knew that somehow he had to make Violet see the light but he had no idea how. Subtlety was never his strong point. A king didn't have time to be subtle—an immortal king on a mission, even less. But apparently regular men had all sorts of time to pussyfoot around. He would have to pussyfoot like a regular man if he had any hope at all.

They were at a charming place called Franklin Park. The newspaper had told him it was the month of May and the green grass and lush trees almost made him feel at home. Taka breathed the fresh, clean air and felt his resolve return to him as though nature was rewarding his effort. That was, until they sat down on a blanket Violet had pulled from the car trunk and his concentration scattered at the sight of her copper brown legs in the insanely short pants stretched out before her. He'd tried to ignore the healthy, moist skin since she'd first emerged from the bedroom but here she was, flaunting the legs again; her calves a song in smoothness, her thighs silky with just the right amount of curve, hinting at the round behind that sat on top. It was almost cruel the way she taunted him.

"Boy, you were serious about liking my body, huh?"

He looked up quickly to find her knowing smirk. Darned if her mischievous grin wasn't as attractive as her legs.

"I do not notice," he bluffed, pulling off his own coat as he was suddenly hotter despite the breeze. He folded it by his side with stiff hands before responding, resisting the need to raise his voice again. "What matter is it to notice? It will be gone soon enough. You will be rid of the burden of your insufficient body before you can say 'snap, snap.'" There. Managed to get it out without allowing her to see how upset it made him. He was well on his way.

"Gee, King, I'd almost think it was your body I was changing the way you're making such a big deal. I don't hate it. I just want it thinner. Sue me. Forgive me for wanting to be able to eat freely for a change."

It was his body! Violet pulled her knees up to wrap her arms around them, reeling in his gaze to the expanse of skin and the lovely face on top. *Do not lose focus,* he scolded himself.

"You are depriving yourself of food now?" he asked; a delayed reaction to a point she'd just made. The slap on his arm that followed told him he'd said something wrong. He rushed to try to fix whatever offense he'd caused. "There was not a single woman in my village smaller than you. Or rather, looking at your frame it seems similar to a village woman I used to know who was about your size."

"Really? You mean I would have been the skinniest in your whole village?"

Backfire. The woman was incredibly adept at turning his words against him to further her own goal. She wasn't the smallest woman in his village, but he certainly wouldn't admit to the lie now; she would only use that against him as well.

"I do not know why women cannot be more like men. So long as we are strong and able to battle we do not fuss over the amount of food we eat."

"Don't get me started on why women can't, and shouldn't, be more like men, King." A lock of hair fell over her cheek and he zoomed in on it. It was as black as night and countered the cinnamon skin of her cheek so lovingly, he was disappointed that she beat him in moving it off her face to tuck behind her ear. Instead he cleared his voice and looked around them at the trees and the people passing by.

"So you say there are places like this throughout the city? Parks? Just for people to come enjoy nature?"

"Mhmm. I don't get out here much but I do like it."

"Situated thus I almost forget we are near to the city."

"We're in the middle of the city, King; surrounded by it."

"Hmm." He nodded. "And what animals do you have in this city? Lions? Wildebeests?"

Violet snorted, her pretty nose wrinkling with mirth. "Only wildebeests I've seen around here are of the two-legged variety." At his questioning look, she clarified, "No, no wildebeests. We have squirrels and rabbits. I've heard some people in the rural areas have deer. I've heard rumor of coyote. Some people keep snakes as pets."

Surely she was joking. "Those are not animals. Those are rodents, harmless critters and cursed serpents of the underworld. You have no tigers? No panthers? No crazed chimpanzees?"

"I hear in some forest areas they have bears," she said hopefully.

This explained a lot. He'd been in cities all over the world but had little time to ask about animal life. Back in Jaha, animals lived in concert with the growth of the community. They were always aware of them and prepared to be visited at any time. No wonder things were so easy these days. No wonder the men were so soft. They had nothing to worry about other than tripping over a crack in the pavement.

"Ah well, it is not your fault you have no serious game. It is for the best. Most likely the Almighty has adapted your environment for the safety of the women and children as

I doubt your men could survive a hunt, anyway. Throw a lion or a panther in this city and the entire population would be wiped out in a week."

"Whoa," Violet laughed. "Number one, you have a serious attitude problem when it comes to men. Today's men are not punks. At least not all of them."

"A valiant effort to defend your worthless men."

"Number two, we women are more than able to take care of ourselves. We don't need no friggin' male protection."

Taka could not help the amusement at her proclamation. Perhaps this particular woman could take out a lion or two. He could easily see her staring down a lion, proclaiming, "You don't friggin' scare me!" Violet went on, a look of unabashed boasting on her face. In his day they called it talking each other up. Whatever it was called, the fierce expression on her face proved her to be a master of the bluff.

"Heck, I've taken karate. I've got a gun and I know how to use it, buster. Violet Jackson knows how to take care of herself. I'm a force to be reckoned with. And as for this lack of animal thing? The fact is, we managed to clear out all but the most harmless. Those bison and antelope: troublemakers. We took care of them, all right. They won't be messing with us anytime soon."

Of course, since he came from a stone she would assume he knew nothing about American history, but he'd once emerged with his stone in the hands of a Sioux chief years before the West was won.

"So the murder of the bison had nothing to do with the attempted murder of the people native to this land?"

She looked at him a long moment, eyes narrowing. He could see her brain ticking trying to decide whether to keep this particular bluff going. She was certainly determined. Ambitious, even when wrong. Valiant to the end.

The countenance of a queen; any man would be fortunate to have Violet Jackson backing them up.

"Okay, okay." She rolled her eyes. "I give. The bison thing, a horrible thing. But the antelope? We took care of them, for sure."

"The antelope still exist in the Southwest; at least antelope as they are known to you."

"Are you serious? How do you know that?"

He shrugged. "I get around. This is my first time in this particular region but I have been in the United States. I understand there are lions and tigers, elephants and panthers in the West. I have seen a photo of a man battling a lion with a chair. Brave man, indeed."

Violet snickered. "I hate to break this to you, King, but you've just described a circus. They weren't battling those animals; they were training them for entertainment. I hate circuses. There's something freaky about an elephant in a ruffle skirt." She took a deep breath of clean, fresh air to erase the image from her mind. "My goodness, it's a beautiful day. I really should get out more."

But Taka was still trying to make sense of the animals-for-entertainment comment. Surely she wasn't serious? Violet had a wicked sense of humor. Yes, simply further tomfoolery.

The sun looked pretty upon her softened face. It was relaxed in a way he hadn't seen since arriving. A smile curled her lips.

"What has happened that makes you smile so?"

"Ah, King, it was a wonderful morning and I'm in a good mood."

"A good enough mood that you can call me by my given name?"

Of course she wouldn't, just because he'd asked her to. He should have told her he liked to be called King and surely she would take to calling him by his name. Or, perhaps she would simply go back to calling him a genie.

"Well, okay. If it's important to you. What was it, again?"

At his look she broke into more pretty laughter. She was getting quite a bellyful at his expense but he was willing to tolerate it if it allowed him to hear the sound.

"Okay, okay. Taka. Taka. Taaaakaaaa." She rolled it around on her tongue. "Not so bad once you get used to it."

He nodded in assent and appreciation. "Thank you," he said.

"No problem. So, what do you want to do today?"

"I do not know. We can talk?"

"Now, you know we can barely do that without getting into an argument. I'm surprised one of us hasn't pinned the other to the ground already. I mean, it's been awhile since you've called me an idiot and I told you to take a flying leap. That's a record."

"I have never called you an idiot!"

"You referred to my actions as 'idiocy.'"

"It is hardly the same thing. What do you expect me to call it when all you do is—"

She picked up her arm and looked at her wrist time-piece. "Time! Now we know we can last twenty minutes but that is the absolute limit. But it doesn't matter because today I am in a good mood. Remember what you told me before about knowing glory and misery? I'm usually somewhere in between, but I'll be darned if I'm not feeling a little glory right about now."

"Yes? Tell me what news you have so I may be happy with you, then."

"I had an excellent meeting this morning."

"Ah, this is some success with your career that makes you glow."

"Something good is coming. I can feel it." She gave him a sly look. "Besides you, that is."

Taka chuckled softly. "Ah, you must love your business if a good day at work makes you forget what a pain I am to you."

"So we should do something. I was thinking, if you want to see a play or something I could try to get us tickets tonight. Or maybe a hockey game? I've never been but I hear they're fun."

"I think I'd like to stay home tonight, if you don't mind. Perhaps you can stay home too? If you do not have plans, that is."

"But you don't get out much, wouldn't you like to see a movie or go to a club?"

"Violet, you do not have to take me out to entertain me. I enjoy spending time with you. I enjoy just being with you, even if I do a bad job of showing it."

He didn't know for sure but he could swear she blushed. It was a fleeting look of surprise and pleasure that made her pretty face even prettier.

They watched a couple walk by with a baby in a stroller. Taka could not take his eyes off the three of them.

"Did you have children?" Violet asked.

"No. My wife and I were not blessed. And you, do you want them?"

"Sure. Maybe. Someday."

"You do not sound convinced."

"No, I want them, but first I have to get married."

"To Jerome?"

"Of course," she drawled giving him a sideways warning look which he rightly interpreted.

"And then you'll give him lots of little mealy-mouthed babies and live happily ever after?" The way she rolled her eyes told him he'd probably said something wrong. "Forgive me. I did not mean to sound so . . ."

"Yes, you did."

"Yes, I did, but I did not mean to make light of you or your offspring. I intended only to make light of the dung beetle you would mate with. It is my nature to express my opinion, whether or not I am asked. I do not know how to, what is the expression? Beat around the bush?"

"Be tactful, you mean?"

"Um, how do I say, lie for the sake of peace?"

"Mind your own business, you mean?"

"I cannot, what is that term, blow smoke up one's rear side?"

"I have no idea where you pick this stuff up; you live in a rock for cripes' sake! Let's just agree that you sure don't know how to keep your mouth shut and leave it at that."

"All right. I admit it freely, but I tell you something I know, Violet, immortal to mortal: it is human nature to assume a day will follow the one that exists but we are not guaranteed that day. People die but regret never does. You are an intelligent, lively woman. Any man would be blessed to have you. Do not bind yourself to a man who does not love you or bind your children to a father who does not covet that position. And if ever you are in doubt of where you stand in a relationship I suggest one simple question: if you knew you did not have tomorrow, would you want him by your side today?"

Her serious eyes on him were satisfying because they told him that she heard him.

"Taka, I used to dream about the man I would want to live my life with; you know, back when I was young and dumb and didn't realize that men had fragile egos, wandering body parts, and were determined to make my life a living nightmare? Oh yes, I made a list." She looked off into the distance with a smile on her face. "He would have to be man enough to be with me, if you know what I mean. Determined, a little bullheaded. No pushover."

"Strong of character."

"Exactly. He wouldn't be a wuss but he wouldn't knock old ladies over in the street."

"Kindhearted but no weakling?"

"Yes. He couldn't just want to sit at home all the time watching TV, he'd want to try things."

"Adventurous?"

"That's a good way to put it. And he most certainly would love food and appreciate the finer things."

"Zest for life? Good cook? Lover of the arts?" She looked at him in surprise and he went on eagerly. "You know my mother taught me to cook. I didn't have to most of the time because my wife did it but I know how to make a good meal, enjoy a good glass of wine, literature, theater."

Her look of confusion shut down his rambling. He cleared his throat and did his own bluffing. "I know what you mean about the list. When I became a man at twelve—"

"You became a man at twelve?" she interrupted, eyes wide.

"No, no, not in the way of today. We had an initiation ceremony and I became a man. That very day I began looking at the girls in my village to find a possible mate, but my future mate was already there. Oh, she was only a girl, she had not yet had her initiation into womanhood; but I knew her well. She had alternately been my childhood friend and nemesis for all my days. I adored her. By the time we were teens and she blossomed into full womanly ripeness I was besotted with her. I could not look at her without wanting to taste her exquisite skin, pined for the scent of her, fell asleep dreaming about the sound of her voice, the curl of her hair, the pleasure I longed to give her on the riverbank under a full, low moon with the smell of jasmine scenting our coupling and the sweet warm air to sing the tale of our love." He cleared his voice as his memory made it husky

with forgotten desire, sneaking a look at Violet to find her
eyes intent upon him.

"I digress. As I was saying, she met every single requirement I could ever want in a woman. Why, as king I had men
give me advice every day about how to run my kingdom but
my wife was my greatest advisor, even though she could not
officially hold that station. She was very good at seeing
the true character of people. She was very good at getting
to the heart of a situation. With very little information she
could figure out almost any—"

"Intelligent?"

"Yes, very. And she had this way of getting her point
across and it would not be offensive."

"Funny? Clever?"

"Very. And a way of cutting to the heart of a matter."

"Quick witted? Impatient?"

"Infinitely. I am a large man, sometimes I frighten
people simply by my size, but she—"

"Wasn't intimidated at all?"

"Not in the least. I was a king, but to her . . ."

"You were just a man?"

Taka looked at her and nodded, "Yes. And it was . . .
wonderful. She was my lover and my best friend. I loved
her boundlessly. I cannot describe how difficult it was to
lose her. Losing her was like losing my leg."

"Did you say losing her was like losing your leg? Come
on, King, surely you can come up with an analogy more
romantic than that. That's like saying losing her was like
losing your horse or your wagon: something sturdy and
boring."

"I am no poet. I am clumsy sometimes with my words.
I only mean to say, I cannot stand tall without her. I
cannot move forward without her support. And much
like a missing limb the place she used to occupy in my
life throbs with memory of what once was, wails with the

pain of what will never be, racks my whole being with quakes of sorrow that never still." He sighed as the breeze crossed his face. "But occasionally the pain quiets when I am out of my stone and I feel a moment of happiness. Today, the pain is almost forgotten. Until I speak of it, that is."

He looked at Violet and she gave him a gentle smile in return. His heart sang.

"Thank you for today, Violet. Will you allow me to do something for you? In gratitude and celebration?"

Her eyes widened in surprise but then she shrugged and he bounded up easily, saying only, "I will be right back. Wait for me here."

He almost couldn't contain his excitement as he went off over the green grass in search of his treasure.

Violet watched Taka make his way in large strides over the grass and chided herself for being struck still by the sight of him, tall and strong and so amazingly male. She was still tingling from the way Taka had spoken to her, looking at her like she was the most precious gem in the world. Sometimes during their conversation she would feel his eyes on her and know desire burned in him. Other times she would catch him in a look so gentle and searching it made her want to cry. At one point she was absolutely sure he would reach out, stroke the hair from her face.

Get a grip, Violet! He's a genie!

She had to keep saying it to herself over and over or she would forget, as she was looking at him more and more like a regular man every minute. His description about the loss of his wife, well, it almost did her in.

This would not do for either of them. If they didn't rein in the lust this would only end in heartache when he disappeared from her life in a plume of smoke. He was already mourning his wife; Violet didn't miss the fact that

176 Ava Bleu

the poor man superimposed all of Violet's qualities onto the memory of his betrothed. She almost felt bad for his wife the way he so obviously wanted Violet. It was as if he couldn't allow himself to want Violet unless he somehow wrapped her in the same paper as his deceased wife. It was tragic, really.

She couldn't help a malicious smile of a conquering heroine.

She leaned back on the blanket, soaking in the sights, when her genie finally came back into view. He strode toward her with a look of satisfaction on his face and his hands full of flowers, their stems still crusted with clumps of soil.

"What's going on?" She laughed as his face opened with happiness upon seeing her.

"My wife used to love me to braid flowers into her hair. I am going to do that for you now."

"What?" Violet croaked as he came toward her with the flowers. "You can't be serious."

"I am more than serious, woman. I know you received flowers yesterday, but they were from Him. These are from me. Now lean back against me and do not give me a hard time."

Violet blinked as suddenly he was behind her on his knees, dropping the little pile of flowers beside him to begin to probe her hair.

"Whoa, wait a minute. It's a nice thought but those flowers are still dirty."

He picked up one, brushing the soil from the end. "I needed to retain the stem for the braiding."

"And what do you know about braiding? I don't know a single man who knows how to braid hair."

"Questioning my manhood? That will not deter me as I am more than confident of my manhood and I am sure the pleasure you receive will cease all objection. Another lesson from my mother. My father would have bellowed throughout the hills had he known." Violet watched as he methodically removed the dirt from the stems. The flowers looked like violets. He remembered.

She scavenged in her purse for some antibacterial hand gel to no avail. By the time he was combing his big, soil-smudged fingers through her perfumed, relaxed hair, she was too overcome by surprise and the romance of the gesture to protest. She allowed her shoulders to rest against his chest. Who braided flowers into anyone's hair these days? But it was certainly nice to lean back against him. His scent was spicy and earthy and entirely too pleasant. She could lie like that all day.

His large fingers were barely a whisper over her scalp. He worked quickly, thoroughly, and she was drunk with the sweetness of it all. She could get used to this.

He came around to look at her, twisting his head this way and that to see his progress. She smiled to match his. "Bella," he said kissing the tips of two fingers.

"Stop it. You keep telling me I'm beautiful I'm going to have to kiss you to shut you up." And, she meant it, though she was horrified she'd allowed her inside thoughts to come outside. He didn't seem to mind if his flush of joy was any indication.

"Then I will tell you of your beauty all night."

Flirt. Violet laughed and dug around in her purse for her mirror. She hadn't had her hair braided since before her own initiation into womanhood: the chemical relaxing of her natural curls at fourteen.

"Goodness." The colorful blossoms were woven loosely but complemented her skin tone. Eventually they would fall out; the straight strands were not able to hold a flower like her natural hair would have been. But he took care to utilize the stems to hold them, tying them in as well. For now it was lovely.

She twisted her head to and fro, enraptured by the simple beauty of a few flowers. "These are really beautiful, Taka. Where did you find them?"

"I walked all around this park and I could not find a single worthy blossom so finally I went into the hothouse and found just what I was looking for. And if the jealousy on the faces of the others was any indication, I found the best blooms. All those people were just walking around looking, none with the fortitude to make up their minds. Well, I had no problem picking my favorites: violets just as we had in mother Africa."

Violet snapped the mirror closed and looked at his handsome, clueless face. "You mean the display in the conservatory?"

"Yes, the hothouse around the bend."

It only took about half a second to determine what he had done.

She stood and gathered the blanket, speaking to him gently. "Taka, I think we need to go now. Hurry, please." But she was not quite quick enough as, alas, she spied two men looking their way: one in shorts and flip-flops with a scowl on his face and the other in an official parks outfit complete with badge. The flip-flop man pointed at Taka and Violet turned to her friendly giant with one command.

"Taka, run."

"What?"

"Run!"

She took off for the car, a sideways glance confirming the guard was taking chase. But soon enough the massive form of a running genie blocked that view, striding beside her and then passing, kicking up dirt along the way. She was about to curse him for leaving her in the dust when he came to a skidding halt at the car and opened his two hands to her, tilted toward the sky in a classic baseball catcher stance. She responded by lobbing the car keys in an overhand toss he caught effortlessly. By the time she reached the car the driver's door was unlocked and open, waiting for her, the key in the ignition and the engine idling, and the genie was in the passenger seat. He'd even belted himself in!

She tossed the blanket on the back seat, buckled, and made a magnificent screech peeling out of the parking lot. One look in the rearview at the perturbed arm-folded stance of the indignant pedestrian told her the two men had giving up chase very shortly after its start.

"What a run." Taka breathed like he'd just taken a light morning jog. "I haven't had a good run in a long while; feels good to these rusty limbs," he said, breathing heavily beside her.

She checked her mirror and saw the guard watching them, a little notepad and pencil in his hands jotting down her identity. She didn't have the heart to tell Taka that her license plate was as good as a honing device. Surely it would take them at least a day to track her down if they were so inclined, and by that time the genie would be safe in his stone. She panted out the exhaustion of a woman unused to running, managing to fog up her rearview mirror and drive at the same time as he continued without a care.

"But I do not understand. Why did we run? I only picked flowers. I thought you said the nature was for us to enjoy."

"To look at, yes, not to steal," she said making a herculean effort to get her breathing under control. She really should start exercising, or something. "I'll have to send them a check or a note of apology or a basket of flowers. Okay, maybe flowers is a bad idea."

"I do not steal," he said indignantly. "I saw others scuffing the grass with their bicycles, drinking freely from the fountain. How is it you accuse me of theft?"

"Let me put it this way," Violet blew air over her perspiring forehead. "What if a neighboring village had a bunch of lovely flowers that caught your eye?"

"If the rotten scoundrels who neighbored me ever came upon the ability to grow any living item worth my interest they should send me a scroll of thanks for noticing and a mule with a bow tied around its neck as a gift for my magnanimity."

"Obviously no love lost between you and your neighbors. So, in that case, what if you just cleaned out all of their flowerbeds and took their flowers as your own? Wouldn't that start a little trouble?"

Hesitation, then: "Perhaps I should send a note of apology. You should have told me. I would have explained my error man to man; we did not need to run as if we'd done wrong. It was an honest mistake."

"Well, maybe for someone who is unaware of how civilized society works but I couldn't take the risk that you could explain yourself without getting yourself sent to the loony bin. And, there's the fact that I have one wish left and I cannot make it with you in jail or being taken down by two guys in a park. What if they'd decided on a little rough justice? They could have pinned you down until the police came to take you away. They could have pinned us both down and taken the flowers back, and I really like these flowers. They could have . . ."

Violet stopped her rambling as the visual of the two men trying to take down her genie filled her head. Any way she sliced it, it didn't compute. In fact, the notion of the two ice cream soft men overcoming her king was so ridiculous it was laughable. She looked over to Taka and found he was doing just that, trying to hide laughter behind quivering lips, his personal attempt at humility. She lasted only two seconds before they both burst into raucous laughter.

Finally Violet composed herself enough to wipe the tears of mirth from her eyes. "Taka, you are fun to be around."

"As are you, Violet Jackson." He sobered and did the same. They watched the streets pass and when he spoke again the humor was gone, replaced by thoughtful introspection. "In my day it was common to go to battle and take what you wanted from another village or kingdom. It was how we grew our own. But there were rules to battle. Any kingdom I had designs on knew my intent, knew to prepare a defense. We did not ravage women or kill babies like some of our neighbors did, and our slaves were treated with respect, able to earn their freedom. As all warriors, I was bred for battle but it was not bloodlust that drove me; it was the honest fight against the worthy foe. My people were decent people; honest, hardworking, decent people. It is important to me that you know this. I am no thief; I simply did not understand. I will go back to Africa myself, if I have the chance, to replenish what damage I have done to the hothouse today. I would not have you ashamed of me or my actions when you remember me. I would not bring dishonor upon your name or make your life difficult in any way."

Violet looked at the worry lines between his brows, the pinched look on his strong face. It hurt her to see him so troubled and she drew her eyes back to the road so he couldn't see the effect he had upon her.

"But know, as well," he continued, his tone hardening, "no living man had ever attempt to pull flowers from your hair that I have placed there, not while I live and breathe. Not while I am conscious and alert. Not if he expects to continue living and breathing, himself. With everything in me I would defend you, Violet. I was not able to save my wife. I will not let that happen again. I will not allow a woman I care about to be hurt like that again. I will not shame my family, my title, or my people ever again. I will not let you down in that way. That is my word."

Violet knew his words were heartfelt. She knew they were true to the depths of her soul. And despite knowing that the woman he had loved came to an untimely end, she couldn't help a little jealousy toward the woman who held his heart. No one had ever loved her so completely. Not even close.

"Taka, I don't know what happened all those years ago, but I tell you without a doubt you are the best man I know. If you loved your wife half as much as I believe you do, you have nothing to be sorry for or ashamed about. You keep talking about what you lost; what about what she lost in you? I imagine to a woman loved by you, losing you would be the worst torture she could endure. No woman loved by you could lose that love lightly. That's more important than anything you think you didn't do or couldn't do. If you loved her, she knew it. If you loved her, she could never forget it. A woman knows these things. If you loved her, she was the luckiest woman on earth, no matter what came later. But that's just my humble opinion."

She couldn't look at him but it wasn't long before she felt his hand rest softly upon hers on the wheel. Hands as strong and gentle as any she'd ever felt. Hands of a man who had been hurt soul deep. Hands of a man she cared about more than a little. A genie, a king . . . a friend. Hands of a man more special than anything the real world had to offer. Hands of a man she knew she'd never have. And that fact finally caused her eyes to tear up.

She let go of the wheel for just a moment, just long enough to grasp his hand tightly, before letting go to clutch the firm certainty of the steering wheel.

Chapter 17

"You know I hate this place a little more every time I walk through the door. I mean, look at it," Violet said, opening the door to her apartment and tossing her purse on a table. "This is no home. I don't even want to put pictures on the wall. I hate it here. I'm an interior decorator and I have no desire to make this place even remotely appealing."

Taka looked around, finally noticing the starkness of the room. "You are right. It does not have your sparkling personality."

"No, it doesn't. I'm waiting, Taka. Waiting for enough money to buy the house I want. And I will get it, too. Believe me."

"I do believe you." He sat down beside her.

"Hey." She turned to him. "You want to see my work? I've won awards, you know. I was in a magazine last year for some work I did for this woman on the north side. Want to see?"

She had such an open look of excitement—her face an open invitation where before she had been closed off and defensive—Taka could not help but agree. "Certainly."

Violet popped up, walked over to a table, and picked up a photo album, bringing it back to sit beside him again. She placed it on the coffee table and opened it.

"I keep photos of every job I do." She turned a page and showed him snapshots of different rooms in different houses. As she described each, her finger moving over the page, her face grew more animated with each photo. Taka watched her intently. He noted how excited she was describing her designs, recognized the hunger in her eyes as she spoke because he'd seen it in the eyes of his men after each battle. He knew it was in his own when, after each win, he would glow with esteem and pride, filled with an indescribable sense of accomplishment. He was seeing the same in her. It was just as Ani had said: her kingdom was her company.

"And this one I did for a congressman. And this one is the one I won for."

Taka pulled his eyes from her face to look down at the album and a full, glossy photo of a room. The colors were striking: golds, reds, purples, and violets. Accents of beads and stones. Pillows embroidered in lush velvets and silks. Tapestries with bold prints, splashes of orange.

"The colors . . ." he started hesitantly. He wanted to scream for joy. The colors were the same that had filled their home. He reached out and flipped quickly through the pages at the photos he hadn't paid attention to, and back to the award-winning design. "The rooms are all so . . . warm. So inviting."

Violet blushed with pleasure. "Yes. I believe in the use of color. So many designers today use color only as an accent. I think color shouldn't be an accent to life; color *is* life."

Taka looked at her deeply now, seeing so much more. Her face was so open and vulnerable, when she turned to him her eyes were so full of pleasure he wanted to gasp. He wanted to reach out to her and call out, "Zahara, are you there?" For only Zahara knew that he had asked for her hand in marriage under a sky blooming with the colors of that photo. Only Zahara knew that he'd had the fantastic brooch fashioned for her because after accepting his offer she'd looked up at the setting sun, pointed to the sky, and said, "Look, Taka. The sky has given us a ribbon of scarlet."

He'd looked up and did indeed see a strip of bright red in the midst of a panel of pink in the sky. The red was the color of the ruby contained in the brooch that would be his vessel. The red and pink intertwined, ending in a stroke of brilliant blue.

"And there, have you ever seen such a beautiful color in all the world? It is a gift to us, my king. The sky is celebrating our love."

Taka choked down his emotion as he remembered the other color, so beautiful and rare it did not have a name; and he didn't even attempt to find a gem to match it. He remembered this now as he looked deeply into the face of the woman who held his wife's spirit.

"It is . . . breathtakingly beautiful," he said today.

"Thank you," Violet responded, finally pulling her gaze from the photo to look into his eyes.

Taka felt his heart pound as he recognized a glimmer of awareness in the depth of her eyes. He felt something in her reach to him, he saw something in her open toward him; but, then, just as quickly it disappeared and she closed herself once again. He felt a sharp sliver of disappointment as she shifted uncomfortably.

"Goodness, King, for a moment there you almost did me in with those eyes of yours. Do you seduce every woman who rubs your stone?" she asked.

Taka straightened as well, looking deeply into her eyes. She was going to shut him down over and over again. Every time he got close she closed her heart to him. Well, if he only had one day left, he would darn sure say his name. She would hear it loud and clear so that forever it would ring in her ears, live in her dreams. He would say it so her soul would recognize and rejoice even if she couldn't.

"Hear me well. My name is Taka Olufemi. Not genie, not King; Taka. If I am seducing you it is your fault, you enjoyed rubbing my stone so much you did it twice. I am only a man. Even I do not know how to resist double provocation."

Chapter 18

Across town, a distraught Brenda sat at a table in a restaurant with Jerome. She fidgeted with her water, nervously. "Thank you for coming. I appreciate it."

"What's this about? I don't have a lot of time. What, you thinking about hooking up with me or something? That's something that can be arranged." He smiled.

Brenda's head pulled back in confusion. "What are you talking about? I'm here about Violet."

"Yeah, yeah. Of course."

"She's lying to you. Just like she lied to me."

His eyes narrowed. "Lying about what?"

"She told me she was happy for me and what does she do? She goes out and steals my account. My account!"

"You mean that big money deal? Wow."

"It was as good as done and she goes behind my back and convinces Bickman to hire her company. How low is that? She didn't even have the decency to tell me. Her secretary told me!"

"Well, what can I say, Brenda? It's not like you didn't stab her in the back too. You stole her technique and passed it off as yours."

Brenda turned a withering glance to him and hissed, "Don't get all high and mighty with me. Oh, I bet you're feeling pretty smug thinking about all that money you're going to get when you're married. Don't get too happy. She already told me she's gonna write up a pre-nup. And don't think she'll be free with her money when you're married, either. She's gonna dole it out to you like a pimp to a trick."

Jerome's face fell. "Hey."

"And you shouldn't even be thinking about marrying her anyway with what she's doing." She looked away slyly knowing he would fall into the trap.

"What are you talking about?"

"I would have told you sooner but she swore me to secrecy and I thought she was my friend. But that man staying with her, he isn't related to her. She's just got that tall, fine man staying with her, and lying to you about it."

Jerome stiffened. "What you talking about? Who is he?"

"I don't know. And she didn't know him until yesterday,"

"Naw, you don't know what you're talking about. She spent last night with me."

"Okay then, if you say so. If things are good between you and Violet and you have no doubts at all, then I'll leave it alone. All I have to say is, whatever happened last night, she went right back to her stud this morning."

She took a sip of water, knowing that her words were making their way through his brain. She didn't know how things were between Violet and Jerome, but she'd taken a stab that all was not right. She saw his face darken with anger and knew she'd gambled right.

"Wait a minute! Tell me exactly what she told you about him. She told you she was stepping out on me?"

"Worse. She was playing games. Told me she met this guy who was making all her wishes come true. Tried to make out that he was a genie or something but I saw right through that. He's a genie all right. A genie in bed. She's not at work because I called over there. She's back at her apartment right now, I bet, working that genie out of his lamp, if you know what I mean."

"Son of a b . . ." He stormed out of the restaurant and Brenda sighed.

She'd done it. She'd gotten back at Violet. She'd done exactly what she'd set out to do. Though as she sipped her water she felt an odd, empty feeling where satisfaction should have been.

Chapter 19

Violet was on the sofa, in a cautious mood, and she blamed Taka for it.

Everything had been going along fine until he'd done the bum-rush on her. One second they were talking about her designs, and the next second, wham! Her emotions raced through her when she saw the intensity in his eyes. She'd never in all her days been privy to such a look. It was one of those looks they have in movies, so ridiculously intense you know it's fake. But it wasn't fake with him. And it pissed her off!

Clearly an effort to intimidate her, throw her off her game. Clearly designed to make her question every look she'd ever received by any man at any time in her life. She knew she would never in a thousand years forget that look. It would have been so easy to simply allow her lips to meld with his, to taste those lips, to outline the provocative curve with the tip of her tongue.

But, finally, Violet had come to her senses. There was no way in the world she was going to get involved with this man. No matter what his name was he was a genie, for God's sake! Of course, he'd had to have the last word, making a flippant reply about double provocation. First, that was a tease if ever she'd heard one. Second, who even talked like that? Third, how was it he could make the corniest things sound sexy?

She sat glaring at him from under hooded lids as he looked through a newspaper, his face serious in contemplation. Oh, sure, now he was trying to play hard to get. Talking nonsense about some foot trip he'd taken earlier, asking about jobs. Boy, he was good. She kneaded a throw pillow with vigor.

"I don't know why you're stressing over all this," she said. "What kind of job can you hold being out of your rock three days at a pop? And why would you want to work at all?"

"I do not know. Maybe someday I will be able to live as a normal man again and I should be prepared. I miss work. I miss being useful."

"You're useful, I guess. If you ask me, giving wishes is one of the best jobs in the world. You just have to learn how to actually make them happen and you'll have it made."

At his further look and eye roll Violet laughed. He could eye roll her all he wanted; she'd made two wishes and had yet to see a return.

"You would not like granting wishes," he said. "It is never as easy as it seems and when people are not clear they can do untold damage to themselves. Besides, if it meant you could not run your business and live the life you want, it would lose its appeal. And then you would resent it. Maybe even resent the people you are trying to help."

Violet looked at him sideways. "Like you resent me? Is that why you're trying to make things difficult for me?"

He folded the paper closed. "You have no need to be suspicious of me." He stood and walked back over to sit beside her in the danger zone. Violet immediately grew hot around the ears, exacerbated when he took one of her hot hands in his equally hot one. "I am not your enemy. I am doing all I can to protect you."

Violet watched the back of her hand as he used his other to stroke it, making little squiggly lines and circles

on it. She listed toward him as she watched, fascinated
by the flight pattern of his fingertip. Hypnotized by his
earthy, spicy male scent and the sheer size of his massive
hand caressing hers.

She swallowed hard. He was starting again. She didn't
know what to do. A day ago she would have snatched her
hand away, but a day ago she would never have thought
the big man could be so gentle. And now that she knew he
wanted to get into her pants, that put a whole new spin
on things. Heck, she was tempted to sleep with him just
to win their little battle of wills and show him who was
running things.

The phone rang and Violet jumped to reach for it over
the sofa, happy to break contact. "Yeah, hi, Carol. No, not
today. I just don't feel like it, that's why. What? What do
you mean she found out? You told her? Who told you to
do that? Who do you work for, her or me? Never mind."
She hung up, and then reached over to turn off the ringer.
Her face alternated between glee and horror. "That was
my assistant. I got the account I bid for this morning.
I took it back from Brenda. She stole it from me and I
stole it right back." Smile. "And Brenda knows." Frown.
"Crap."

"She was bound to learn sometime," Taka said.

"Yes, but I wanted to decide how she found out. You're
right; I should fire that sneaky secretary of mine. But the
good news: I'm loaded, or at least I'm in the process of
becoming loaded. Not only is he happy with my designs,
InStyle called already. I'm getting a spread. Oh, and
the press is already calling because the word is I've got the
contract for his hotels, too. I'm going to have to call Tracy
to confirm, but not right now. I just want to enjoy this
for today. I'm set, Taka." She sat stock straight, only her
hands fidgeting and her head shaking slightly with shock.
"Oh my God, I can't believe it."

Her heart was too full to allow her head to think straight. So many years she'd dreamed of just this moment. She'd always wondered who would be by her side to share her success when it came. She'd assumed it would be Jerome. A silly assumption since they rarely spent downtime together and when they were alone they didn't have that much to talk about. She was surprised at how happy she was that it was Taka sitting next to her.

"I am glad to see you happy," he said.

"Aren't you proud of me? I worked hard for this."

Taka's mouth pinched, he hesitated, but then continued. "Did you? Is this an accomplishment you worked for?"

"What do you mean? Of course I worked for it. I've been trying to get something like this for years, I told you, and . . ." She stopped, her smile fading. Elation dropped as quickly as a sinking stone; her eyes falling from his quickly so he could not see the hurt he'd caused. "Oh, you think you did this?"

"You did not have this one day ago," he said simply.

"So you don't think I'm good enough to pull this off on my own?"

"You did not pull it off on your own so I can only deduce if I had not come along you would still be in the same shape as before, chasing your friend around trying to beat her at her own game."

"That's low, King. That's really low. I've worked hard for a long time; you have no idea how hard. The only reason she got that contract was because she stole it from me."

"I do not fault your resourcefulness or your talent, Violet. I only wonder why it is you chose to play such a dangerous game at all. You are too good to be in the mud, messing your talent with the taint of trickery."

"You sound like you think the fact that Brenda is a witch is my fault. Never mind. Just forget it."

How could she have allowed herself to be lulled into forgetting what a pompous, judgmental jerk he could be? Her previously hot flesh chilled down to arctic weather and the cold front ushered in a gust of good sense on the northerly front, with a few sprinkles of lingering disappointment.

"Why did you even come anyway?" she continued. "You told me I had three wishes and every time I make one you fuss at me. If this is what you're usually like no wonder you only get out of your rock for a few minutes each time. I know you're a decent person under all this distemper but no one would ever know because unless you want to get into their pants, you would never lighten up enough for them to see it. Who could tolerate your nagging without an upside?" She walked into the kitchen, reaching for a bag of potato chips. She opened it and pulled a chip out to crunch in her mouth, stopping mid-chew at his stare. "What?"

The frustration on his face would have been laughable had she been in the mood. She could see him burning like a volcano to spew another round of unwanted lecture her way. The man had no self-control when it came to giving her unwanted advice.

Instead he shook his head, grinding out, "I am hungry, and you have nothing but play food to eat."

Talk about avoidance and denial. Just like a man. Just because she told him to shove his advice he had to start whining and pouting like a baby.

She tilted the bag his way and he gave her a dirty look. She slapped the bag on the counter and put her hands on her hips.

"There is plenty of food here." She jerked open the freezer to prove her point. "Look: Salisbury steak, fried chicken, enchiladas, what more could you want?" she asked, pulling each frozen dinner out of the freezer as she mentioned it and watched his face scrunch in disgust.

"There is ice covering those boxes. If there is food inside it cannot be edible. First, eggs covered in hot peppers to break my fast. Now, shattering chips from a bag and boxes of items frozen over from the tundra. I am a warrior; I cannot eat soft-man gruel. Are you trying to kill me, woman?"

"Your problem, genie, is that you're just a prima donna," she told him. "All this griping and it's only . . . My goodness, is it really five?" Then she sighed. "Okay, look, I promised you pizza this morning, didn't I?" At his silence she followed with, "That's a large piece of dough with some sauce and—"

"I know what a pizza is but somehow I doubt what you will feed me will be comparable to the pizza I have eaten at the table of my Roman friends, so I respectfully decline." He might as well have crossed his arms and poked out his bottom lip.

"You said you didn't want to eat out, King." Her voice sounded grave with warning, even to her. "What do you want? Do you want me to take you to the store or something so you can pick out your own frozen meals?"

"The market?" He brightened immediately. "I would like a healthy piece of fish. A green vegetable, maybe. I can cook it myself. I am an excellent cook, I told you."

What a pain he was being. Violet didn't know why she cared what he ate. She was tempted to serve him the frozen two-year-old enchiladas after the way he'd insulted her, but never let it be said Violet Jackson wasn't a compassionate soul, when she wanted to be. And maybe if he got something he liked he'd be easier to live with.

"Well, I suppose it can't hurt." She looked him over, giving in to the momentary surge of generosity. "You drive."

Taka's brows went up. "Me?"

"Why not? If you screw up we're both in trouble, so you better watch yourself, genie. I'm too pretty to go to prison."

The idea of having a decent piece of fish and getting behind the wheel were apparently too much for him to resist because before she knew it he said, "Let's go. Yes, I will drive. Do not worry, I shall be very careful." He pulled on his coat, reached in the pocket, and pulled out some money, looking at it in amazement. Ani had giving him a fraction of a fraction of currency. It wasn't all the riches of his village but it was enough, he hoped, for a good meal. "Come. Today we will dine and celebrate your good fortune and the day. I am happy for you, Violet. Truly. And I am happy to spend this time with you and I am glad to know you."

Boy, what a little freedom, a few bucks, and promise of a good meal could do to a man.

And so in minutes Violet found herself sitting in the passenger seat of her own car, strapped in, wondering if her insurance would cover her if this maniac drove them into a tree. Good thing she was going to be rich and could cover the property damage.

Amazingly, his lessons from yesterday had stuck like glue. He drove the car surprisingly well and didn't speed once, despite her impatience at the way he adhered to the limit.

Violet blew air up her bangs in frustration. Bull pucky. She was more anxious at the way he followed the law than she would have been if he'd been doing doughnuts in the middle of Livingston Avenue. She was likely to croak from a burst blood vessel due to stress of trying to get to the friggin' market with a genie at the wheel.

"For God's sake, you were moving faster when we were driving over that patch of dirt yesterday. You moved

faster when you ran to the car this morning. Can you pick
it up a little, grandpa?"

"You mock me to coerce me to move faster."

"Well, is it working?"

"Does it feel like it is working?" Taka gave her a
patronizing look and continued to inch his way along,
taking special care to stop a mile short of red lights and
pedestrians. If anything, they might have been moving
even slower. She could be wrong, but she thought they
were going backward. The police threw people in the
pokey for that, too.

Finally, after what seemed like hours later to Violet,
they pulled into the lot in front of the North Market. She
undid her seat belt and moved to get up. He looked at her,
his expression stopping her. "What?"

"May I go alone?"

Violet noticed the eagerness on his face. The man
wanted some freedom. He'd had a little of it and now he
was fiending like an addict, loving the taste and feel of it.
She almost felt like her baby bird was testing its wings.
Only her baby bird was close to seven feet and could
flatten anything in his path with little effort. Her baby
bird had shoulders as wide as the Olentangy River and
skin the color of a coconut husk. Her cold front thawed as
a tropic breeze rolled through.

"Are you all right?" he asked.

"Fine, fine." She waved away his concern with her
hand. "Look, you go on. I'll stay here. No biggie."

Taka gave her a look of such pure gratitude she almost
flinched. Then he reached over and laid a hand on hers,
pulling it up to his lips to press a kiss against the back. "I
shall be back shortly, okay?" he said. Then he left the car,
leaving her doubly flushed inside.

His use of the word "okay" made her smile. She was
obviously a good influence on the man. She was mod-

ernizing him but good. One day out of the stone and he was driving like a pro, using modern vernacular, and asserting his independence. All on her watch. She was a genius. Then why was she feeling that niggling finger of doubt?

Because she was an idiot!

In a day and age where a good woman couldn't keep a man to save her life, here she had a great man, and she as good as gave him the tools to get away from her. And she was a little less good than some women she'd known. Even now, he was probably chatting up single women in the market, impressing them with his modern vernacular and tales of his superior driving skills. And she could only imagine if he could drive a car that well, what he could do with that superb body of his. Women would be all over him like pit bulls on sirloin!

And why should she care? That was simple. Because he was her responsibility. Sure, he was a genie and all, but somebody had to look out for the guy. If he showed up with an STD or something, the Big Kahuna would be plenty pissed with her, and if she wasn't looking after her immortal soul, who would? The king was just too innocent to understand women of today. Why, if she were a single woman walking around the market and saw a magnificent-looking being such as Taka walking around, being gentleman-like, buying fresh fish in order to cook for some woman waiting at home, she would do everything in her power to change his priorities. She would make it her goal to conquer that particular natural wonder in record time. And by nightfall, she would have him demonstrating those wonderful manual dexterity skills all over her satin sheets. If she were single, that is. And if he was a man and not a make-believe character.

It seemed to take forever but finally he returned.

"Done already?" she asked as he got in, a triumphant look on his face, putting his bags in back.

"I am. Shall we go home?"

Home. Violet liked the sound of that. She smiled as he started the motor and pulled out of the lot.

Chapter 20

Skeeter sat on a lawn chair behind his Uncle Euclid's ranch home and looked at the elderly man who had stopped midsentence. He couldn't tell if the old man had paused to think or simply fallen asleep again with his eyes open, but just as he reached up to poke him the octogenarian gave him a rheumy-eyed glare.

"Don't you be poking me with those sharp fingers of yours, boy. Make me have to go upside your behind."

Skeeter was sixty-eight but, to 102-year-old Euclid, he was still an upstart whippersnapper.

"I'm just trying to get you to go on with what you was saying, Uncle."

"Sayin'? Who was saying what?"

"You was! About the village that disappeared, remember?"

"Oh, yeah. Stop interrupting me, boy! Listen. That town was run by that king what's-his-name. Tanya, something like that. And my daddy told me that king was some kind of mean. Oh, people were super scared of him 'cause he killed folks without a care. Lopped off one man's head just for saying hi!" He drew one shaky finger across his neck and displayed a comical look of horror to contribute to the story telling. "So my daddy's daddy's daddy, well, he helped take care a him. Went to the village one night to kill that king and free the people and what you think he found? The king done killed all his own people! 'Cept for his wife. The wife killed herself out of horror at the kinda evil man she married. Couldn't take it!"

"Uhn uhn uhn." Skeeter shook his head with the shame of it. "And what then, Uncle Euclid?"

"Well, then God was so mad at him, so disgusted, He was gonna send him straight down to the devil and be done with him but He got sidetracked. Tanya spits in his eye, laughs, and says, 'You can't do nothin' to me, everybody's dead.' So's God says"—at this point Uncle Euclid adopted an evil squinty-eyed glare and raised that finger again to point at the air in front of him in his best improvised version of the Almighty admonishing the king—"'I sent all these good men from these other towns to come in here and save your people and you done already killed them! Ooooh, I'm so mad at you, Tanya, I'm so mad I could spit! I got somethin' I can do to you, boy. I'll take care a you real good. I'ma go upside your behind!' He said it just like that there."

Skeeter listened to the same story he'd been told all his life but had never paid attention to. It was a tale of a lost village passed down through generations, a tale he had never believed until that day and the man built like a mountain came into his store with an eye on a bowl. It looked like the same pattern of a cup Skeeter had seen in his great-grandfather's hands as a young boy. The cup was part of the tale of their African ancestors. Skeeter had always just thought it was a made-up story about a thrift shop item, until the big man had come into the store today and picked up what could have been a matching piece with memory and intensity in his eyes. A big man with a heavy accent and the assumption that Skeeter was a thief.

"You listening to me, boy? I oughta rap you over your head, disrespecting your elders. Why I oughta—"

"See you later, Uncle Euclid." Skeeter had already risen, kissed the old man on the head, and planned his next move. He knew some people in New York who knew some people in Africa. He'd gotten all he was going to get from the old man. Surely his historian friend could give him a little more than tall tales.

Chapter 21

An hour later Taka sat at the kitchen table, polishing off what had been the best meal he'd had in 400 years. The fish had baked to tender perfection, the shrimp had baked in garlic, butter, lemon, and parsley, and the vegetables had been steamed in a handy device Violet called a "bamboo steamer" and tossed with butter and more lemon. For dessert, he'd found some cheesecake and fresh berries. And for Violet, he'd stopped by a stand and purchased a slab of barbecued pork ribs, with extra sauce on the side, after seeing what she'd had for dinner the night before. Even now she was licking her last bone clean.

"I love these ribs," she said, washing down the meal with a mouthful of wine he'd chosen. She didn't know much about wine but this wine went perfectly with ribs. "Best ribs in Columbus."

"I saw how much you seemed to enjoy the pork yesterday and when I passed the stand the smell reached out to me. It smells almost like the fragrant stew of my village. I would have made the stew for myself had my stomach not already been twisting with torturous hunger pains; the stew takes several hours to simmer and I had no time. So you like the pork ribcage? I was afraid since you had them last night at the restaurant you would be tired of them."

"Uhn uhn. Never tired of ribs," she said over her last good chew. She stretched and sighed as he carried their plates to the trash can, scraping them. She then loaded them into another machine, added liquid soap, and turned it on.

As curious as he was about the machine, Taka was thinking more about Violet. Earlier in the day when she had found out about the contract she'd won over her friend, he could not help but question how it came about, even though part of him warned him to keep his mouth shut. It wasn't that he wanted to dash her pride, it was only that he wanted her to know what he had learned the hard way: sometimes when it seems we are overly talented it is only because the Almighty has paved the way for us. But perhaps it hadn't been his place to try to force his own lessons upon her.

He watched as she wiped down the kitchenette and frowned in his effort to choose the right words. "I feel I may have . . . I think earlier when I questioned the source of your good fortune, I might have . . . I may have made you feel badly. I am sorry I did that."

Violet leaned against the counter, a knowing smile on her face. "Are you apologizing to me, King?"

"You call me 'King' or 'genie' when I annoy you. Can you call me Taka again? It is preferable to me."

"Well, that depends. Are you apologizing to me, King?"

His lips tugged upward on their own. She was an extremely stubborn woman. "I fed you, didn't I? I made you groan with pleasure over the saucy pig carcass and the sweet wine. I even tried to clean."

"And?" She smiled beguilingly and he had a difficult time not chuckling at her brash arrogance, enchanted by the way her smooth cheeks rose when she smiled making her eyes sparkle even more. Oh, she was a wonder when she was not caught up in the mundane. She was beautiful and fun.

"All right! Yes. I apologize."

"Mhmm? And?" she prompted.

Ah, but she was a cocky female. "I was rude and I was wrong. There. Are you happy now?"

Violet clapped her hands and laughed. She pitched forward and clasped him around his waist. "Yes! You should admit to being wrong more often, Taka, it would do wonders for our relationship."

Taka froze. Violet was holding him, her arms barely able to make it around his solid mass, but she was grasping him all the same. Every fiber of his being told him to grasp her back. A beautiful woman in his arms. His body was stirring again after 400 years of abstinence. If he did not do something soon, the decision would be made for him. But he couldn't simply pounce on the woman. What woman would want a man who would jump on her simply because he desired to do so? He wanted her to want him as much or it was no good to him.

His stillness finally transmitted its way to Violet. She was holding but there was no holding reciprocated. She was actually itching to feel him up a little. But he apparently hadn't learned the cardinal rule of "hug and be hugged" because he was as tense as a tree. Now she was standing there looking stupid. She raised her head slowly, and was immediately captured by the look on Taka's face. It held no cockiness or arrogance. Only bald desire.

She should be a lady and step away, but the desire to wiggle just a little, to press her womanly assets against him in wanton abandon, just to see what he'd do, was overwhelming. He made the decision for them, stepping back, holding her arms loosely in his hands. She swallowed her disappointment and let him change the subject.

"In my day, a celebration always included dancing. Would you like to dance?"

Dance? They *had* been dancing. The oldest, best dance known to man. Violet looked at him in confusion. She didn't understand this man. She knew she'd felt the telltale sign of desire for a flicker of a blink before he'd pulled away. She'd never had an aroused man voluntarily pull away from her before, never in her life.

Taka took her hands and clasped them waiting, it seemed, for her to accept or decline. And she would do one or the other as soon as she figured out what was going on.

He'd stepped away from her. Even though he wanted her. And it wasn't like he had any options to get it anywhere else. It didn't make any sense. Men just didn't do that kind of thing. Men didn't have that kind of self-control. It was almost like he was one of those things that used to be that thing they don't have anymore, something gone the way of the bison and the . . . what was it called? A gentle . . . gentle something. *Oh yeah, a gentleman.*

In that moment, she didn't know how or why, but a feeling swept over her so intensely she blinked. In that moment she felt something she'd never felt in any relationship. Valued. It made her give him a shaky smile. It made her knees wobble. It made her feel helpless with desire and powerful with the knowledge that he desired her just as much but was man enough to deny himself in order to be respectful of her. Gary would never have done that. Jerome would have bedded her last night, vomiting and all. But this man, this man, was different. She wanted to giggle like a schoolgirl.

Taka seemed a little shaky himself but summoned up a little smile. The effort, a strange-looking smile on one side, made Violet finally give a breathless, nervous laugh.

"I have a better idea," she said. "Why don't you show me how you danced way back in your time?"

He nodded. "I will do our victory dance. For when we won in battle."

Victory dance? Violet thought. When he stripped off his shirt and tossed it onto a chair, moving the small table and chairs out of the way, she should have been prepared for something special. She stepped back to give him room and her eyes widened when he jumped in the air. She almost put her hands up to prevent being body slammed, but his entire body, over 200 pounds of muscle, landed in front of her in a crouch, as deftly as a ballerina. His hands rested on his knees as he gave her a look that made her want to go running for the hills. Then, from his throat, a sound started out low and then some tongue quivering made it into a yell. Then he raised one leg and stomped it down. He raised the other and did the same. These repeated, increasing in frequency while his yell blended into a semblance of rhythm. Then he straightened slightly, bowed at the waist and bounced his torso up and down in rhythm, alternately bending his knees or moving this way or that, his hand up to shield his eyes from the imaginary sun or to cup over his ear for an imaginary sound. And then his arm would sweep before him and she could almost envision a lush expanse of land before him.

She realized the sounds from his throat were both music and words, his yells blending into shouts in some foreign language, every other word punctuated by a stomp or a clap. She'd heard some Africans speak before but she'd never heard this tongue. She'd even seen some African dance, but never anything like this. He began to move in a circle, his head bobbing, his hands gestured to the sides, then before and behind, holding an imaginary weapon with a grip so tight and purposeful the muscles and tendons in his arm and shoulder bulged and flexed with the movement. Everything was done with such intensity that a trickle of perspiration made its way down his face and a light sheen of moisture began to develop on his satiny dark skin so that she noticed things she hadn't before: the many little scars that were sprinkled over his torso. It was easy to miss them next to the beauty of the dark mahogany velvet skin, but perhaps his form in motion brought things to light.

Violet watched, eyes wide. This was some crazy stuff she was seeing. Crazy good. As she watched, amazed, she felt herself getting warmer. There was something about his strength and intensity, something about the primal energy from his movement and the seriousness of his task, something about the way he used his words to convey his meaning. She could see him in battle, leading his men, riding off to victory, with a voice that could be heard for hundreds of miles, and a bearing that could be felt far beyond.

It wasn't right that a modern woman should get so hot over a brute, macho man such as him, but getting hot she was. Taka was so into his dance that by the time he gave his final whoop, jumping into the air to end again in his crouch, chest heaving with the exertion and sweat streaming, he didn't notice Violet was no longer watching. She was, instead, leaning on the sink, having poured herself a glass of water, dipping her fingers into it to pat it along her forehead.

"You all right?" Taka asked between breaths as he straightened.

"I'm fine," Violet said in a voice too high, refusing to look at him. What kind of stupid question was that? No, she was not all right. She was all horny was what she was. For a man who lived in a rock! It would take her days to get the image of him out of her head. Now if he would just keep his distance, she would be fine, she thought, patting more water on her fevered cheeks.

"That is a good idea," Taka said, coming up beside her to pour himself a glass. Violet nearly groaned when she felt his heated body beside her. What was the man trying to do, drive her crazy? He didn't know how close he was to having the rest of his clothes ripped right from his body.

Taka gulped the water and breathed in relief. "Ah, I did not remember how good it felt to celebrate."

Violet cracked a glance at him, and asked grudgingly, knowing she was only making things harder for herself, "What were you saying, in that other language?"

He finished his water and set the glass down turning to her. "I was saying that our kingdom was victorious, that we were the best and fiercest in the land. That no army to the east, west, north, or south could defeat us because our greatest weapon is our honor." He took a breath, thinking. "It is an arrogance dance, but in our times, arrogance was needed. If another army felt you were weak in any way they would attack. We kept them at bay because they feared us."

Finally, Violet's skin was back at room temperature. "Well, what happened then? Where did your people go? Why haven't I heard of them before? Why haven't I heard that language before?"

He paused so long before answering Violet looked up at him and then regretted the question because of the raw pain on his face.

"I'm sorry, Taka. I didn't mean to be so tactless."

"You have no need to apologize. It is odd. As a king I could not allow myself to feel emotion often. But now, it is so close to the surface the slightest prick brings it screaming forth." He gave a small, wry smile. "Your question is fair. You have already gleaned that I let my wife down all those years ago. The full truth is that I let my village down, too. They are all gone. They died because of me, and yet I am here. That is all I can tell you and all there is in the world to tell. So you see, I do not deserve to speak the name of my forgotten village or its people. I should not have spoken our tongue. I am now ashamed to even have danced. Celebration without just cause is sacrilege. Though, I have no doubt they will serve a great celebration for me down below when I come blazing down to my fiery throne, for I have truly earned a place by the side of the evil one."

His eyes were filled with pain and his large shoulders almost bowed under the weight of whatever invisible pressure rested there. Violet had never seen a man so tortured, never known a man with a larger conscience or heart. Such a magnificent person, torn with internal anguish over something, she was certain, could not have been his fault. This man would never act out of malice. She'd never known anyone like him. That fact alone changed what was a solemn moment into one that sparked an unexpected response.

Violet dropped her eyes as her breathing thinned, but raised them again quickly feeling the heat of his stare on her. The dark intensity of his eyes drew her in and she shuddered air into her lungs. He'd been a gentleman with her earlier but she wasn't so sure she could be a lady. She wasn't so sure she wanted to.

She reached up tentatively and touched him softly with the tips of her fingers lightly on the side of his jaw. She trailed slowly down the front of him and heard his intake of breath in response, saw the sudden rise of his chest as he quickly took in air.

Her head told her to slow down, but her little voice had multiplied and was doing *fire it up, Violet, fire it up!* cheers in a round. Her head told her she shouldn't take advantage. And her head was right, right? She didn't want him to think she was forward. She didn't want God to be mad at her. She didn't want to lose Taka's respect. She didn't want—

Violet gasped as he pulled her to him, taking her lips in a kiss that made all wonders cease.

Chapter 22

He was a strong man but even he had his limits. Taka groaned as he pressed his lips to Violet's, feeling her hand stray to its favorite place behind his neck. It settled there as if it were its right, and it was. All parts of him had always been and would forevermore belong to this woman, this spirit, this being who claimed him lifetime and again.

He kissed her as if her lips were air to breathe, practically broke his neck bending to her because he was more than willing to put himself through all sorts of contortions if it brought him to her. Soon his hands were in her hair, testing this new texture, again, feeling and moving around in it so he could remember. He pulled his lips away from hers so he could plunge his nose into her hair and trail it along the side of her neck where the scent of her perfume mixed with the ever-present but faint note of shea butter. Always with the shea butter. Always driving him crazy with shea.

The skin of her neck seemed to glow with gold dust and he bent to taste that too, nibbling, licking, and sucking all around on both sides and around the front until the sound of her moan of pleasure graced his ears. It was different coming from Violet, but it still meant the same. He knew what Zahara liked but wondered if he could find the right way to please Violet, wondered if her body would arch when he licked her just so.

Her cry of desire made his head swim with need. All he wanted at that moment was to pull them both to the ground and love her like he'd longed to love her, like she deserved to be loved. Cherished like she deserved to be cherished. Worshipped by his tongue because she was his queen and he was her servant in all the ways that mattered, man or king.

He reached for the tail of her shirt to pull it upward, suddenly clumsy in his need. And in that millisecond of separation he felt the wall come down between them before he even looked into her eyes. Worse than seeing hesitation in them, he saw closed lids instead. She shook her head silently, eyes squeezed tight as if looking at him were painful to her.

"What are we doing? This is crazy, I'm engaged. We can't."

His hands shook from the effort but he released her shirt, placing his lips against the pulse in her neck once again, hopeful that her body would remember what her head had forgotten.

"You do not want him," he groaned against her perfumed skin, agonizing with need. Her skin in his hands felt so right he was certain it would be a sin to separate.

"I'm committed to"—she hesitated—"my life as it is. Please." She pulled his greedy lips away from her and finally opened her eyes to him.

He wanted to cry from the torture of being parted with her again when his body and soul knew they were made to be cleaved. But in her eyes he saw regret, pain, and doubt were killing the desire.

"I'm sorry for what I started," she said. "I may be a lot of things, Taka, but I've never been a cheat. I'm committed to a relationship with Jerome. That means something to me."

"But you do not love him and he does not love you," he ground out. "When he touches you do you go aflame for him? When he presses his lips against yours do you part them for kisses as sweet as honey? Does your heart pound like galloping horses when he trails his fingers along your skin? Do you moan like you will die from pleasure with him? Has he, or any man, made you feel the way you feel when I touch you?" He was pleased at the flush that made her blush uncomfortably at his words. He already knew the answer but wanted to hear it from her; anything but what she said:

"That's not fair, Taka. You're a king and a genie. You're magic. He's just a man."

Her words were like ice water. She thought the sparks were some sort of spell.

"Fine," he tried. "If I am magic, then let's make magic together. If it is only one night then at least you will have known one night of ecstasy."

"And let you ruin me for any other lover? I mean, Jerome? I'd be crazy to have genie lovin' and then try to go back to a regular man. That'd be torture. Why would I do that to myself? I'd have to be a flaming idiot."

No, he was the idiot for thinking this would work. For two days he'd been preaching to her to do the right thing, banging his head against the wall, and when she finally decided to follow his advice it resulted in denying him access to her. Of all times to listen to his inane advice. It would be funny if it weren't so ridiculously tragic.

He pulled on his forgotten shirt and then poured himself a glass of wine.

"You all right?" she asked.

He heard her behind him but swallowed an entire glassful of Merlot and proceeded to pour a second. "I'm fine. Just fine." Second glass down and he looked at her sideways. It hurt to look at her now. It hurt to know how close he was to loving her and losing her; it could easily go either way and he didn't have a clue what to do.

"Ouch," she said.

He stopped pouring the third glass to look at her. "What is the matter?"

"I don't know, but it's not right." Violet placed a hand on her stomach where the spasm had come from. "I don't know what it is. It's like, a j . . . Oh, wow, there it is again." She stood stock still as another odd flash made its way through her. Then a familiar feeling: kind of like after she ate a couple dozen buffalo wings doused in volcano hot sauce, only magnified.

"Ah," Taka said calmly, filling the rest of his glass. "Does it burn? Pierce? Pulsate? Grind?"

Violet's eyes widened as the spasms changed to pain that was doing precisely the things he was describing. She didn't even get out the question before he said with a sad shake of his head, "It is your wish. It is working."

"Wish?" Violet croaked. "I didn't wish for my body to feel like someone was shoving a hot poker up my butt all the way through my intestines and straight through my belly! What wi . . . ?" Then she remembered and smiled long enough for another spasm to wash it away. "Well, I'm happy it's happening, if that's what's happening, but I really don't feel right."

"It is painful work dropping several sizes in a matter of hours," Taka said.

"If you don't go easy on that wine you're going to have a killer headache in the morning," Violet warned, sitting down at the table opposite while he stared morosely at the half-empty bottle.

"I would have to be a man to have a day-after head-ache."

Violet realized she'd managed to hurt his feelings. She didn't know why he was upset, she was the one who denied herself mystical loving. And now she was just happy she wasn't in the middle of something when the stomach cramps started.

"The spasms will calm eventually. I am certain you will have what you want then: a tiny little body for your little boy of a friend, because he obviously can't handle a magnificent full-grown woman. No, little boys who want to be friends have very little egos and usually little body parts to match."

She watched him down wine like water until the groan of her protesting belly sounded loudly again. "He's not that little and this will all be worth it when we're married. One day I'll laugh at the crazy things I did when I was engaged."

"You are not engaged. You wear no ring."

"It's coming."

"The only way it is coming, woman, is if you go to the jewelry store yourself and buy it. That half-wit you call a fiancé is no more committed to tying himself in marriage to you than a worm is committed to a particular spot in the muck."

"Let's just not talk about Jerome for a little while. Why don't you watch TV while I sit over here and think of my last wish so you can get out of here and torment someone else? Oww." She didn't mean it, of course.

"You don't mean that," he said, maddeningly. He swallowed more wine. "I was bred to be a leader, not a follower; a doer, not a watcher. But I'm being forced to watch a catastrophe. What is it about this man that appeals to you so? If I were to treat you with the casual inattention of a boar would you then allow me into your bed? Perhaps I should start eating soft-man gruel and speaking like an imbecile; would that make you desire me?"

"Oh, Lord, you're drunk. Just what I need, a drunk genie. Some girls have all the luck."

"I am not drunk, I tell you! What I am is mistimed and misplaced. A man without a home, a king without a kingdom!"

Her stomach howled in agreement and Violet grimaced until the wave of pain passed. She then gasped, wiped her brow, reached for the bottle only to pull back with the thought of what her angry stomach would do if she added wine to it.

"There is always a place for a good man."

"And what would you consider a good man? Do you consider the rat dropping a good man? If it takes becoming like him to be considered a man in these times . . ." He shook his head and punctuated his disgust with another glass of wine.

"You're a good man, you're just not real," Violet said, trying to ignore the protest of her esophagus. "King, let's put this subject to bed, shall we? You're a good-looking man and you're an all-round good guy. You have your quirks, but you wouldn't have a problem getting women if you were a man. Now, stop scrounging for compliments."

"And what of my other qualities?"

Violet looked at him hard. "Are you trying to win an award or something?"

"I have always been a hard worker and a good provider. I would need to do that again, for sure, if I were living in this place today. What else is there?"

Violet thought about that. She thought he was already the best man she knew, but what man couldn't afford to improve just a little bit? Where to start? "How about compassion? Understanding? How about the ability to communicate? How about selflessness? And a sense of humor? And affinity with children? How about those things?"

"What about them? I have all those things."

"Well then, king, I'd say you were darned near perfect."

"No, I am missing something. Tell me what is wrong. Tell me the bad things. Please, Violet, you do not need to spare my feelings."

Violet pinched her lips. Rarely had someone asked her to cut them lower than a two dollar dog. She didn't know if she could do it under these circumstances.

"You're arrogant and stubborn, but you already know that," she said, using her fingers to tick off the points. "You treat women like they are second-class citizens. You have no patience, you're always in a bad mood, and you can't stand being wrong. You believe you are better than everyone else and that, somehow, you know what's best for everyone. Oh, and you eat a lot."

"*I* eat a lot?" He snorted.

"Oh, and you're judgmental and you can't stand not to have the last word. And you're a smart aleck."

"*I'm* a smart aleck?"

"Oh, and sometimes you don't know how to be kind to a lady."

"A lady?"

"Enough!" Violet said, pointing at him. "It's exactly that smart mouth of yours I'm talking about."

"Forgive me," he said, not looking as if he wanted forgiveness at all. "You know, back in my day no one would dare speak to me the way you just did. They would find themselves looking up at their shoulders once I'd lobbed off their head."

"Ooooh, scary!" Violet wiggled her hands in mock terror. Her stomach gurgled in protest. "I bet you got plenty of women talking like that."

"How did your friend of a boy talk to get you?"

"Jerome? He didn't get me, I got him."

"What does that mean?"

"It means, I saw him across a crowded club and I decided I wanted him and so I took him."

"I see. That explains it," Taka said knowingly.

"Explains what?"

"Explains why it seems you are the pursuer. Because you are. Why would you want a man you had to chase? A true man, once he has found a woman he wants, will do the chasing, not the other way around. It is the woman's place to allow, or disallow, herself from being caught. You have turned the tables and he is running like a female who has no intention of allowing herself to be contained. Just like a woman, if you find one who does not want you she will never want you, ten or a hundred years from now. You as much as admitted he repulses you and fails miserably in lovemaking; it is ludicrous. When compared to what it could be, surely you see you cheat yourself out of true pleasure?"

Violet slapped the table lightly with her palm. "I have never admitted any such thing. And see there, that's the judgmental part I was talking about."

"I'm supposed to condone the way you shovel garbage into your temple?"

"He's no more garbage than any other man. You just hate Jerome."

"You are right. He is a bug."

"And you're vindictive," she continued.

"Me? I am not vindictive. You are mistaken."

"You are in denial."

"You presume to know me so well after one day?" he said, turning the tables on her.

"You are not all that deep, genie. You're moody and for some reason you hate modern men."

For some reason. "Hate is a strong word."

"Okay, modern men disgust you."

"That is accurate. Am I wrong to be disgusted? Look at them. Where is the dignity, the honor? They skulk around as if they have a right to be lackadaisical. Even the African men I have run into in the last century or so bear no resemblance to my people. The world over, men are becoming more and more shiftless. I say, it is amazing how fast a hard stone will turn a lazy man into a productive citizen. But I suppose that discipline is frowned upon today, if the condition of your men is any indication."

Violet couldn't help but smile at that. But the humor was short-lived as her stomach let out a loud groan and she clenched her middle. "I'm starting to think I should go to the hospital. I don't think I could walk if I tried. Why do I feel so weak?"

"I had hoped it would be an easy transition but it may be one of those difficult ones."

"Difficult ones?" Violet looked at him through bangs that were as lank as she felt. "What's that mean?"

He shrugged. "Most people do not take care with the wish and when it manifests it does so at its own desire. It may take fat or it may take muscle. Once, a very thin man wanted to lose ten pounds. I told him, 'you are insane, ten pounds will put you in the morgue!' but he did not listen. The wish took what little fat he had and made up for the rest with use of some internal organs."

"What?"

Taka waived off her concern. "It is all right, he did not really need the spleen and the appendix would have come out ten years down the line. This wish did save him from a certain future surgery but he could not have known that."

Violet looked at him as she heaved, blowing her bangs up as he nonchalantly sipped his wine. She was right from the start. She was being punished. The genie? A demon for sure. A male succubus; that's right, an incubus. An incubus was sitting across from her swigging Merlot.

"You never said—"

"I told you to be careful."

"Had I known—"

"You did not give me time to explain."

"I can't walk down an aisle like this! I can't enjoy life like this. All I wanted was to be a friggin' size eight!" She moved over slowly and plopped herself onto the sofa, feeling like a sack of potatoes.

Taka walked over to sit next to her. He placed his arm around her shoulder. She hesitated and then squirmed into him, liking the feel of his strength beside her. Everything in her life was changing but she felt she had somehow lost control. And, who knew, she might even lose a spleen. She didn't know what a spleen did but she still wanted to keep hers!

She pressed her face into his shoulder willing herself not to cry and failing miserably.

"Do not cry and streak such a pretty face, woman."

"I just want to be skinny and rich, is that so wrong? I can't believe Brenda is marrying Gary. It's not like I want the jerk; it's the principle. How could he do that?"

"Gary is a fool and cannot see that you are a woman of quality. It is not his fault; it is like a man who cannot tell a chunk of glass from a diamond. It is an inability inherent to the condition of being an idiot."

"You couldn't see that I was a woman of quality. When did you lose your inherent idiot inability?"

"Once again, the comparison is moot; it is like comparing a magnificent baobab to a dry-rotted root: no matter how much water you pour on the rotted root it will never grow life."

"Uhmm, what?"

"The magnificent baobab tree in Africa and the dry-rotted root that is dead? The water being the information that makes the tree grow, like learning more about you has made my understanding grow because I am intelligent and majestic like the baobab. But despite pouring information on the stupid dry-rotted root that is Gary the root will never smarten and grow. You see my point? What has happened to the world that people cannot understand a simple parable? Why, my father *never* answered a question without a story with the inclusion of at least two animals, trickery, and a talking tree."

Violet's quiet laughter was sucked up by the material of his shirt which effectively dried her tears. She looked up into his frowning face and stroked the line between his eyes. "Don't worry, Taka, I understand you. You're saying you were an idiot when you met me and I set you straight. See, no need to get all frustrated."

His face softened and Violet liked the way his chocolate brown eyes melted as well.

"You understand me like no other," he said. "You comfort me, calm me. I am at peace when you are in my arms."

"Is that three-day rule set in stone?" she asked him, softly.

"I'm afraid so."

"I wish you could stay longer. I don't have many friends. It's nice having you around. You're easy to talk to."

"Your impression of me has changed as well?"

"It has. A little." Violet smiled up at him and in that instant was a continuation of where they'd left off before. Her breath caught in her throat as she looked into his deep, brown eyes. A feeling, sharp and fleeting, followed swiftly by an overwhelming desire.

Taka looked into the face of this woman. As many times as he'd kissed Zahara, he'd never seen this particular expression. He'd never felt this particular emotion. The woman in his arms moved in different ways, her facial expressions were different, her eyes even held a different look, completely different from Zahara. And yet as he looked at her moist lips, he wanted to kiss her again, like he'd never wanted to kiss anyone. He came closer to her until he could feel the soft breath from her nose and, then, a loud grumble and a frozen expression on her face ruined the moment.

"Sorry, gotta go." Violet moved up and off the sofa as fast as she could in her debilitated state. When she returned a while later, she padded back over to the sofa, looking a thousand years old. Her shirt bagged over her frame.

"Are you small enough yet?" he asked.

"Who gives a crap? I'm miserable."

"But now you can fit into the orange dress?"

"You can save your 'I told you so.' I don't want to hear it."

"Hmmm, what a peculiar and accurate term. I told you so. I like it."

But he didn't use it when he certainly could have and maybe even should have while all night long she sprinted to the bathroom and back. Each time she returned she huddled into a fetal position on the sofa; each time he wordlessly hooked a finger in a belt loop of her jeans, dragged her over to him and proceeded to hold her while she quaked, shivered, and convulsed to her new, improved size.

"It was a stupid, impulsive wish," Violet gasped, finally. "I don't hate myself enough to make myself sick. I think I'm going to use my last wish to reverse it."

"I will try to remove the wish, if you want me to."

"Can you?" she croaked, feeling the first glimmer of good spirit in the last two hours.

"Actually, only our Father can, but I will ask. You will lose the second wish, regardless."

"That's okay, I'll take my chances. Thank you, Taka."

"You're welcome."

"I'm exhausted. I'd go to bed if I could make the walk back."

Taka stood and scooped her up, sucking in his breath. "Ridiculous! You weigh but a feather! This is what you wanted?" He shook his head, muttering about the silliness of the situation as he carried her into her bedroom and laid her down, pulling the blankets around her. He brushed back the hair from her face and stroked her skin gently.

"Ah, Violet. If only you knew the beauty you hold already. If only you knew your worth."

Violet shivered and shuddered, her teeth clacking together. "We can't all be royalty, Taka. But if you can make me the way I was I will listen to you say 'I told you so' day and night. Will you be comfy out there on the couch? The bed is big enough for two." She hadn't asked him yesterday, but she didn't care yesterday. She saw indecision rage on his face.

"I will be fine on the sofa."

Yes, that was probably best.

She was closing her eyes when she noticed the message light on her answering machine blinking. "One last favor? Will you hit that button on the answering machine and that one to turn the ringer back on? I haven't listened to my messages all day."

He hit both the ringer and the answering machine button and watched warily as a voice spoke from it. The first message was Skeeter. The next two were from media folk who'd caught wind of her coup. The fourth was from Skeeter.

"Okay, okay. I'll give you one thousand one hunnert for the piece, okay? Call me back, Violet!" he asked.

Taka raised his brows. Violet swirled a finger in the vicinity of her temple. Skeeter might as well be crazy if he thought she'd ever give up the brooch now. The next voice was a familiar one.

"Violet, it's Brenda. I thought you were my friend and you went behind my back and stole the Bickman account, after all we've been through together. You stabbed me in the back and I will never forgive you, Violet Jackson. I'll get you back. In fact, I already have. So there."

Violet could barely move but her lips curled in malicious glee. Taka caught the movement and shook his head.

"It wasn't anything she hasn't done to me a thousand times over, Taka. We've been over this."

"And she will do it again and again. Sometimes it is better to lose and move on. Defeat is a hard pill to swallow but it is a part of life. Sometimes we must accept what we cannot change."

Violet summoned up enough indignation to lift her head off the pillow and fire back, "Like you accepted it? Look at you, living in a rock, literally. Don't lecture me about not accepting the bad things in life. You gave up on life." Her head fell back, satisfied.

Taka felt the sting of being properly shut up, but he had to be clear. "You're right. I did not accept my fate. Instead, I have lived an existence far worse. I have lived to see others happy. I have lived to wonder what might have been had I not given up. Even now I work to put my life together when the world has forgotten me and my people ever existed. In all these centuries, perhaps the hardest pill to swallow is that of humility. I am not a god to determine my fate and neither are you to yours."

Violet stung under his admonishing, wounded and angry by his rebuke. He didn't know anything about her life, her struggles, or her fate. He didn't know how difficult it had been to let him into her confidence only to have him throw her problems back into her face.

"Tomorrow you will be gone and I will be left here alone to deal with my life in the best way I see fit," she said, finally closing her eyes as sweat popped on her forehead. "I don't have a kingdom of people to fight for or a lost love to mourn over. I just have me and a friend who hates me and a fiancé who's lusting after that same friend and a business that will survive only if I am cutthroat enough to do what I need to do to make it survive. So if I have to step on Brenda to get what I want I am going to do it. And if I have to marry a man like Jerome to cement my position in society I will do that, too. There's no such thing as the type of world you lived in, Taka. It is history, and so are you. So please, keep your advice to yourself and let me live my life."

Chapter 23

Violet woke the next morning to the smell of coffee. She came into the kitchen walking upright and looking well rested. She smiled at Taka as she approached.

"You removed it, thank you."

Taka looked at her in her jeans and a tee shirt. She was back to her normal weight and she looked beautiful to him. "Our Father removed it. But you cannot have another. You have only one wish left."

"When I woke up this morning, I was in bed. I distinctly remember falling asleep on the bathroom floor after the thousandth trip. Or passing out."

"You are light. It was no trouble."

"I was light, for a brief period of time."

"You are still light, in the right hands."

"Thank you for getting it reversed, after how rude I was last night. I appreciate it."

"Your coffee will be cold."

"Hey, is that the paper?"

"I told you yesterday, you will be having no more problems with your neighbor."

"Wow, you are multitalented. If I had known you were so useful in the beginning I wouldn't have given you such a hard time."

"It was nothing."

"I'm trying to thank you. I don't do it often; will you let me?"

"You don't have to thank me, woman. I would lower myself to my knees without your request if it would convince
my Father to restore the beauty that you hold. I would
scavenge a thousand papers in the morning if it would bring
you happiness. There is no limit to what I would do for you,
Violet."

Violet was silent for a moment, not knowing what to
say. "My, you certainly have a flair for drama."

"Hearing a man tell you of your beauty or value should
not be drama. Not if you have a man who is supposed to
love you."

She was caught up for a moment watching him as he
cut strawberries into pieces to shovel them into parfait
dishes. His large hands doing such delicate work only
made him more masculine.

Taka found her gaze on him disconcerting. She was
once again herself, once again beautiful, but he could not
forget the evening before. He could not forget her words
or the feel of her in his arms. He could not shake the
feeling that her cynicism, her pessimism, was all his fault.
And while she was spouting words that hurt his soul, he
could hear the vulnerability beneath the harshness.

He could also still feel desire he hadn't known for
generations. As she watched him his hands trembled
slightly. He longed for her to come to him and perhaps
place a hand on his, a kiss on his lips, her arms around
him so that he might hold her body to him eagerly. He
knew his wishes would show through his eyes so he did
not look at her. At least, not until she said:

"I have my third wish."

"There is no need for you to wish now. Why not wait
until the end of the day?" he said, anxiously. Suddenly he
had no desire to leave her side. He felt a profound panic
at the thought that Violet could, in one wish, banish him
from her life as completely and quickly as she could utter
the words.

"But I know it now. And I wouldn't have if it weren't for you and what you said last night. I realized that I really want to be in a relationship where I can truly count on my partner. I mean, it's not unreasonable, right?"

"No, it is not," he said, cautiously.

"You had that kind of relationship, didn't you? I mean, it does exist?"

"It does."

"So there's nothing to say Jerome and I can't have it."

Taka felt an overwhelming fear. "Be careful, Violet."

"I mean, everyone wants love, right? Everyone deserves it."

"We have hours; please be careful."

"I've decided." Violet smiled and spread her arms wide. "I want the love of a good man!" And the burden was lifted at the admission. She wasn't made of stone. Of course she'd rather have love than simply an arrangement. She'd like to have a man who doted on her and adored her. Strangely, her conversations with Taka had made her see that. Taka sighed in relief but she was too busy hugging herself with her arms to notice. "Phew! What a weight off my shoulders. I never would have thought of myself as a romantic, but I have to say, you have been a positive influence on me."

Taka looked up to the ceiling, waiting to be zapped off the face of the earth.

"I wouldn't mind being in love. And to not have to lie to my partner. And to truly want to spend time with him. And I tell you, Jerome is a good guy. He just needs motivation, that's all."

Taka felt a moment of surprise followed by a flash of anger. "Jerome? Him, again? Humph. Motivation means nothing to a slug."

"You're not starting again, are you? I thought we reached an understanding."

"I understand that pathetic bag of waste will only drag you down into the swamp with him."

"Thank you for caring, but not all mortal men can be as wonderful as you. And before we start arguing again, I'm going to go change, okay?" Violet left the room and Taka immediately set his knife down and spoke to the ceiling.

"Father, I have asked little of you during my imprisonment and I realize I have no right to ask. After today my fate will be determined. But I ask for Violet. She does not know what she asks for. The only fate worse than condemnation for me is to be condemned knowing that she has bound herself to a man who does not love her. Please, Father, protect her."

The air crackled around him and Ani arrived, sitting at the kitchen table and taking a ripe strawberry to bite into. "You speak to our Father with respect and you address the woman as 'Violet,' easily, without hesitation. I think this is the first time I truly believe you accept her as she is."

"How can I not? As strongly as Zahara was Zahara through and through, Violet is Violet. A different woman, yet . . ."

"The same."

"The same. I respect her. I even understand her."

"You should. She is the epitome of you at the height of your own power. You see with the eyes of a man who rules a country. In these times, a person's life is a country. A person's kingdom is their own environment. A person's enemy is within themselves. And just as during your own reign you focused on things other than what was most important, so does she. She is so busy arranging her life, she fails to see what is important. Love."

"I had a kingdom to run. I did not know how to do it and love at the same time. But I did love. I do love, deeply."

"I know that, Taka. If it makes you feel better, she is just as clueless. She chooses Jerome: a man she can mold into what she believes she needs. Her wish was for the love of a good man, but she said nothing about loving him back. She doesn't even dare love him. She can't. She's hopelessly in love with you."

Taka looked at Ani quickly. Could it be?

"Don't get excited, love isn't always enough and she's relegated you to the status of a cartoon character; don't ask. The bottom line is she is not as blindly naïve as she seems. She's using every trick in her arsenal to block herself from the pain of truly living. The only difference between the two of you? She doesn't have a rock to hide in."

"It's a precious gem."

"Our Father decided he'd had enough of the rock rehabilitation after you. Imagine that."

Taka sat down in a chair, his face speaking an indescribable knowledge. "I made it impossible for both of us, didn't I?"

"The harder we tried, the harder you fought. And all along all I wanted to teach you was that no one is entitled to happiness; it must be earned. Even in grief there is beauty. And death isn't the enemy, only a natural progression. He had much more in store for you, son. You would have loved again."

"Maybe. But after all this, I cannot say I am sorry for holding on to her."

Ani reached out to take Taka's shoulder in a gentle grip. "You wouldn't be the Taka I know and love if you did. Don't ever apologize for love and don't ever regret life's lessons. You have been a hard one to teach, but I feel rays of knowledge are now reaching you. Like water seeping into the roots of a magnificent baobab."

Taka smiled. "Yes, I am hard to teach. But my stubbornness is of my Father."

"I will give Him the steadfast dedication. But the stubbornness, never." Ani smiled. "What happens now is out of your hands. You have the rest of the day to be with her but I warn you, don't make your parting difficult for her. She has to live with her decisions and learn her own lessons. She's made her wish and it still doesn't automatically eliminate you. That's something. You have until the end of the day to determine if it is you she chooses or Jerome."

"He's a vile creature. I cannot believe I am competing against that."

"Watch your mouth, Taka; he's one of our Father's children, as well."

"He must have been having a bad day when He made that one," he groused, earning a cautionary frown. "Just one last question. Why now? Why did He choose this time to bring me to her?"

"Because the last of the people of Jaha have come home. You see, you and Zahara were not the only souls troubled by the brutality of your passing. Some came back one or two times. One came back almost as many times as Zahara before finally forgiving himself. It's the spirit of the man you knew as Kamil."

Taka felt the name down to his toes. Not just a warrior, Kamil was also his best mortal friend. His eyes watered with the knowledge of how his friend must have suffered, as much as he had. "So he has perished now?"

"My, your word choice is all wrong! Your friend died in 1600 AD. His spirit was restless, searching for answers, almost as stubborn as you. But he found those answers in this last life. He found peace and when the body that held his warrior's spirit died this time, his soul finally passed into our Father's Kingdom to be embraced by the rest of the Jahanian people. They all wait, you see. They wait for their king and queen to return. One way or the other your spirits have ended their journey; this is the final incarnation for you both. Do you see, my son?"

Yes, finally he saw. What had his Ani said yesterday? The Almighty wanted Taka to bring Violet back to him and now he understood that if Taka could not make things right no one else could. Violet's spirit had been back many times and this was her last chance. When all was said and done, if they didn't make their way back to each other, Taka would surely get to the underworld first to cool off a prickly seat with his behind in order to offer it to her when she followed: a final gift for his beloved wife. No, he couldn't allow that to happen.

"Today is an important day for you, Taka, and I find I'm in a strange position."

Taka was alarmed as his friend's eyes grew wet. "Ani-weto, what is it, my friend?"

A gentle smile from a gentle soul. "Before you were born our Father told me about a young man who would grow up to be a strong and valiant king. But, as with everything wonderful He has ever created on this earth, evil was going to try to destroy this young, proud man by taking everything he loved. So our Father sent me to help prepare the man. He gave me substance so I could be seen, heard, and felt by my ward.

"That is how it came about that when you were born I whispered into your tiny ear and told you it was safe to open your eyes. When you began to eat I took your food in my hand and showed you how to chew. When you faltered on new legs I held my arms to you so you wouldn't be afraid to walk. When your father died in battle I held you as you cried. When you married Zahara I stood beside you, overjoyed with the love that woman planted in your heart and soul. I was as close to a real father as I ever had the fortune to be. And, inevitably, when that horrible day came when everyone you loved was beset upon by evil I anticipated the overwhelming grief. I even anticipated the anger. But it was my job to make sure you knew you were not alone. I failed you. You felt as if our Father had abandoned you and nothing could have been further from the truth. We were with you every step but still you felt hopeless. I asked our Father's forgiveness long ago. I ask yours, now."

Taka's jaw tensed as he fought the tears that threatened to fall. "I . . . I have nothing to forgive, Ani. You were my friend. I've always known you were there for me. I treated you like I treated Zahara. Because I knew I had your love I knew I could cause you pain. I was hurting and I wanted you to hurt. I wanted Him to hurt. In my arrogance and narcissism I thought I was favored by our Father and blessings were due me. It never occurred to me that I might have been blessed for any other reason. Ani, it is I who ask you for forgiveness. You have been more than a friend to me. And no matter what happens tomorrow, I thank you. And I love you, my dear friend."

Tears fell down Ani's cheeks but he smiled nonetheless. "And I love you. No matter how the story of Taka Olufemi ends, know that I will love you for eternity. Go in peace, my son."

Ani disappeared and for a moment Taka was still. No one had to tell him he had just said good-bye to his friend forever. He felt the loss already, as if a warm blanket that had always lain across his shoulders was slowly peeled away. Ani couldn't help him anymore. His guardian's job was done and Taka had to make his own way from here on and the enormity of his task set in.

How could he do it? How could he save them both? More importantly, how could he save Violet? He would gladly go to the inferno if it would spare her the trip. But he'd used every tactic he knew. He had nothing left.

The sudden knock on the front door drew his eyes but he remained frozen. He had little time left and no plan. And suddenly something as simple as a knock on the door frightened him.

Violet ran back in from the bedroom, tossed him an intimate look of annoyance—he should have answered the door—and then opened it herself. Jerome stepped inside and Taka's heart shriveled.

"Hi, baby!" Violet said, tossing her arms around his neck. But something wasn't right. Taka noticed the stiffness of the man's body and the box by his feet that Violet was too taken with enthusiasm to spy. Finally Violet pulled away to look into the face of the man.

"Did you hear? I got the Bickman account!"

"Oh yeah, I heard. I heard a whole lot of stuff. Spent all night thinking about 'stuff' and getting stuff together." He pulled farther away from Violet, pointedly creating distance. He then pulled the box inside to drop loudly on the floor. "I heard you been holed up here with this guy." He gestured at Taka. "And he ain't even family. That true?"

Violet's face froze while she went into damage control mode. When she unfroze her eyes were wide and innocent. "I don't know who told you that, but that's a blatant lie. I told you, Taka's my cousin."

"Yeah, well Brenda says he ain't."

"Why were you talking to Brenda? You know better than to believe what she says; she's just pissed because I took the account from her."

"That right? 'Cause she says you been lying to me. *Me*."

Violet inspected the look on Jerome's face. He gave her a look like the idea was so close to sacrilegious it hurt him to think it was true. As if lying to him were a sin along the lines of destroying the holy grail. *Pleaasse!* Violet almost wanted to burst his bubble and remind him he wasn't all that but that would be defeating the purpose.

"Now, Jerome." She put her hands on her hips. "Why would I lie to you? You're going to be my husband. You and I are the ones in this relationship; she doesn't have a thing to do with it. And when we get married—"

"Oh, and she says you planning on making me sign a prenuptial agreement to keep me away from your money. How about that?"

"Prenup?" She twisted her face and put her hands up in the air in an "I don't know what you're talking about" expression, all the while thinking, *prenup might not be a bad idea.* Two days ago it didn't matter but today she was wealthy. She might have to slip the page in with some other papers so he wouldn't realize what he was signing, but it could be done.

"Look, baby. I don't know what that skank has been saying to you but she's a liar. She's just upset because of the contract and now she wants to get back at me, that's all. I mean, it's just amazing to see how far desperation will make some women go."

"So you ain't trying to keep no money away from me? I mean, I been supporting you, encouraging you and all that. It'd be whack if you tried to cut me out when all my effort paid off."

"Of course not, honey. What's mine is yours."

"I don't know," he said, doubtfully. His eyes swung up to Taka who was watching the whole scene with a sour face. "What about him?" He gestured with a nod in his direction. "Brenda said you two got something going."

"That's a lie," Violet said emphatically.

"He really your cousin?"

"Absolutely."

Jerome looked at Violet's face, inspecting it closely. He seemed to relax a little, seemed to be believing her. She almost wanted to smile but she would have to save that for later. Later she would smile, laugh, and do her own victory dance over Brenda's dead, size-negative-two carcass.

"So, y'all ain't got nothing going up in here? 'Cause, you wouldn't let me have none the other night. What was that about if it wasn't about him?"

Violet felt a flash of embarrassment. "You don't have to tell our romantic business, Jerome, it's embarrassing."

"I'm just saying, I didn't get none. I want to make sure it ain't 'cause of some other guy up in here."

"How many times do I have to tell you? He's my cousin. This is all completely innocent and Brenda is a vindictive witch."

He looked at her longer, trying to gauge her honesty in her eyes.

From where he stood, Taka watched as well. He had to admit, she was good. He would believe her too, if he didn't know her so well. As Jerome would know her if he spent half a second trying to get to know her. Taka hung his head in frustration and Jerome caught the movement.

"Hey," the man said, looking at Taka, then at Violet. Finally he focused on Taka's tormented eyes. "You tell me. She telling the truth?"

Violet's comfort visibly fled. "I told you the truth, Jerome."

"I asked him," Jerome said, staring him down. "You all honorable and crap like that. You her cousin or what?"

Violet turned to look at Taka and he returned the stare. Her eyes screamed for him to back her up. Her face was panicked. He did not want to make things difficult for her.

Jerome was her choice, apparently. Jerome was what she wanted, so who was he to meddle in that? She had proven time and again that she was bound and determined to destroy herself, and His Father had told him it was not his place to sway her. So he could leave here today, satisfied that he had done all he could. He could go away finally putting to rest the idea that he was her savior. All he had to do was back her up.

He looked at her large, brown, pleading eyes. He looked at Jerome's beady, stupid ones. He asked himself what he could live with. He couldn't decide for her, but he could decide for himself. It wasn't a question, really. He'd been many things in his life, but he'd never been a liar.

"I am no blood relation to Violet," he said firmly but softly. The simple statement went off like a gun in the silent room. It might as well have been a gunshot the way Jerome began flailing his arms, yelling, and screaming about what a tramp Violet was and how trifling she was and how she was no good and wasn't worth anything and never would be. Violet was busy trying to avoid the flailing and get her arms around his neck at the same time to convince him otherwise. Taka was wishing he could be anywhere else so as not to have to see this.

"You a liar!" Jerome yelled, pushing her away. "You calling Brenda a skank; you a skank!"

"No, no, it's not like that, Jerome, really! Nothing's going on between us. Nothing could, I love you!"

"You a liar!" He finally tired of her trying to touch him and moved forward, pushing her away. She fell back onto her behind and Taka sprang forward to push as well, only this time and with the amount of force, Jerome's back slammed against the door with a loud bang. Taka's adrenalin surged with his anger and when Jerome attempted to right himself, he slammed him again into the door.

"Don't ever lay your hands on her!" Taka yelled.

"Screw you, man!" Jerome yelled back, coming at Taka with his fists. Taka reached back to gain some foundation behind a punch he would land on Jerome's jaw, a punch a long time coming, when he felt Violet's hand on his arm. She had scrambled up and nearly catapulted onto his back trying to stop the fist and the inevitable punch. Taka twisted and looked at her, despair in his voice.

"Why would you stop me? He pushed you to the ground!"

"Leave us alone to fix this!"

Jerome had shaken himself free by then, and managed to place an arm's length from himself and Taka. He shook himself off and opened the front door. "Ain't nothing to fix, Violet. It's over."

"No. Don't say that," Violet said, feverish thoughts running through her head. She didn't know what was worse, the scene that had just happened or the thought that everything was slipping through her fingers. "We can make this better, baby. We can fix this."

Jerome shook his head, trying to hide embarrassment and humiliation. He pointed to Taka. "You crazy," and then to Violet, "and you a ho. See ya!" Then he turned and walked out, posturing all the way and slamming the door behind.

Violet stood stock still for a moment, her face a mask of shock. She blinked in confusion, looking lost and dazed. Taka looked at her and was surprised to see sobering pain. No, she had not loved Jerome, but she had invested in him. And apparently that investment had just gone cold.

She looked at Taka, her face hardening into a mask. "You did this."

He wanted to take credit because he knew breaking up with Jerome was the best thing for her but he would give anything to remove the wounded look from her eyes. Yet another scar on her already scarred soul. "I did nothing."

"You never liked him but he was going to be my husband. All you had to do was back me up, that's all you had to do. That's . . ." She stopped suddenly and staggered over to pull open a drawer and Taka watched while she pulled out a paper bag, her color going high and perspiration popping on her forehead.

"What is the matter? What is wrong with your breathing?"

"Your fault," she gasped, putting the bag to her face and breathing in and out, crazily. "You betrayed"—in and out—"me!"

"I could not lie."

In and out like a bellows. "You ruined"—in and out—"everything!"

"I ruined nothing."

She took some more deep breaths and finally pulled the bag away, sighing in a normal breath again. When she looked at him her face was flushed and her eyes raw. "My final wish . . . You were supposed to give me that one last thing."

"It was not my wish to give. My Father, our Father—"

"Isn't that convenient; whenever things go wrong you blame Him. But I blame you. I blame you!" She stalked over to him and used her two arms to push him, just as she had been pushed, but he didn't budge. She pushed him again, frustration making her try harder when it was obvious she could make no headway against him. "Why couldn't you just leave me be? Why'd you have to ruin my life?"

Taka felt his heart tear and break even as her anger washed over him. "You do not love him. You only wanted to play with him."

"So what? You think I haven't been played with a thousand times? It was my turn, don't you understand? It was my turn to have the upper hand!"

"That is what it would have been?" he snapped. "The upper hand? Living with a man you did not love? That would make you powerful?"

"I asked you to make him love me."

"That power is beyond me, and, I am certain, beyond all that is holy."

"I hate you. And I'm sick and tired of you lecturing about love. You don't know what love is. Your love is dead just like you are! Just like your people and your kingdom and the wife you claim to love so much!"

She said the words and knew they were cruel; and even saw them hit home as his eyes flashed with pain, but she didn't care. She wouldn't soften to him after he'd ruined her dreams. It was time someone said it.

"Shall I show you what love is?" Taka asked. "Would you like to see real love? Would you like to see what is important?"

"Yes! You know so much, show me your dead love!"

Taka looked up to the ceiling, his body tense with the gravity of what could be his final prayer. "One last time, Father. Please, I beg you, take us home one last time!"

Violet gasped as Taka grasped her around the waist and pulled her close. Around them the air swirled madly. She looked around her kitchen but it was fast fading into gray, the floor dropping from beneath them as they twirled up, still entwined, to the ceiling, an extra-wide plume of smoke that hovered in her small apartment before shooting into the stone that fell off the table with the force of their spirits catapulting inside.

Chapter 24

Violet's eyes were pressed closed and she held him tightly until finally, she felt something under her feet. She opened her eyes into Taka's chest and blinked several times before noticing that he no longer wore the nondescript clothes and coat he'd worn previously, but seeing instead dark blue silk. She stepped away slightly and found his entire dress was different. There were vibrant silks wrapped over him from head to toe, with his chest partially bare. He wore chains of gold and silver. He even wore a gold head dressing on his regal head. Where before he'd been dressed as a man, now he was dressed as a . . . king. Her eyes widened, looking him up and down. "What is this?" she asked, trembling.

"This is my home. This is my source of love. This is the environment that gave me my strength. And look." He turned her around gently and she saw she was in a large room with pillars beyond which opened up to the outdoors, resplendent with green trees and pastures. But he was facing her to a tall piece of glass and as she approached she thought she was looking at a painting behind a frame. She saw the colors of the silks and the delicate draping of the fabric before she saw the full image, but as she stepped closer she saw she was looking into a mirror and the woman in magnificent dress with the headdress on her head was she.

"This is the Great Hall at Jaha. And these are my people." He clapped his hands together as he'd done in his time, half expecting silence to follow. But his Father was kind. At the sound of his clap, people began to spill into the hall, rushing to greet him. People he knew! As Taka stood there, friends, and family came in a rush, some walking and some running in their haste to get to him, happy to see him after such a long spell. Taka laughed out loud, in the booming laugh that had been stilled for so long, as tears streamed over his cheeks and down his face. He looked upon the people who had filled the happiest days of his life. Were they spirits or apparitions? No matter. When his father ran in and his mother came shortly after, tears in her eyes, and cupped his cheeks in her hands, he didn't care if she was an apparition. He held her and cried with her and smiled at her gentle words. Cried as he had not cried since he was a child held in her sweet arms.

Someone started playing music with the introduction of a loud drumbeat that vibrated the hall and sounded out for miles around. A cheer went up as people began to dance. More people rushed in with food, so much food it seemed beyond belief. And fruits of the most exotic nature. Wines, baked foods, potatoes and yams and lentils, coconuts and mangos, dates and figs: platters upon platters of food.

Violet turned in a circle watching the pandemonium around her. She felt as if she were on a spinning top: a ride too fast and hectic to stop. Her eyes took in the sights and colors, the people rushing about, the sounds of the music enveloping the whole world, it seemed. Seconds later she felt someone grab her hand and looked up, happy for the lifeline, anything to stop the ride. Taka stood there beside her.

"Let's eat," he said. He sat at one end of a large table and she sat at the other, embarrassed, but eating up the attention. "A toast!" Taka boomed, his large voice easily carrying down the length of the table and throughout the hall. "To friends, wise men and children, nurturers and warriors. I did not know how blessed I was. Every man should have a piece of the happiness I feel at this moment, and he will know that no matter what comes after, he has truly tasted paradise. For even one moment of this love is a gift." He paused, his words coming from his soul. "A toast to the Almighty who allowed me this license so that I may do what I never thought I could ever do, and that is to tell each one of you how you have graced me, how you have honored me, how you have filled me with your dignity and your pride.

"I fear I have not been as strong as you. And because of that I must ask you now for your forgiveness. In my weakness, I failed you all. It is time again for me to behave as a king and admit my fault. I should have accepted the challenge to move on so that in me you could still live on in history. I should have raised my voice to tell the world of each and every one of you." He reached beside him to take the hand of a woman with a kind face. "The kindest woman who ever lived birthed me." He kissed her hand and looked to his other side. "The bravest man in the land raised me. The heavens sent the most gracious of its angels to care for me." He then looked across the table, his gaze searing. "And the most beautiful, gentle, intelligent creature that the Almighty saw fit to create married me."

Violet blushed as his words rang down her spine. Try as she might, she could not break his eye contact or his hold on her. She felt as if at this moment he spoke directly to her. And then she realized that he was allowing her to feel the love he had felt for his wife. A wife who she suddenly realized was missing.

Tears came unbidden to her eyes and her fingers trembled. It was too intimate a moment to share with her, a stranger, and yet she wanted this moment. This and a thousand more. This feeling, she'd never known it existed. Being a part of Taka's heart was like being in the eye of a storm, and so much more.

And then, the sunlight started to fade and the music and laughter slowed. She watched as the people gathered outside the hall and Taka asked if horses were ready. Then, he turned to the group, facing them. Violet felt his hand grasp hers and looked at him. His handsome face was solemn and Violet wished she could, for just one moment, offer some solace. She knew these people were the people he mourned and that somehow he had transported her to some dream of his. She also knew he had allowed her to sit in the place of his wife so that she may feel what it felt to be loved. And yet, there was something lacing his sadness that transported it beyond normal grief. Something that had catapulted him into a depression that lasted centuries.

"There are no words," he started in his booming voice, but his voice choked. He was saying good-bye, that was obvious. And she didn't know why she should be the one to step in for him, but she felt she should. After the terrible things she had said just this morning about these people, she felt she should.

She squeezed his hand. At his questioning gaze she moved forward, clearing her throat. She didn't plan the words, they seemed to flow freely from her lips coming from a place so deep within she almost felt they came from another. Her eyes filled with silent tears as she spoke.

"I feel your love deep within me. I also feel your joy. Please know that I see your faces each and every day." Now, why did she say that? It wasn't what she meant to say. She looked at Taka's head which hung in grief. She touched his coarse hair gently. "This man has been in pain but you have helped him to see that he needn't be any longer. He is a good and honorable man, a proud and just king: the burden is not his to bear." Taka looked up at her, tears in his eyes, but she was too deep into her speech now. "His journey adrift is over, my friends and family. It is time for him to be at peace." She turned to him and whispered softly, "Forgive yourself, Taka. Forgive yourself and be born anew. It is time."

Taka moaned his relief. He fell to his knees before her, grasped her waist to cry into it, to sob to her like he'd never sobbed in his life. He almost kissed her feet for freeing him, but he knew, even now, that Zahara was no more. Her spirit may indeed be in the woman before him, but the woman before him was not Zahara. The part that had been his wife was gone, at peace. *It is time:* Zahara's final words to him. And now it was just him and Violet and if he were to fall apart now, it would only frighten her. Violet: the woman who had reawakened his heart to new love. The woman he wanted in his life. He was finally free.

Taka nodded and stood, then spoke to the group. "Our Father bless you all," he said. There were hugs and laughter around. They were all well and happy, so much different from what he had expected. Kamil came to him and he clutched his friend in an embrace, grateful to see the peace and happiness in the eyes of his second-in-command.

He had thought that by their quick and violent deaths they would be tortured souls, and he had been eager to torture himself as well. Now he knew, he'd been foolish to believe that His Father would do anything less than embrace his loved ones. Now he believed what Ani said. Now he understood, no matter what harm was done to them by evil men, He was the ultimate equalizer. His was the final word. Taka should have trusted.

He turned to Violet who was standing like wood beside
him, a dazed look on her face. Still, she did not understand
what was happening. The words had been as much a
surprise to her as to him. But that was okay. Now they
could start anew.

He turned her around and before them, between the
columns, were two black stallions. "Shall we ride?" he
asked.

Of all the things he regretted in his life, the biggest was
that he had not shared one last ride with Zahara. Today,
he would give her that ride and he would say good-bye to
the wife he knew.

Violet shook her head. "I've never ridden," she said,
eyes wide. Three days ago he would have been crushed.
Zahara rode as if she were born on a horse. But this was
not Zahara. This was Violet. And it was okay.

"Then we will ride one horse together," he said. She
moved forward hesitantly and allowed herself to be
placed onto the horse, with him behind her. Once atop
she could not help but smile as she stroked the beautiful
fur of the animal.

"Don't let me go," she told Taka.

"Never," he promised. They rode away from the hall as
the others waved. They rode away from smiling, beatific
faces. They rode until the hall was a speck and they were
surrounded by green velvet hills. They rode until the
setting sun caused an explosion in the sky. Taka stopped
and pointed up. "Look. A Jahanian sunset."

"Jahanian sunset?"

"There is no other like it on earth. See the colors? See
the shades? It is unique in all the world."

She had nothing to say because she was stunned by
the palette before her. The colors were so brilliant they
seemed unreal. Her vision was perfect but never had she
seen a vision like the one before her.

"There," he pointed to a particular brilliant shade. "That is the true color of violet. It cannot be duplicated. It cannot be captured. And it is not seen any longer on this earth. It disappeared with my people. It is legend now. Violet: a shade of heavenly beauty. Named by my wife many moons ago. And now, held by you."

Violet froze. Was it possible?

They left the area and rode back to the palace at a fast clip. Taka knew when he returned the Great Hall would be empty. 400 years ago at sunset his people had been massacred. Tonight at sunset his people were at peace, as was he, finally.

As they got off the horse, Violet did not ask where the people went. It was obvious to her that this fantasy into which Taka had transported her was simply going into another phase. He took her hand and a bottle of wine from the table and they walked together through the magnificent halls and into a large room that opened onto the night sky, which still shone brilliant through the pillars. In the center of the room was a large bed covered with a million pillows of different colors. Surrounding it were panels of delicate colored silk that billowed softly in the breeze. The colors were just like those of the sunset. The room was so beautiful she wished she'd designed it herself.

A light movement in the corner drew Violet's eyes and there on a small stool sat a little man holding what appeared to be an ancient guitar. Taka saw him and smiled. "My friend, as always your timing is perfect."

"Yes, I have been sent to play one last song. One last Jahanian tune. It is the love step for you and your lady."

Taka turned to Violet and said softly. "Jahanian music, unique as well. We will never hear this melody again, Violet, so enjoy it."

He turned to her, almost shyly, taking her into his arms and pulling her so close their eyes couldn't meet, but even better was the mingling of their halting, nervous breaths, the subtle shock of Violet's hand on his shoulder, and his arm encircling her waist so completely and intimately. With his other hand he held hers and the warmth in his palm was soothing. For a moment they stood just like that: she resting her forehead against his chin and he trying to keep his heartbeat steady with her so close. The only sound being the soft swish of the silk panels in the evening breeze and their breathing, as if the whole world had stopped and the only thing that mattered was their breathing together. The sound suddenly took such meaning. The sound suddenly sounded as much like life as the Great Hall filled with noise and people had. Even more.

And then the musician began to pluck at the strings of his instrument. At first it sounded like little more than child's play. But almost as in magic the sound began to meld into a tune as gentle as the night air. Taka moved his feet and Violet followed in a gentle sway that brought them together, two wisps entwining and floating together in nature. They almost felt relief at being able to collapse against each other for dear life. Finally, Taka stopped and simply held her, so gently she wanted to cry. In his arms, she felt reverence; a love she'd never known existed.

"Violet?" he asked, concerned. "Are you all right?"

She stood still, blinking and looking around. The guitarist was gone. The only sound was once again the shift of the silk panels in the wind. They sounded incredibly loud. She felt as if there was thunder rumbling in her ears. She felt as if something rumbled within her. And then she became afraid. Fear began to claw its coldness into her blood.

Violet reached up and grabbed Taka's head with her two hands and pulled it down to press her lips harshly against his. He kissed her back eagerly. Her hands went around him like a vice and she used all her body weight to topple them both onto the bed with its mountain of pillows.

Taka fell onto the bed, having been caught off guard. He righted himself while Violet pulled the pillows that had tumbled down upon her off of her. Then she reached up to pull him to her again, and Taka willingly gave her another kiss, luxuriating in the taste of her lips and the feel of her. Violet. He didn't know when had he fallen in love with Violet, but he loved her with all his heart. And now, he finally felt she was feeling the same.

He bent in to kiss her again, his eyes full of love.

"Taka."

"What, sweet woman?"

"Is this the part where you show me what love is? 'Cause I'm ready. You were right: one night of ecstasy won't hurt anything. Tomorrow Jerome will forgive me but we're broken up tonight. You've had me all hot and bothered for days now, stop teasing me."

Taka pulled back slightly. Her tone, her face, the cold look in her eyes . . .

She sat up to look at him. "For God's sake, don't stop now. The dancing, the music, the food: that was the best foreplay I've ever had. No one can say you don't put on a good show."

Taka reared back as if a bucket of water had been thrown into his face. His hurt was too great to mask. "That is all this has been to you? A show?"

"What do you want me to say?" Violet said with a lift of her chin despite a trembling voice. "You told me you had some pretty good parlor tricks, but I never imagined all this."

Taka looked at her, desperation in his eyes, his voice pleading. "You cannot mean those words. You cannot really be so disrespectful of what you have experienced here. You cannot truly have forgotten everything. I do not believe no shred of memory remains. Violet," he said her name urgently, pleading. "When you silence yourself in the morning, when you close your eyes and open your mind and consciousness to the great beyond, somewhere in the silence, in the openness, do you not see me there? Someplace in the quiet and the peacefulness, do you not hear my voice calling out? Some small place in the corners of your mind and your thoughts, do you not feel me there, Violet?"

Violet didn't know why she should feel such an onslaught of emotion at his words, but she looked away so she didn't have to see the pain in his eyes. "When I close my eyes to meditate I feel nothing, I'm sorry to say. I see nothing. I just do it so I can tell people I do, so I can sound enlightened. It helps to get customers. Why would I be listening for any-thing? Why would I want to look for anything, seeing you like this, hearing the pain in your voice? Why would I want that? Why would anyone want that? Why would anyone want to know whatever horrors . . . Look, I don't know what you want from me. I'm just a regular woman."

But her words and her actions told him otherwise. Finally, he understood. "No, that is not true." He turned away and climbed off the bed, standing to stare into the night sky, now settling into navy blue. "You know what I want and you are determined not to give it to me. You forgive but you do not forget. Perhaps it is my fault and my mistake to think that you would trust me again, and allow me in again, after I failed so dreadfully before."

"I don't know what you're talking about. Look, I don't like to see you hurting, but I don't know what to do.

Why don't you come back over here and kiss me again? Isn't that what you were going to do? It's our last night together; let's spend it pleasuring each other. Come on, it's the least you could do since you didn't grant my last wish."

He whirled to pin her with his stare. "I did grant your wish, Violet, or rather our Father granted your wish! You asked for the love of a good man, and here I am, loving you! Wanting to love you! Begging to love you!"

"Love me? You won't even touch me. And all this pomp and circumstance is nice but it's not real. It's a cartoon. Fantasy. It's smoke and mirrors."

"Smoke and mirrors?" He raised his hand to the room. "This was our home. This experience tonight was but a snapshot. That song, it was a song created for me and my wife for our wedding night. This place was decorated by my wife in love and filled with all I cherished, but this place is not what I cherished most. And love, it is not merely in how many times I press my lips to yours or in a thousand nights of passion." His voice softened. "Love is in my eyes when I look at you. Love is what makes a man travel hundreds of years to have a second chance to make it right. I didn't understand before. I do now. That is what I want for you, Violet. That is what I have asked our Father to give you after I have gone. Perhaps there is still hope for you, if not me."

He turned, wearily, back to the night air looking at the last streak of pink on the horizon. "The king I was tonight was not the king I was then. I wouldn't stop for the five minutes it took just to dance with my wife the way I did with you a few minutes ago. This palace, my kingdom, every treasure I owned was great, but it was not what was important. In my wife was my home. I should have protected it. I should have worshipped it. I should have let it rest in peace. I know that now. And by bringing you here, it was not to show you all the things I had. It was to show you that I have found a new home in you. That my heart lives in you. You are my home, Violet, more than this place or this time. Where you are, I am home."

He took a tired sigh. "Life doesn't wait. It doesn't stop, nor should it. I had paradise in my hands and I put it aside to run a kingdom. Now, I look at you and I see my kingdom and I'm ready to live life today. To love, today. To enjoy the gift that stands before me now so I never need regret another thing in life."

Violet's heart began to beat even though she didn't know why. That fear she'd tried to cover was back now that she heard his words. She didn't understand any of it except the fact that Taka was hurting, and she was terrified despite her best effort to shrug off the feeling.

"I don't know what you want, Taka. I'm sorry I disappointed you, but I can't give you what you're looking for. I don't believe in love. And this . . . I'm glad it meant something to you but it was just a nice day trip for me. I wish you the best, Taka, truly I do. And I hope your next awakening will be more fulfilling," she said honestly, missing him already.

"There is no next awakening, Violet, this is my last. And don't worry over me for I have made peace with my Father and it is time. I am finally weary of immortality. I am ready to place myself in His hands and to give up control. I am ready to submit and ask for His mercy and grace. I am tired, Violet, so tired. I am ready to go."

A sudden wind kicked up and the intensity and force of the billowing curtains into the dawning night drew their attention and when Violet looked back into Taka's face the worry lines between his eyes were gone. His strong face relaxed. It was as if a lifetime of burden had fallen away, somehow, and she saw him as he must have looked as a young man so long ago. Strong and fierce, without fear, without regret, so handsome in his vitality it made her smile, so hopeful for the future it made her long to share it with him.

"Violet, do not be afraid of what is to come," he said softly in a voice gruff with some unspoken emotion. "If our Father will allow, I will watch over you all the rest of your life. The days ahead may be difficult, but if any part of me or your memory of me makes its way back into your soul, if any little bit of you can trust in me or in love again, please know that I will be here for you always, for I have never loved another. All those years ago, I thought He was cruel for taking you from me. Now I see I am the cruel one, cruel to ask you to remember the horror of that day. I am a selfish man. I wanted you too much to think about what I have been asking of you. You do not have to relive this memory, my queen. I understand. If it allows your beautiful, gentle soul not to have to feel the trauma of the day you were torn from this place, I am glad to be forgotten. I want only joy for you, no more pain. No more. I release you, my darling. It is all right to let me go." He smiled gently even while his eyes sparkled with unshed tears. "Violet, the color of my heaven. Remember me, my love. I shall always remember you."

Chapter 25

1600 AD: Jaha, West Africa

Zahara strode into the Great Hall, picking up the skirt of the long tunic that bared one arm completely and bunched with gathered material at her bosom. The shells of her necklace would look far better lying against her brown shea butter–slathered skin than against the fabric of her dress, but past experience told her that a public adjustment of her bodice to achieve this end would not be appreciated by the villagers. She would have to find another way to generate the sparkle in her husband's eyes. Instead, she gently cupped the ruby pin at her shoulder, the memory of her husband's awkward delivery of the extravagant gift making her blush.

She nodded to passersby and smiled, head held high. They could disapprove all they wanted; disapproval had never stopped her from loving Taka before and it wouldn't now. With a quick movement she looked both ways before pulling at her top to reveal a little more skin before pulling back the panel of silk that separated him from the hall, stepping through into the circle of the king's privacy. He read from a scroll in his hands, a wrinkle marring the area between his thick brows. From this vantage she could look at him like she so loved to do.

He wore a chain of shells to match her own; and a chain of gold link pounded specifically for him lay against his own bare chest. She swallowed, as always, at the display of his wide shoulders and arms corded with muscles earned through battle and hard work. Overall, a fierce visage, but in happiness he would change. Once in a while his mouth, which rarely curved, would form a smile and those who witnessed it would feel blessed by having seen it transform the fierce and intimidating leader into a large, warm, and human man. The fact that it was so rare made its sight all that more valuable. Occasionally, he would laugh a loud booming sound, a laugh from his gut that would sound across the Great Hall and into the adjoining palace, and sometimes across the land with its deep baritone. Rumor had it that people in the next village would stop when they heard the ground rumble because they knew King Taka was laughing, and it was a glorious sound indeed.

Zahara saw his smile more than most and felt his laughter as viscerally as if it were her own. She also felt the tenseness that coursed through him. Today his face knew no hint of gentleness, held no memory of softness. Zahara would do her best to change his disposition.

King Taka felt Zahara enter and though his concentration changed to annoyance, he didn't snap as was his right to do. He could never snap at her; never this woman. She was the most stubborn, insolent, determined woman he knew, but that was exactly why he'd married her. And why he knew that ordering her about was tantamount to waving a red flag for battle. Instead, he sighed without raising his head as he felt her move to his side, leaning against the table to place her face in his line of vision.

"Put it down, Taka. You promised." She leaned over farther, her body blocking his view.

"This is important business, my love," he said, keeping his temper in check. She was lovely, as always. Her eyes were a deep mink brown framed by lashes and brows of the same color. Her skin was the color of the drink that was made with sassafras and licorice root, and tasted as good: both sweet and warm at the same time. He was drawn to taste it right now, thrilled at the sight of the soft pink shells of her necklace lying against her skin just above the fabric of her dress. He knew he had only to drop the one offending shoulder of fabric to have her beauty before him. He imagined taking her naked into his arms, her perfect body round in all the places that made a woman different from a man. Breasts large enough to cup with still more to overflow; hips and a backside that swayed when she walked and made him long to be cradled within; the thin layer of padding that told the world she was robust and healthy, a woman loved enough to be well fed and beautiful enough to know her own power. She was stunning. But he was king. Usually this made him happy, but for the few times it forced him to deny the thing he wanted most.

"I know I promised you. But you know you married a king."

"A king without a stroke of leisure in his whole body," she said. "It's a beautiful day, husband. I want to go out and run in the fields. I want to go out and ride our horses in the sunshine. You used to do that with me." The lilt in her voice and its soft timbre made him vibrate with desire. As always.

"I am so busy, Zahara. Tomorrow, I promise," he said firmly to strengthen his own resolve.

"I don't know that I believe your promises anymore, my love."

Taka felt a flash of annoyance, wishing she were not so stubborn. "You have to leave. Go, busy yourself with something. I thought you and your maid were beading purses."

He saw a flash in her mink brown eyes. "Do not condescend to me, Taka Olufemi. I bead in my spare time but

I am not a child to be easily amused by small stones and bright colors."

"I am king. I cannot humor you whenever you grow bored."

"If you humored me one-tenth of the times I grow bored I would be satisfied."

"If you do not go away I will call the guards and tell them you are harassing the king."

"And you would allow them to take me away in chains, my king? And what would you do about the injuries?"

"Injuries?"

"Yes. The injuries I would cause biting, slapping, and kicking you until they reach me. Do not even jest; you would never call your guards on me. Because you love me."

She was right and he knew it was clearly reflected in his eyes. When he looked upon her his insides dissolved in fiery heat. The sight of her caused him to burn from within. She told him once that in their most passionate moments his eyes would seem to fill with smoke, blaze with intensity. He believed her. The smokiness that revealed his desire was like the smoke from an evening camp: only a small measure of the true source of heat. He could barely look at her now without burning alive.

"If you know I love you why do you torture me?" he said, aching to plant his lips on hers, knowing they would taste even sweeter than the deep red berries that had stained them the same fetching color as the brooch on her shoulder.

"Perhaps I want to hear you say it. Perhaps I want you to regale me with stories of your love for me like a proper husband should."

"I will tell you all you want this evening. Right now, I am busy."

"But right now is when I want to hear it."

"Must you fight me at every turn?"

"Of course. We fell in love fighting, and if I'm not mistaken I beat your royal behind soundly."

"I was merely a child."

"Oh, the scandal. The future king, whipped to tears by a common girl."

The memory made his lip turn slightly at the corner. "A common girl with scruffy knees and hair that a thousand beads and a million pots of precious oil couldn't tame."

She pulled a braid from her headdress to twirl in his face. "My parents were scandalized. They wanted to send me away, you know. They hoped that by the time I came back to the village you would forget that I had disrespected your little royal backside."

"I never would have forgotten."

"Neither would I."

"Neither did this village. I had to work doubly hard to prove myself with the men. I had to fight twice as many fights. I had to prove that I was a worthy warrior so that I could lead them into battle."

"So, you see, it is to my credit that you are the bravest man in the kingdom." Zahara reached up to kiss him, disappointment on her face when he didn't meet her halfway. He hardened his face and voice to her, the only way he knew to end this flirtation.

"You must go, Zahara."

"Just one minute more."

"There is rumor of forces coming from the north. We need to prepare." Her shoulders fell in defeat and Taka was both satisfied and disappointed that he had won this battle of wills.

"Will you dine with me this evening, then?"

"We will dine with you."

"Will we have guests again?"

"Our allies. They will aid us in strengthening our defense. With our villages working together we will be unstoppable."

"Do you trust them?"

"Not all, but they are not foolish. If we can help them survive, it is to their benefit to keep us happy as well. They will assist us. But you needn't worry about these things; if you do not want to dine with the guests I will keep a guard posted with you until I can come to you this evening."

"And tomorrow we will ride?"

"Tomorrow, my love."

"One kiss before I busy myself playing with children's amusements?" She placed a hand on the back of his head and her lips pouted in anticipation of the kiss he longed to give her. He removed it gently and wondered which of them felt the loss more keenly. He would make it up to her. Tonight, tomorrow, a thousand times over. He would make her smile twice for every time he disappointed her. But he couldn't now.

"One kiss will lead to two, which will lead to more; it always does. Save me a kiss for this evening?"

"I will be asleep when you come to bed."

"I will kiss you anyway. You are more agreeable when you sleep."

She smiled. "Don't disappoint me, my king. Without your love and your kisses I am lost. Deny me and I will be angry. I would hate to have to injure you yet again."

"I don't mind being injured by you, my heart. You make up so sweetly afterward."

Chapter 26

Violet sat up in bed gasping for air, drenched in sweat. The dream she'd just had, it was gone, but her heart still beat from the impact. She looked around but the bedroom was empty. Sun struggled through her window blinds. She showered and put on a face mask. She came out of the bedroom to walk across the living room and into the kitchen for coffee that was steaming in the pot. She went to the front door, opened it, retrieved her paper, and came back inside. All the while feeling as if something were missing.

She stopped with her coffee halfway to her lips. She forgot to meditate. She should meditate. She really needed to. How odd. But suddenly someone was banging on the door and she went to it. She noticed a box on the ground near the door and was looking at it, trying to determine how her things got into a box, when she opened the door to Jerome.

Oh, yeah, the boyfriend. He stood there, entitlement and indignation on his face. "Look, things were said yesterday that maybe shouldn't have been said. I was probably a little hasty. I got to thinking about it and I realize you love me. But my feelings were hurt. I mean, you can't expect me to sit around while you got another man, making a fool of me and all."

Violet took a two-handed sip of coffee. She knew who he was but what he was saying didn't make any sense.

"So I was thinking I could probably forgive you and all if, maybe, you show I can trust you a little. He ain't here, is he?"

He who? Violet was trying but her head was in a fog and it was like he was speaking but nothing meant anything. It was gobbledygook. It was Jerome, but she didn't really want to see him. She didn't want him there.

She looked down at the box with her things and realized the items were those she left at his place, including a toothbrush tossed haphazardly across a silk blouse. Tossed there like it didn't matter if toothpaste rubbed off on a $200 blouse. It wasn't like she was rolling in money that she could afford to ruin a blouse over nonsense. Toothpaste would probably come out at the dry cleaner, but it was the point.

"Sorry 'bout that," he said, apparently having followed her thought process. "I was angry, you know. But like I was saying, I could probably forgive you."

She couldn't recall what she might need forgiving for but she knew with certainty she didn't care. She sipped her coffee and looked at him again. She wasn't attracted to him in the least. Had never been. So why was she with him? Oh yeah, the Brenda Competition.

She took another sip.

"All I think I need is to be able to trust you," he continued. "So I think you should just go ahead and let me share ownership in your business. I mean, that way we could always trust one another and it would prove to me that you are worthy to be my wife. Because after yesterday I really thought about cutting you loose, Violet. I really did."

She didn't know what ridiculousness he was spouting. Her head was telling her to listen, to pay attention; it could be a good prospect. But this little voice was saying something else. It was saying:

"Truth is, Jerome, I don't want you. I can barely stand the sound of your voice. I had to force myself to make love to you and then I had to squeeze my eyes shut to get through it. You were only ever an acquisition to me. I was with you because I knew I could control you. I would never give you access to my business and I'm done giving you access to me. You're a jerk with itty bitty little boy equipment and my chunky butt deserves better than you. So you can take your forgiveness and shove it. I'd rather be alone than put up with you for another minute. Fact is, if for some reason I were to drop off the face of the earth tomorrow, I would be sorely disappointed if I had spent today with you. It would be a waste of a perfectly good day. Please leave and don't come back. And that's not a tease; I really mean it. Good-bye."

Then she realized she'd spoken out loud. Jerome's shocked face contorted with anger as he slowly came out of it.

"What the—"

Violet used one hand to slam the door and shrugged. *Oh well, good riddance to bad rubbish.*

She put her coffee down and went into the bedroom to sit cross-legged on her bed to get back to meditation. Her brow furrowed with her effort to focus. She was so spacey this morning.

She sat on the bed with her legs crossed, closed her eyes, and breathed deeply. She had to admit, as always, the cleansing breaths felt good. She allowed her mind to be free and open, allowed her thoughts to drift away on a cloud, so peaceful, so gentle. There! This was where she usually stopped. No point in going any further. Nirvana did not have a place in her morning toilette. She didn't have the time or inclination for it. At least, usually she didn't. Today, she felt some part of her urging her to remain just a little longer. Nirvana was teasing the edges of her consciousness.

She should really get dressed. She would be thrown completely off her schedule if she stayed any longer. But her heart wasn't in any rush and unlike every other morning, she wanted to linger. She wanted to fall into the peace that promised to envelop her. She wanted to be cradled by the warmth she felt lingering in the depths of her consciousness. She longed to stay in the softness that existed, so different from what awaited her once she opened her eyes. She wanted to hold on to the feeling of acceptance, understanding, love. Last night's dream teased the edge of her consciousness like a book waiting for the last chapter read. Right there on the edge, she could almost feel it.

Violet's head screamed for her to open her eyes so she didn't have to see or feel the emotions that threatened to come but her heart would not let her. Instead, she probed gently into the unknown recesses of her brain and the images came to her quickly like snapshots with no rhyme, reason, or order.

Herself and a man in a palace. Oh yes, the genie. It was coming back to her now, the last few days he'd stayed with her. The genie and the brooch and the wishes. The brooch was in her head now. Big and gaudy and fake looking. Old. But then, new. Fresh and shined. Being handed to her as a gift. Feeling overwhelmed. The largest known ruby in the world, cut specifically for her as a wedding gift. Curious. She wasn't married. But there she was standing next to a man with a headdress. She looked at him: tall, big, and strong, his serious face softened by joy and love, his voice booming with laughter. A strong, powerful man beside her; valiant warrior, brave fighter in battle, raised to lead and . . .

She felt reticence when people came as guests; so many people with eyes that would not look into hers. But Taka said it was okay, so it must be. She sat at the large table and finished eating, looking forward to the end of the meal, and her husband smiled at her from the other end. That's who he was, the husband! Her husband? But how? No time to figure it out because now she sees the sword, sees it slice into her beloved so quickly she barely has a chance to realize what is happening. Her blood grows cold as the steel is pulled roughly from his body, as if he were merely a goat to slaughter. As if he were not her king; the most wonderful man she'd ever known.

Pandemonium, screaming, running, blood . . .

He reaches toward her but someone grabs her around the waist and she's being dragged up and away from her husband's loving arms. She panics as she's pulled away because her husband can't stand and he's struggling so to get to her. She sees his life's blood flowing and he's struggling with all his might to stand.

No, my darling, don't move! If he stays still perhaps he will not lose so much blood. She fights to go back to him, fights to hold him, knowing that he will die alone if she doesn't get to him. She fights with all her strength and it isn't until her attacker gets tired of her struggle and wraps large hands around her throat that she realizes she should fear for her life, too.

Feeling the air restricted, Zahara raises her head, tries to push him away from her but only manages to inch her head up slightly to see her husband lying still in his own blood. Even though she can't breathe, she can cry. The pain—losing the man of her heart, her friend, lover, and soul mate—why that pain is even greater than that of the denial of air to her desperate lungs. She reaches out to her love, whom she will never see again, his name soundless on her lips.

Violet's eyes whipped open. Gasping for air, her face bathed with sweat for the second time, her limbs trembling, Violet called out, hoarse, with only one word on her lips: "Taka."

The bell of the antique shop tinkled as Violet ran inside like a madwoman. Skeeter's eyes lit up with pleasure. "Did you change your mind? I'll write you out a check for a thousand!"

Violet gave him a dirty look. "I thought you said eleven hundred, Skeeter." Then she shook her head, had to stay focused. "Never mind that. Tell me what you know about the brooch."

Skeeter put on his poker face again. "I don't know what you're talking about."

Her tenuous grip on control had expired. She leaped across the counter to grab the old man by his shirt front, pulling him to her and speaking in a hoarse tone. "I have spent beaucoup bucks in this place, old man. Now when I ask you for a favor you dummy up and try to play me? Uhn, uhn. Here's what's going to happen. You're going to tell me what you know about that brooch or I'm going to reach into your spindly chest and pull out that peach pit you call a heart and shove it up your shriveled behind. Got it?"

Skeeter looked at her, eyes big. "Well, when you put it that way . . ." Violet released him and he straightened his shirt, struggling to save face. "Okay, I found a little information on it."

A few minutes later they were sitting at a little antique table, two chairs pulled up to it and papers, photos, and letters spread on the table. The brooch was sitting there as well since Violet had decided Skeeter was sufficiently terrorized that he wouldn't try to steal it. He admired it, holding it in his fingers.

"I thought right away it might be Jahanian. There aren't many artifacts left but the few that have been found have a distinctive style. Had a bowl in here day before yesterday I suspected was Jahanian too, but I didn't know until some guy came looking at it. None of it can be substantiated, of course. All these articles and papers mostly debunk the idea of a lost civilization of this magnitude. They easier believe in Atlantis than Jaha. Only a few diehards believe otherwise and that's because of stories we got on our folks' knee. Thought they were just stories."

Violet nodded, still shaky from her morning's meditation. The vision was so real, the details so chilling it stunned her. And then snippets of last night's adventure with the genie. She had assumed she had been possessed in some way. Now she wasn't so sure. She had to know the truth.

"I don't understand. How can a complete civilization be lost?"

"Oh, that's easy. Just wipe out all the people, all the literature, and any architecture, and it's gone. Only word of mouth left. Of course, that's just exactly why no one credits Jaha with anything: no proof. But every once in a while a piece turns up somewhere that is unlike any other piece from anywhere. People start saying it don't make sense. And then somebody who has heard about Jaha starts to looking at it and wondering again. But really, among the historians, it's all just legend."

"What exactly is the legend?" Violet asked.

"Well, they say Jaha was to Africa what the Roman Empire was to western civilization. You see, King Taka Olufemi had become this monster of power and he was crazy with it. Surrounding villages, they were planning to put him out of power but he up and killed all his own people. Maniac. At least that's what some people say."

That wasn't what she'd seen in the vision. She remembered the table, the wine, the sudden attack on the king. Skeeter's story didn't compute. "And what do the others say?"

He looked hesitant to answer but fear was a wonderful motivator. He swatted the air with disgust. "It's nonsense. Anybody that got family come down the line will tell you all about King Taka."

"Humor me with the nonsense, Skeeter."

"Well, they say other villages were envious, that when he invited them into his home *they* massacred everyone."

"How horrible," she said, shivering.

"How untrue. Truth is he was power hungry and couldn't stand not being in charge so he killed his own. And when they died the sunsets died with 'em. Yessiree, they say them sunsets were the most beautiful God ever made. And his wife was so horrified she up and killed herself and God imprisoned him forever in that brooch."

"And the other story?" She sighed. He pursed his lips. "You're testing my patience, Skeeter."

"Okay, okay. The other story is that the death of his wife sent him over the edge. That's where that brooch part comes in. It was a wedding gift to his wife. When she was murdered, he and God had a huge fight. He said he didn't want to live without her. God said, 'Okay, buddy, then you're stuck in this brooch granting wishes for eternity.' Legend says that he is trapped until he finds the spirit of his queen. And if she accepts him, he lives as a mortal. If she denies him, he is condemned to burn forever. If she's smart she'll keep that boy right in that rock."

Violet froze. He'd allowed her to sit in the place of his wife. Everyone at the celebration had embraced her as if she were one of them. Violet felt her stomach roll and her lips muttered the words, "What do you know about his wife?"

"Hardly nothing. But I sent away for some info based on a lead, and I finally got something in the mail yesterday. I called you."

"Yeah, yeah. What'd you get?"

"Hmm, it was right here." He shoved some papers aside and found an envelope. "Oh, here it is. Haven't even had time to look at it." He tore it open and pulled out a folded sheet of paper. Even from the back they could see it was a drawing. "They didn't have cameras back then. This guy sent me a copy of a drawing he has." He unfolded the page and stopped, stunned. But Violet did not even need to see it. She knew.

He turned the page to her, his old hands shaking with fear. "My Lord, this . . . this looks just like . . . like . . . you."

She looked at the page to see her own likeness adorned in a headdress, the brooch pinned to the top. The photo must have been from an art history book, as the caption read only: "Unknown African Queen, believed to be a seventeenth century work."

Unknown African Queen.

No!

She wasn't possessed by the spirit of his dead wife, she *was* his dead wife. Those weren't visions, those were memories. Last night wasn't a senseless adventure with a mad genie; last night was the final chapter in the life of a king, a man who had once been her husband. Taka, beloved king of Jaha, the jewel in the crown of West Africa, her home. All those people hugging her, kissing her, saying good-bye in Taka's home, those weren't strangers. They were her friends and family, too. A whole village of people who loved her despite the mess she was. And she'd looked right through them, every one of them. All along she was the betrayer. She had denied herself the gift of love all this time. She had defamed the very thought of it instead of cherishing it. She had known it utterly, completely, and unceasingly and still chose to turn her back on it. She had betrayed herself.

And Taka. He'd known her. He'd tried everything to reach her. Her love, he had given his heart, put himself and his life in her hands. He had come to find her. He had given up his mortality to search for her and she had turned him away and hurt him. Her king. Her heart.

She opened her mouth to speak, and then burst into tears. She stood quickly, grabbed the brooch, and ran out of the shop.

Chapter 27

Violet sat in her apartment, the blinds closed, a used paper bag at her feet. She'd come straight from the antique shop to run home and curl up on the sofa. All the bits and pieces had fallen into place and by the time she got home she knew everything.

How could she have forgotten? How could she have ignored the signs? How could she have ignored the little voice inside her telling her that something about Taka was familiar, special? And screw all that past stuff; how could she have allowed the man she loved to simply walk out of her life? Yes, she loved him. She loved the genie. She loved his big, arrogant, crabby self. Just as he was.

She looked around the room and noticed another bag on a table. She opened it up and inside lay a bowl carved like lace. The second her fingers touched the wood she felt a stab of bittersweet emotion so strong tears sprang to her eyes immediately. She recognized this bowl! It was carved by the women who prepared for religious celebration. A collection that was scattered to the wind, and yet, somehow, Taka had found it. Like a homing beacon, he had been able to zoom in on a relic of his kingdom. And yet she, who had been queen, had lost all memory of her past as easily as if it were nothing. How many relics of her people had she passed time and again at Skeeter's? How many sacred mementos had she allowed to slip away due to ignorance and cowardice? She was not worthy of being queen.

She saw a sheet of paper on the floor, apparently having floated there from under the bowl. She reached to pick it up. It was an employment application. Taka had started to fill it out. He'd written his name. That was as far as he'd gotten. How was a man supposed to fill out an application when he had no skills in this time? Why would he even have tried? Her lips shook with the threat of new tears as she realized he'd actually been trying to find a way to stay, trying to plan a career, to be with her. And she'd chased him away. Two days of trying to make her see, competing with the likes of Jerome, two days of begging her to remember how good the good could be and on the third day she ran him off.

A knock on the door jolted her but she decided to ignore it, hoping they would go away. Someone knocked harder and her face scrunched in irritation. She wiped her eyes, took a deep breath, put the paper and bowl down, and answered the door to Brenda. Without being invited, the woman walked into her apartment and started talking.

"I know you don't want to talk to me. Just listen."

"Get out."

"I was just so hurt by what you did."

"I don't need this right now, Brenda."

"Just hear me out, Violet. For once," Brenda pleaded.

Violet threw up her arms but sat and listened.

"I shouldn't have done it. I knew I shouldn't have done it," Brenda said.

"For pity's sake, Brenda, Jerome and I were bound to break up someday."

"Not just that. I shouldn't have stolen your technique and I shouldn't have stolen Gary. Those were not nice things to do."

"Gary is water under the bridge. You can have him."

"I shouldn't have taken him in the first place. I shouldn't have even looked at him, and then I never would have gotten involved with him. And every day I talked to you about it like it was nothing, and it wasn't nothing. It was something. I hurt you and it was wrong. Despite that you said it didn't matter, I knew deep down it did."

"Why are you bringing this up?"

"I woke up this morning, expecting to be happy because I'd gotten back at you, but I wasn't. I couldn't stop thinking about you and Jerome. But worse, I couldn't stop thinking about what was going on now with you and that other guy and feeling guilty for siccing Jerome on him."

"What?"

"That other guy. Jerome said he was coming over here to kick his butt. Did he hurt him?"

"Jerome hurt Taka? Jerome?" Violet could not help the laughter from bubbling out of her lips. Ridiculous. But even more ridiculous was how quickly the laughter turned to tears. To her own horror she was sobbing like there was no tomorrow.

Brenda froze, not knowing what to do. "What?"

"I . . . I've made such a mess of things. He's gone."

"The genie?"

"He had three days to grant my wishes and I chased him away last night and . . . Oh, forget it. You don't believe me anyway. And why should you? We've been lying to each other and stabbing each other in the back for years."

Brenda sat down beside her. "Have we, really? But we're friends."

"Friends don't behave that way, Brenda. The truth is, I've always been jealous of you and I've done everything I could to outshine you. I'm jealous of your money and your family, and up until yesterday I still hated you for Gary. There, I've said it."

"I'm jealous of you too. I will forever be known as the woman who took your castoff. I'll never be a better decorator. And now, this. This genie fantasy you've got going."

"It's not a fantasy, Brenda. He's real."

"Well, maybe I shouldn't say this. But you're lucky to be rid of Jerome. He was always looking at my butt."

"Thank you, Brenda, that makes me feel better."

"Look, I don't want to spend all my time competing with you anymore. It's exhausting. I want you to know, Gary wasn't just a competition. We really do love each other. And I really do want you in my wedding."

"Honey, look at me. Do I look like I could be happy for anyone right now? I just broke up with my boyfriend; you don't want me at a wedding."

"But that's not what's making you look like that, is it? It's the other one. The one who looked at you like you hung the moon. If you ask me, that's what broke you and Jerome up. He looked at you like he'd give you the world if he could. Jerome couldn't compete with that."

"He's gone. He's gone and I never got to tell him how I really felt. I was just so scared, Brenda. I was too scared to take the risk to love." The tears started again. Brenda looked at her, and then, awkwardly, she reached over to give Violet a stiff, sincere hug. The women clung to each other and finally Brenda pulled away and spoke sternly.

"I'm going to teach you something for a change, Violet. As hard as you work to beat me at everything, you need to work just as hard to get him back."

"But he's gone!"

"I don't care if he's a genie, a medicine man, whatever the heck he is, you get him back!"

"You know, I've never been in love like this before. I thought I fell with Gary but it wasn't like this. I didn't even realize what I was feeling until he was gone."

"Well, that's it then. Now that you've felt it, you can't go back, right?"

"There's a lot you don't know, Brenda."

"I know all I need to know. Now are you going to sit in this apartment crying or are you going to get your man back?"

An hour later Brenda was gone, and Violet was sitting on a park bench, eyes ragged and wet, hands trembling.

When Brenda had issued her challenge, she'd immediately decided she was going to get Taka back, no matter what. But after racking her brain, rubbing the stone until her palms were red and would surely be callused in the morning, and just plain yelling at it, nothing had happened. That was when she realized she had no clue how to get Taka back.

She'd come to the park where she'd found the brooch, defeated and demoralized. After the way she'd treated him, he probably didn't want to come back. Or worse, if what Skeeter had said was true, she'd probably condemned him herself. All because she'd been a coward. Too afraid to admit her feelings for him. Too afraid to hope that she should be allowed something as simple and magnificent as to be loved by someone and to love in return. Too sure that she had nothing to offer.

She dropped her face into her hands as a sob tore through her frame. She almost scared herself; it'd been so long since she really cried she didn't know the sound of a good belly buster anymore. When she pulled her hands away to take a deep breath, she spoke to the gray sky.

"I don't know how to reach you but I think you should know what I feel. I lied when I said I never knew you were there. Every morning when I close my eyes and reach for something, I feel you in the peace that comes to me. And when I sleep sometimes I dream of a man in shadows who calls out to me and takes my hand and promises me the love of a thousand lifetimes. I taught myself to ignore those dreams, and any other that came along. I couldn't bear to imagine something so beautiful and wake to a reality that didn't have you." She took another tremulous breath and went on. "I can't go back now that I know what love really is. And I know I have no right to ask you back. But I want you to know, wherever you are, my heart will always remember that you are my home. You are my only love."

But it was too late to talk to Taka. He was beyond her now. For the first time in a long time, she looked to the gentle sky for answers. "Dear Lord, I know I have no right to ask for a favor. I haven't prayed in a long time. But if you're there, if you're really there like Taka said, I can't see why you'd make me love him and then take him. But if he's gone for real, please tell him I love him. He didn't ask for much but I at least owe him the truth. I couldn't give it to him last night but I tell you to my depths I have never known a better man and I love him. I love him. Oh, God, please forgive me."

Violet finished, dropping her eyes to her lap. She felt her eardrums pop and an electricity surround her. The hairs on the back of her neck stood up. She looked around and jumped when she saw a dark-skinned woman sitting calmly next to her, hands crossed. The woman smiled at her.

"Now, are you sure about that love thing? You kids today toss that word around so much, who can tell?" She smiled a teasing smile then noticed Violet's expression. "Don't be frightened, Violet, I'm Aniweta. I'm a messenger sent from our Heavenly Father." Violet knew she was staring at the woman like she was crazy. But a second ago she hadn't been there. She materialized just like on TV. Ani sighed. "I miss the days when I could talk to my wards face to face. Nowadays, everybody's scared of us. I have to whisper to people because if I straight talk to them they go running into caves thinking they're crazy. I ask you, what is so crazy about talking to an angel? It's the most logical, rational thing in the world. Taka never had a problem with it. He talks to me, yells at me, cusses me . . ."

Violet said the first thing that came to her mind. "He said you were a man."

"Yes, yes. I let the men see me as a man so they won't be frightened. You know how easily men can scare. And you, you look at me as if you've seen a ghost and yet you have your own angel that has been with you for all your life."

"No, that can't be. I pray. No one ever answers," Violet said, both doubtful and dubious. The woman laughed prettily. "Oh, your angel speaks to you all the time and our Father is constantly shouting in your ear. You go through all sorts of calisthenics to avoid listening to anything they have to say. The only reason I'm here is because of Taka. Our Father decided the only one you would listen to is that man of yours so he brought Taka here. Kind of like a giant cotton swab to clean out your ears so you can hear Him. And he was right. You're a little late but you never would have asked for His help had it not been for your king. The two of you are so much alike, it's spooky. Both so determined to get what you want you block out anything you don't want to hear, even the truth. Every choice you made our Father tried to place you on the right path, and every time you seemed bound and determined to convince everyone that power was the most important thing."

"It is. You should know, Miss I Come and Go as I Please."

Ani smiled. "My, you are even feistier than Zahara. Yes, you are a good match for each other." Violet felt a tingling in her toes and Ani's eyes brightened noticeably.

Suddenly, Ani's posture seemed to change, and the air seemed to swell around her. When she spoke next, Violet was certain, somehow, that it wasn't Ani she was listening to.

"Do you know what Taka learned? He had all the power, child, and it was taken from him. That was when he realized what was truly of value."

"A . . . Aniweta?" Violet stuttered softly. She didn't know why she was frightened now, the woman looked the same. But she was different.

"You know who I am, daughter. You have heard my voice and felt my love. Did you not?"

This was it, she thought. All her years of praying; all her years of hope and anger and doubt about God. All her years of thinking she knew who God was and what He was about. Now, God was here talking to her, and not in some abstract kind of way, but face to face like a person. She wanted to be mature and ask smart questions because this chance may never come again. She wanted to be respectful and humble. But in this moment, sitting there, gone was the epiphany she'd just had this morning about being grateful for what she'd had. All she could feel now was what she'd lost, again.

"Why did you take so much from me if you love me so much?" Violet whispered.

"I didn't take it. Evil took it. If I didn't love you so much, my child, I never would have given it to you in the first place. You have lost a great deal and your pain is real. But there is more left for you, Violet, if you allow there to be. There is more to this life than just existing. There is beauty. There is joy. There is hope and happiness, longing and regret, all of it worth feeling. All of it worth the lesson. I will sum it up by saying this: with my power I give you life and free will. I don't ask for much in return. I ask only one question: do you love life enough to hold on to it with everything you have? For by loving life you love me."

"But how could you punish him the way you did? Not only did you make him a prisoner, you allowed them to destroy his home. He doesn't even have the satisfaction of being spoken of in history books. He might as well not have existed."

"He, he, he; don't you mean you, as well? That's part of the problem: you always did put him before yourself. Do you truly believe that if it is not written about it did not exist? Have I not taught you anything? The history is in here." She pointed to Violet's heart. "Taka Olufemi, the Jaha Kingdom, mother Africa lives inside you. My son spent so many years so proud of his birthright. But my pride was not in what was inherited by him; that was simply given to him. My pride was in the attributes that he worked for: courage, pride, loyalty. When I look at Taka I see a kingdom within a man. I taught him strength and honor and dignity. And yes, he could be arrogant and sexist, but he also had a kind, pure, loving heart to temper those negative qualities. When Taka lost so much, he chose to hate the life I had given him. To hate his Father. It was his free will to do so, but it was his anger speaking. I knew eventually he would repent for the right reason. I offered him a chance. He did not budge in his insistence on finding you even if it meant he might never find you. He chose that over the chance to rebuild his life and rebuild Jaha. And while I would not have had that for him I had to allow him to experience what he has. I had to teach him that no love is greater than life. And no death is greater than love. It all has its place. He knows that now."

"What is my lesson?"

"Child, the lessons do not end, not for as long as you walk the earth. When the lessons are over you come home to me. And for one such as yourself, well, lessons abound.

You passed one test today. You opened your heart to another. You made it easier for your friend, Brenda, to be a better person. You brought her one step closer to me. That was a fine thing to do."

"She came to me crying. What was I supposed to do?"

"What were you tempted to do?"

"Slap her face and send her on her way."

"Well, there we are. Progress."

Taka cracked his eyes open and saw the roof of the Great Hall. He raised his head and searing pain drew his head to strain and his eyes to search for the source, finding it in the sword wound in his side that was spilling blood as if it never intended to stop. He dropped back and tried to lick dry, cracked lips, but his tongue was like a shriveled prune in his mouth and dried blood the only flavor.

He felt like he'd been there a thousand years waiting to die. He was back where he started. Back to that awful day. He knew if he looked around he would see the bodies of his friends and family but he had no desire to look. His limbs were weak and useless, his body drained of the nectar that sustained it, and yet he would stay there a thousand years more if it could delay the inevitable.

"Inevitable? There is no such word."

Taka's weak heart leapt with happiness and he tried to grin at the entity he could only hear.

"F . . . Father, I thought you had forgotten me here." His voice had dried up like his tongue. Despite being devoid of moisture a tear leaked from Taka's eye and streaked down the side of his face slowly.

"I do not forget mine, child."

"It seems my time has come to pass and I accept my fate. I have failed you and myself."

"Hush, son. Sit up and speak to me."

Taka could no more sit up than he could speak. Beyond pain now, his body was no longer under his power. But once again he had forgotten to whom he was speaking. A tingle started in his feet and moved upward, erasing numbness as it went along. The pain that followed was a blessing because at least he could feel again, but soon that was gone as well. Taka tested his neck and there was no pain. Finally he moved, sitting forward propping himself on his arms. And there before him, the vision he'd longed to see. It was Ani with the sparkle in his eye. It was his Father. Another lone tear moved down his face as he smiled gently.

"Once again, I underestimate you."

"Some things never change." The Almighty shrugged, offering a smile of his own. "But other things must."

"You give me my legs back so that I may walk into the underworld?"

"Anxious to get there, are you?"

Taka laughed at that, moving up onto his legs, firm once again. "I do not hold anxiety any longer. Nothing left to be anxious after if I cannot have her."

"You are ready to accept your fate, then? No argument? No complaint?"

"I have complained and argued enough. The task was left to me and I failed. I am not a man to blame my failure on others. It is over. I am ready."

"You do know it would have been difficult for you, had she accepted you. How could a man such as you have possibly gotten along in the modern world? Why, the only job they want to give you is manual labor; they cannot see that you are a king. How dare they?"

"My pride got the better of me. I would have accepted manual labor. I would shovel cow dung if it would give me opportunity to better myself and the respect of my woman."

"But they don't see your intelligence, don't realize how educated you are."

"An educated man does not need to announce he is so; he just is."

"But the resume, what a hassle."

"Yes, but I would have found a way. I do not know how but I would have found a way."

"But the world treats you as if you are a criminal; your brown skin makes you the target for whoever decides you are not worthy. It is dangerous simply for you to walk down the street. What a horrible time to live as a man of dark hue."

"Every time I emerged from my stone it seemed I was more hated for my color, more maligned and reviled. But what could be worse than what my fellow Africans endured at the hands of the world shortly after . . . ? Those villages that rose against me to massacre my own—and other innocent, neighboring villages—fell to the very people we were to fight against. I read about it. They were sold; some sold each other. They were traded and treated inhumanely for hundreds of years. Hundreds. But they survived. So people can look at my dark skin and do their best to treat me like the animal they think I am, but I know if those people could endure, so could I. If my love could endure, we could endure together. I would never have been alone if I had the most valuable of gifts beside me. With her love and your grace we would have prospered."

"Humph," the Almighty blustered, seemingly indignant on his behalf. "But Violet, she could not possibly understand what it is like for a great man: the pressures, the stress. You would certainly have had to lay down the law, show her that as a woman she is best served just to listen to you."

"Violet does not have to listen to me or anyone. She is an intelligent, independent woman. Have you seen her business? On her own she has done what many men can't, has built a company and a reputation to be envied. She is talented and resourceful."

"She is no king or queen."

"She is king and queen, ruler and leader of herself. She is no one's second."

"But she would have to be yours, correct?"

"What madness is this coming from you? I mean no disrespect but I would never want Violet to be second to me and it angers me to hear you suggest it. That is not her place."

"You wanted it to be before."

"This is a different time and a different place! I would not have understood things could or should be different back then, but this is not 'before.' I am not the man I was then and Violet is not Zahara! Sir." The Almighty's face grew serene at that point but Taka was too disturbed to try to analyze his Father's moods. "Why do you provoke me thus when all is already lost? I realize I have failed; do not taunt me with what might have been but cannot be. Nothing else in existence pains me as much as the prospect of what might have been had I been man enough to make it so."

"Sometimes what looks like failure is anything but. If you had it to do over again, Taka, what would you want for Violet? What would you want for yourself?"

Taka winced at the emotions that simple question generated. He looked around, smelled the acrid smoke, looked over to where his love lay still.

"I cannot say I would not follow her to the ends of the earth. Selfishly, I would do it because I want what I want. In whatever form she takes I love the spirit I knew as Zahara *and* Violet. You made such a splendid soul in such beautiful form both inside and out, Father, how could I not love her? Would I do it again? Yes, if only for a brief time to spend with her. Should I? That, I cannot answer. I have done so much damage, I cannot help but wonder what might have happened had I released her from the start. But, you see, I had to hold on. I do not know who I am without her. The most powerful man in the land, ha. I was never anything without her. That is my truth and my wound to bear."

"Taka, the acknowledgment is not the wound. The acknowledgment is always the start of the mending. I will tell you who you are without her. You are strong. You are compassionate. You are brave and courageous. You are proud and intelligent. You are a king among men. I say this without hesitation for all that you were and all that you have become through four hundred years of patience, determination, and hope. My son, you are splendid, to me. Those attributes that Zahara loved are the same attributes that will wake you in the morning. Your love for your wife made you a better man. Let it make you strong, now. Let it embolden you. Let it carry you. And when you feel weak and your memories are not enough, come to me. I will remind you who you are, Taka Olufemi. In the darkest of times you are still my child. You have not fallen into the hands of my enemy. Far from it. You have proven yourself to be the man so many men envied. You have proven yourself to be the warrior you were meant to be. I am proud of you, Taka."

Taka let the tears fall but he wasn't sad. Not anymore. He lowered himself to his knees and even though the smoke still lingered and human death still surrounded him, he felt a palpable weight lift from his shoulders. His family, friends, and loved ones were not stuck in this place of death. They were free and soaring and would be waiting for him when he came home. This tragedy was horrific but it wasn't all that remained of them. The truth of them, the goodness of them, was everlasting.

At that moment he knew his life was changed. He committed the bittersweet scene around him to memory and then lifted his head to speak to the Source of Creation. "If you are proud of me then I am satisfied, for nothing else matters. I am sorry for before. I thought you did not care enough about my people or about my pain and now I know we are all in your care, and all in safekeeping there. Father, forgive my ignorance and selfishness. I am a stubborn man but I am no longer a fool. Forgive me for breaking whatever future might have been for me and for my love."

The Almighty smiled. "You ask what might have happened if you had released her? It is no mystery. It is a simple answer and it has never changed. You would have found each other again, Taka Olufemi, as soul mates always do. And eventually you would have gone home to spend eternity by her side. My children never die; they just journey until they come home. My blessed Son made it so. As for your soul mate, your love will be a beacon to her. Not a beacon to a sad, restless soul, but a tether to a comforting, peaceful, and loving soul. And someday you will have all that you wish. Provided that is her wish, of course."

Taka could not help the smile that cracked his face. "Of course. I am smart enough not to presume that will be an easy task. But I have always been a man willing to step to a challenge. The harder won the better."

"I would expect nothing less, my son."

"I mean, I know I kind of pushed him away but I was just scared. You saw what happened with Gary; how was I supposed to know it wouldn't happen again? And I had

Jerome, I mean, I *had Jerome,* and Taka came along and just swiped that away like it was nothing. I was angry." Violet shrugged and looked to the Almighty for commiseration and when none came she went on. "Anyone would be angry; he just came on like gangbusters and I am not used to that. I mean, I have to stand my ground, right? But I love him. But I didn't know who he was. Why couldn't he just tell me? Why couldn't he just be straight from the beginning and we never would have had our little misunderstanding?" She stopped to breathe and found the Almighty's eyes on her, patiently.

"Are you done?" the Source asked.

Violet tried to hold it in. She kept reminding herself that even though it looked like a harmless angel beside her, God was speaking through that harmless angel. She should be reasonable, humble, keep her mouth shut. "No, I want him back!" Tears burst from her eyes and she catapulted herself at the figure before she even realized what she was doing, realized what she was doing and backed off quickly, hands up. "Sorry. Am I allowed to . . . ?"

"I invented hugs, daughter, of course you can."

She breathed a sigh of relief and continued to grasp, pleasantly surprised when arms clutched her back. She was suddenly bathed in comfort. It was as if she'd been hugged by her mother or father. It was as if she were a toddler again feeling loved and safe and warm. It was like every worry she'd ever had was gone. When she pulled away she was sorry, wanted to go back in to continue to be held by those arms. Wanted to go back where it was safe, again.

"I am always here for you, daughter. No matter how far you roam you need only to come back to me."

"I don't know how," she croaked. "Every time I hear that little voice it tells me to do something dangerous. What if I do it again? What if I put everything I have into something and it gets taken away?"

"Nothing that is yours can ever be taken. People die, yes, but only their bodies. The important part lives on. Love doesn't die. Spirits don't die. My blessed Son made it so. Taka chose a path I did not plan for him, but his journey should prove one thing to you: evil can never triumph over love. He gave up his life to follow you, daughter. He begged me for that chance."

"And how do I know it's me he wants and not her? The queen, I mean? I heard the legend; maybe he just wants to stay out of the heat."

"You've been talking to Skeeter, haven't you? Skeeter is a man. I am God. Who are you going to believe?"

She cracked a look at the All Powerful, trying not to let her doubt show. Ani's face merely looked back with a patient, knowing smile. "Taka really loves me? Me? Violet Jackson? I've been known to be . . . not so easy."

"How could you be easy? You were trying to keep the pain at bay. So you found men who didn't value you, friends who didn't care for you; you made a life for yourself void of all the connections that could nurture your heart. I understand, but that is not my plan for you. You are my child. You were made to love and be loved. And your love will be as splendid to you as you are to me."

"God, I'm not splendid in any way," she said quietly. "Didn't you see what I did? I was going to marry Jerome just to keep him like a Chia Pet. And I was going to do horrible things to Brenda. I mean, she's a friggin' size negative two, for cripes' sake. Why couldn't you have made me a size negative two? She's rich. She took Gary. She stole my technique. She has everything. It's not fair. Can you blame me for wanting to body slam her?"

"I am aware my enemy takes great joy in providing you with many colorful options for doing away with Brenda." Violet wasn't sure but she thought she saw humor on Ani's face. "But you must be strong. Nothing Brenda does escapes my notice. And it is not in you to do bodily harm to anyone; at least, not much. You have more of me in you than my enemy, this I know."

"You're not mad at me, then?"

"I don't ask my children to be perfect. Only my blessed Son is perfect. You may have heard of Him: kind, easy to talk to, and much more patient than I am, I must admit. My human children"—the Almighty shrugged—"are flawed, as I know they will be. But these last few days you cared for a man you didn't remember, fed him, helped him feel welcome and comfortable, shared your life and dreams with him. You took a former king hardened by centuries of resentment and you nursed his heart to life again. You made him happy to be alive again. Not as the woman he used to know, but as the woman you are today. I know who you are, daughter. You, Violet Jackson, are the only person who could have saved my son. You are more than worthy of Taka's love. You are more than worthy of anyone's love. You are the only one who doesn't know this."

Violet grew still and felt the tears well in her eyes. This flew in the face of all she had ever felt possible. Maybe the love was worth the uncertainty life had to offer? Maybe the love would make the difficult parts not so much so? Maybe the love would fill the emptiness?

"Can you bring Taka back?" she croaked.

The Almighty shrugged. "Loving is an active job. Love won't stay where it is not wanted. If I drop a piece of it on the ground it is up to you to pick it up. If I speak to you and tell you, 'Look, there it is,' it is up to you to listen. If I point to it and shine a light on it, it is up to you to step out of your fear and grasp it. If you ignore love's beacon it may not show you the way again. Love is a living thing, Violet. It goes where it is wanted. Do you want it enough to step past your fear and go after it? Do you want it enough to take it as it comes?"

The breeze against her hair was the only sound in the world as she looked into the face of the Almighty. What He was asking was a greater thing than she'd ever done. She realized now how strong her fear was. And because of that she knew how deeply she loved.

"I will try with all that is in me to trust in love and trust in you."

Ani's face smiled. "And you will pray? Check in with me and let me know how you are doing? Talk to me even when you are not in trouble?"

"Yes, yes!" Violet laughed, brushing away errant moisture from her cheeks. "Man, my stepfather wasn't as demanding as you are."

"Of course he wasn't. He is a good man but I am your Creator. I love you more."

That quieted her for a moment and she felt the warmth of emotion flow through her. But she had a few more things to cover first. "When you talk to me, can you talk a little louder so I can hear you? I'm used to ignoring you; it's going to take some practice to pay attention."

"You don't say?"

"Maybe wave a flag or two so I know it's you? I mean, I don't want to be tricked by you-know-who. He already knows I'm easily influenced and prone to sinful behavior. And I know you don't think I would really hurt anybody, but Brenda may need a little—"

"Violet."

"Yes?"

"Just try. If not for yourself then for me. Yours has the potential to be one of my greatest romances yet. I would really like it if the two of you would not make a mess of it. You are both stubborn and moody and temperamental and—"

"Hey, we're splendid, remember?"

"Oh yes, that, too." The Almighty smiled, leaned over, and cupped Violet's face in Ani's hands. "Go in peace, my child. The wrong is right again. Say hallelujah." She leaned forward to kiss Violet's eyelids one at a time and as Violet lost sense of the world only one word was on her lips:

"Hallelujah."

Chapter 28

The sound of the tinkling bell in Skeeter's shop shook Violet awake and she blinked the haze from her mind. She stood in the doorway but had absolutely no idea how she'd gotten there. It took her a moment to notice a weight in her hand and then she glanced down to see a brooch in her palm. Yes, the brooch she'd found earlier today at lunch in Bicentennial Park! It sparkled in her hand, beguilingly. The day's events came back to her quickly. That's right: she was here to find out about the brooch but darned if she was going to sell it. It twinkled at her like a wink. She liked it.

Stepping to the counter, Skeeter greeted her by insulting her and her mama but Violet wasn't deterred. She saw the greed in his eyes.

The bell tinkled with the entrance of another shopper but Skeeter was too engrossed in squinting at her jewelry to notice. He looked long and hard and finally straightened up, putting on his poker face.

"Paste," he said surely.

"What? Doesn't look like paste to me. How are your glasses, your prescription up to date?"

"Don't need twenty-twenty to tell paste. I'll give you . . . one hunnert for it."

One hundred, her behind. "Really, Skeeter? You'd do that for me? I don't know, seems wrong to ask you to come out of pocket for anything, considering it's just paste."

"It's all right. I know a lady likes to buy up all my junk. She'll give me two hunnert and everybody's happy."

Humph. Violet knew a con when she smelled it and the old man was smelling like a super-sized con. She glared at him while he stared at the brooch, unable to mask the greed in his eyes.

"You seem awfully interested, Skeeter. So either you're handing me a line or there's something you aren't telling me."

His eyes came back up and Violet could see indecision in them.

"I'm trying to do you a favor, is all. This piece here, I think I may know what it is but it's nothing but bad luck. Ain't worth nothing but it sure can cause some trouble. Ain't nothing. Just give it to me and—"

"Listen, old man, I have spent much money in this place. I've had a long day, all I've had to eat is one little hot dog with a little sauerkraut, and my best friend stole my account by stealing my technique. This piece of jewelry is the only bright spot in an otherwise crappy day and I do not have the patience." She leaned forward to take his cotton shirt in her palms. "You tell me the darned story or I will reach into your spindly old chest, pull out that peach pit you call a heart, and shove it up your shriveled old butt!"

Skeeter swallowed hard. "Well, when you put it that way . . ." Violet released him and smoothed her hair while he smoothed his shirt. "It's just a story I heard on my daddy's knee from his daddy's daddy's daddy's . . . you get the picture. 'Bout this garnet. Way back when there was this African writer guy wrote up all these stories 'bout how people come and killed off his people. Wrote up all these elaborate tales about how wonderful and special his people was, made up a language and everything. People loved them stories but there wasn't no real sign them people ever existed in the first place. I know 'cause my kinfolk was some of the people he lied on. 'Cause of his lies folks didn't want to trade with my people, wouldn't talk to them, wouldn't give them no jobs; it was plain wrong. Got people believing them lies, too. They say God was so mad that man lied on all them good people He trapped his soul in a rock and if you rub it and say his name three times old Olufemi will jump out and kill you, just like that man on that movie named after that game, Candy Land."

"You mean *Candyman?*" Violet asked.

"That's the one. You say Olufemi three times, see don't that crazy man pop out of that rock and kill up everybody!"

"Well, that's interesting, Skeeter, because that would mean this rock is more valuable than you're telling me, just as I suspected."

"Ain't no value in it, gal, other than valuable bad luck. I'm trying to do you a favor. One hunnert."

Of all the dirty-handed tricks. It wasn't like they were friends, but she'd given Skeeter good money over the years and here he was trying to scam her. It was the principle. He needed a little comeuppance and maybe he would think twice about scamming Violet Jackson again. She tossed him a nonchalant look.

"You know what I think, Skeeter? I think we should just test this baby out. I mean, if it's not the rock you think it is no need to worry, right? Let's find out!" She tried to blind him with a smile and while holding the brooch in one palm, closed her eyes, rubbed her fingers over the stone furiously, and said, "Olufemi, Olufemi, Olufemi," so fast she could hear Skeeter's gasp of surprise. She couldn't help but smirk. *That'll teach the old cheat.*

"Let me guess," a deep voice intoned. "Somebody in here is besmirching my name again, huh?"

Violet opened her eyes and hopped with surprise to see a man standing beside her.

"Good God!" A yell and a crash as Skeeter dove under the counter.

"Please get up, sir, and explain this," the man said, plopping a wooden bowl on the counter. He was tall and broad and his face was a profile in annoyance but that didn't make him any less attractive. "If I had a dollar for every . . ." he started to grouse and then turned to her and did a double take.

If she weren't so cool-headed Violet would have gasped at the impact of looking at him straight on. His face was imposing; too strong in structure and fierce in its scowl to be classically handsome. But it was full of character and animation, strong and proud and sturdy. And his eyes—deep, dark eyes set under prominent brows—were striking. His full, sensuous lips held promise. She was dumbstruck for reasons she couldn't begin to define. But if she was dumb he was stupefied if the way he was looking at her was any indication.

"Get out of here, evil spirit!" Skeeter screamed from below the counter, releasing Violet from her trance. She looked down at her brooch.

"You mean that ridiculous story is true? Man, I would not have guessed that." *Hey, if the story was true . . .* "You mean you're Olufemi? He wasn't right about that part where you kill up everybody, was he? I should warn you, I'll put up a fight."

His face relaxed and she caught a glimpse of handsome. *Why, this man would light up a room if he smiled,* she thought. His lips wiggled as if he were coming close to doing just that.

"I didn't walk out of that stone," he said as if the accusation weren't new to him. "I walked in through the front door while the two of you were preoccupied.

Yes, I am Taka Olufemi, the twelfth, and I've heard that story a thousand times; it precedes me in certain circles, especially in the U.S." He glanced down at the brooch in her hand and was transfixed, again. He straightened a little, cocked his head sideways. "Hey, that looks like it might really be the Olufemi stone. I'll be . . ."

"Don't act like you don't know," Skeeter said, inching up slowly, obviously ready to duck if the man popped off.

"I don't. I've never actually seen it, only heard the stories like every other person in my family. It's legend."

"Wait a minute," Violet said. "You said the story wasn't true. You said you walked in the front door."

His eyes swung up at her again and Violet felt the sweep of his interest, a palpable, intimidating, glorious thing. He looked at her as if gold dripped from her tongue. He gazed at her like she was a precious jewel. His lips curled in a true smile, this time, and her libido cranked up to 425 Fahrenheit.

"Actually, miss, there are two stories about the Olufemi stone: one is the lie drummed up by the murderers and the other one is the truth, passed down through the generations from King Taka himself. I know the truth. He is my namesake, after all. The truth has nothing to do with a murdering king popping out of a stone to kill people."

"He wasn't no king!" Skeeter cried, indignant. "My daddy's daddy's daddy's, you get the picture, told us all about him. Spreading lies. Ruining good people's names on stories. My kinfolk had to leave the homeland 'cause they got so much grief after all the lies. Lots of them, run out of the motherland 'cause of crazy Olufemi and the fools who believed him."

"Oh, what a shame," Taka said, giving a wry, dismissive glance to Skeeter. "I'm sure the motherland mourned the loss of families of murderers and liars. And what a gift for the New World, you are." His face hardened. "I knew I disliked you the second I walked in the door. I heard you trying to cheat this lovely woman out of her valuables. And this bowl right here, $1.99? This is a Jahanian artifact. Number one: you shouldn't even have it. Number two: you insult my Jahanian ancestors by undervaluing it. In fact, it is an abomination that you even laid hands on it at all. You're as crooked as your kinfolk, old man. Somebody ought to take you out back and beat the dignity and honor back into you. Back in the day, thieves were dragged around through piles of cow crap until the spirit moved them to find their manhood again. You should be on your knees begging the good Lord to bring that back to you instead of worrying about a man popping out of a stone. But I see the apple doesn't fall far from the tree. Like your daddy's daddy's daddy's, you get the picture, like son. I know one thing: if what you believe is true maybe you should slow down on badmouthing me or my kinfolk in my presence."

Violet's lips itched to curl at the corners. He was passionate and determined. He was fiercely protective of his birthright. He was almost ruthless. He was just her type. Her libido kicked up to 500 but she played it cool. Her libido wasn't running things; she was.

He turned back to Violet and just like that his face softened when he looked at her. He leaned an elbow on the glass-top counter to smile at her, but Skeeter was still stinging with indignation.

"You can't threaten me! I'll call the po po on you, boy!"

"Call the po po, old man. I'd like to hear what they say about some of the items you have in here. That bowl was stolen; it's likely not the only thing."

"What are you talkin' 'bout? I got that bowl from my cousin who says they mass market those bowls overseas. Ain't nothing in here stole." But the man named Taka was once again looking at her and Violet ordered her stomach to cease flip-flopping, despite her overwhelming urge to lean a matching arm on the counter just to sidle closer to him. She resisted.

"I know his name, and you know my name," Taka Olufemi said. "What's yours?" Simple question. She didn't know why it got the butterflies all jumping around in her stomach. Probably the way he said it, sensual and sexy-like.

"Name's Violet," Skeeter's gruff voice responded. "To hear the name you'd think she was a nice lady, with a name like that. That'd be a wrong thought. Mean as the day is long. Uncouth and bad rearing, you ask me."

"Violet is a lovely name. It suits you. About that brooch in your hand, Violet; the only thing I've seen are drawings from years past."

"How many years?"

"Ah, four hundred, give or take a day."

"And no one's found this thing, yet? Let me guess, you want it? I suppose you think this belongs in your family? What are you going to offer me, $125?"

"I'll give you $130!" Skeeter countered.

His eyes told the truth. "Well, legend says it's supposed to roam free to find its owner. And there's always the museum where his journals are preserved; they would probably like it to go along with the other things."

"Ain't no things, it was a lie I told you," Skeeter groused.

"Well, somebody needs to tell the people restoring the artifacts they found last month. Broke ground to build a shopping mall and, lo and behold, they discover, oh, only a couple thousand pieces of artifacts and a burial ground with the remains of a couple hundred people. Just like the Olufemi journals claimed, just like the other fools in the region believed. The hidden burial ground of Jaha. Go figure. Turns out the stories weren't just stories, after all."

"That's impossible! That can't be!"

"Mr. Olufemi," Violet interrupted Skeeter's blathering. "No point in this small talk. If the brooch was stolen I will inform the police that I found it, in full sight of a hot dog vendor in the park. As compelling as your story is, I wasn't born yesterday. I know what you want and you're not going to get—"

The chirping of her cell phone stopped her intended rant cold and she walked away, briskly, fishing her phone from her purse and putting it to her ear to hear her boyfriend Jerome's annoying voice. Two seconds into the conversation and she was sorry she did.

"What do you mean you want part ownership of my company? Are you insane?" Violet couldn't believe what she was hearing. Marriage and a prenuptial? Minor cost and doable. Sharing part of a company she had built from the ground up? Priceless. Impossible. "I don't care what you've been thinking."

"But it's like you said," Jerome continued. "We'll be getting married anyway. What's yours is mine and what's . . . You know how it goes. Look, why don't we talk about it tomorrow? We got that dinner with Brenda and Gary, so we'll talk about it before that. And try to wear something cute so you don't look heavy next to Brenda. Not that green dress; shows too much cottage cheese. You know, you could lose a pound or two. I'm just sayin'."

Violet, Violet, why do you put up with it? her inner voice admonished. Her eyes flowed unwillingly to the stranger trading barbs with Skeeter. Now, that was a man. *Don't you know him from somewhere?* Boy, her little voice was talking up a storm, today.

"So you think about it," Jerome was saying. "I know we can work something out, baby. You play your cards right and we'll see about that ring."

Violet blinked as a wash of rage flowed through her body and blinded her, momentarily. Was it possible this loser was holding the promise of marriage out as a carrot to get her to hand over the keys to her kingdom? Could it be he thought she was stupid or pathetic enough to put up with that? Oh, sure, she made him feel like he was the man but that was only to shut him up and keep him at her beck and call. Suddenly having him at her beck and call didn't seem all that attractive anymore. Stomach turning, really. Heck, she'd rather be alone. She didn't want to wake up one day sorry for all this time she was spending on a loser. If, by some horrible twist of fate, she got hit by a truck tomorrow her ghost would be truly sorry she'd wasted today on him, for sure.

She sighed. She was tired. Tired of the game playing and trying to one-up everyone. *Don't do anything drastic, Violet,* logic told her.

"Jerome, there is no way I would ever allow you near my business. I'm sorry, this is partially my fault, really. I let you think you are more important to me than you actually are. In fact, I don't even want you near me. In fact, I fake it in bed. Either that or I have to pretend you're someone else to even let you touch me. I can barely stand the sound of your voice. That 'in out in out' way you breathe really irks me. You've got weak, little boy arms. I know you stare at Brenda's butt when I'm not looking. And so, you know what? I deserve better. I'm not going to punish myself one second more by forcing myself to stay in this sham of a relationship so let's just do ourselves a favor and consider this thing a wrap. Don't call me. Don't e-mail. Don't text. Mail my things to me; don't even bother stopping by! 'Kay?"

She didn't realize she'd raised her voice but when she disconnected and put the phone away both men were looking at her. Taka smiled appreciatively doing all sorts of wiggly things to her nether regions.

"A woman who knows what she wants. I like that," the stranger said.

"Crazy woman, you mean," Skeeter supplied.

"Feisty. Commanding. Confident," Taka replied.

"Mean. Irritating. Annoying," Skeeter translated.

"Fed up. Bored. Done," Violet finished. She opened her hand to look at the prize again, placing it on the counter where they all stared at it, appreciatively. "Sorry, gentlemen, I'm not parting with my jewelry so get a good look while you can. Skeeter, you can keep your bad mojo and you . . ." She looked the stranger up and down and tried not to linger inappropriately. It was hard. *He* didn't have little boy arms. "You are just out of luck. I'm sorry I'm usurping your family's precious heirloom but finders keepers. How did you even know it was here, anyway? I didn't tell anyone about it."

"I didn't. I just saw this place as I was driving by. I'm only here in town because I'm renovating my office building and a friend told me his new designer has this great technique of using fabric to paint the walls. They're doing a story about it in *InStyle* magazine."

"You. Have. Got. To. Be. Kidding. Me."

"No, I'm not kidding. Ron says this woman knows her stuff. Do you know this Brenda something-or-other from Odyssey Designs?"

Skeeter laughed the laugh of the inconsiderate.

Violet hiccupped: a warning of a hyperventilation fit to come. She took a small sip of air and willed her lungs not to go berserk. "I know Brenda. Yes. Yes, I do. Brenda is a good friend of mine. But you have to understand. While I respect Brenda and love her like a sister, she is a complete witch. That technique you're talking about? Mine. Do you know how difficult it is to stand here and listen to you go on and on about a technique she stole from me? I patented the Melting technique for cripes' sake. I should string her up by her skinny little ankles and play Ping-Pong with that hard little nugget she calls a head. Better yet, I should trample her freakish size-negative-two body until she screams to the world what a lying, backstabbing—"

"Want to discuss it over dinner?" Mr. Handsome Stranger interrupted with a beguiling smile. Just like a man to use a vulnerable moment to jump on an opportunity.

"Just like a man," Violet said. "You think you can use this to get into my pants you've got another think coming, mister. You've already messed up, siding with my enemy . . . I mean, my friend, Brenda. And just because I'm single and available and you are tall and strong and sexy doesn't mean I'm attracted to you."

"That's fair," he said. "Lovely Violet, I'll forget your friend's name entirely if that's going to be an obstacle to getting to know you better. Any woman worth having is worth working for and I'm not one to shy away from a challenge."

"If a brick wall is a challenge." She waved a hand up and down in front of her to pantomime the obstruction. "Yes, there is a serious challenge here. I am done with men weighing me down. I am done with men who think they can just ride my coattails. I've worked hard for what I have. So what I'm not a size negative two?"

"I like a healthier woman, myself." He shrugged. "I'm a big guy, wouldn't know what to do with a tiny lady."

"Oh, I'm not intimidated by your size. A good right hook or a Smith & Wesson evens the playing field just fine. So what if I talk a lot?"

"I happen to like a good conversation."

"I am not dumbing myself down for a man ever, ever again. I am done setting myself up for failure. I am finished inviting losers into my life."

He smiled. "Then my timing is perfect. I don't have a
single strand of loser DNA in my entire makeup. Techni-
cally, I'm royalty. I'm not conceited but I am a catch."

"Humph," Violet said.

Skeeter couldn't stand it any longer. "If y'all two are
finished making googly eyes at each other how's about
you get the heck out of my store? Give me a headache.
Unless you want to sell me that brooch? I'll give you one
hunnert and fifty, that's my final offer."

Violet rolled her eyes at him. "If you offered one
thousand fifty I still wouldn't sell it to you, Skeeter. You're
a thief and a con man. Your practices are unethical and
inexcusable. You should be shut down or run out of town.
I can barely stomach you. I'll see you next week."

"Okay, see you next week, then." He gave a friendly
hand up in good-bye. "I'm gonna finish up in back and
when I get back out here I expect the two of you gone." He
headed to the back and then turned back to Taka. "Do you
want this bowl or not?"

"No, you keep it, Skeet. I'm not going to be involved
in purchasing illegally smuggled cultural artifacts, even
if they are part of my birthright. If I were you, when the
folks at U.S. Immigration and Customs Enforcement call
to ask about that bowl I suggest you point them to the
source because it's a felony to steal from an archeological
dig for personal profit."

Skeeter stared at Taka a long moment, then: "I gotta
make a call." He shuffled to the back faster than he'd
come out front.

"Oh, dear," Violet said. "He's a pain in the rear, but he's
old and helpless."

"He's old, all right," he groused, his frown following
Skeeter until he disappeared from sight. When he turned
back to Violet again his face was relaxed and happy like
she was the precious jewel he was trying to swindle from

her. "And you, you haven't told me what you think of the brooch. Holding on pretty tight. Mind if I take a closer look at it?"

"I'd rather you didn't." Violet saw his onyx brown hand reaching for her jewelry and she, instinctively, did the same. She got to the brooch first and his hand clasped hers, instead. His hand clasped hers and in her mind's eye the hand was in a different time and place. In her head she was standing at an altar, so full of love and hope tears were frozen in her eyes. Violet looked at the stranger beside her in the dark jacket and open button-down shirt and suddenly she pictured him just as majestic, only dressed in a heavy silk robe over a bare chest, a crown on his head, and love in his eyes.

She snatched her hand away and the brooch went skittering to the floor, but she left it there, backing away from it, and him. He bent to pick it up, turned it over in his hand, and, from where he was crouched, looked up at her. His face was a combination of confusion, wonder, and emotion.

"My God, the legend is true. King Taka's writings, all true."

Danger, Violet Jackson, her head screamed. *Remember him,* said a little voice.

Suddenly the big man didn't seem so harmless. Crouching there, his furrowed brow in a worried face meant more because, instinctively, she knew he wasn't a stranger. She didn't know what he was or who he was, but something told her he had the potential to cause her insurmountable pain.

"Holy . . . Are you seeing what I'm seeing?" he said, standing slowly. "Are you remembering what I'm remembering?"

She backed away until she ran flush into a table and there was no place left to go. She could barely see him but for trying to ignore the images flashing through her mind. She couldn't allow herself to look at them, not any of them. And she didn't want to look at him. It seemed no place was safe.

"Stay away from me. I don't know who you are but I don't want what you're selling. Just stay over there. Or, better yet, take that cursed piece of jewelry and go."

She watched his face go through a metamorphosis of emotion. Something was happening within him, maybe the same thing that was trying to happen within her. But unlike her panic, when finally his face settled it was into a calm, peaceful expression. When next he focused on her his eyes lit as if he were a child in a roomful of Christmas presents. He reached a hand out toward her and she flinched. Concern washed over his features.

"Can't you see? Can't you remember?" he asked. "Aren't the memories coming to you, love?"

Chapter 29

"I . . . I . . . Please leave me alone," she croaked, weakly.

Taka quickly assessed the situation and realized any excitement he was feeling or wanted to express would have to take a back seat because Violet looked like a deer in headlights. It didn't matter that he felt more alive, held more memories, and carried more hope than he'd ever had before; none of that mattered if she wasn't in the same state of mind with him.

He dropped his hand and looked at her a long moment, working up something to say, when Violet gasped with a sudden, breathy hiccup. The burnished copper skin of her face flushed and it was immediately apparent she was having a hard time breathing, but trying to keep an eye on him while doing so.

"What's wrong?" he asked, quickly. "Are you sick? Asthmatic?"

"No, no, not really." She gasped and put her hand behind her to lean her weight on the table. "Just need . . . a minute." But her breathing was coming faster now.

He watched her, helplessly. A minute ago he'd merely been Taka Olufemi XII with only the stories and legends of his ancestor who claimed to have been a king. He'd been fascinated by those stories as a child, memorized some of the journals. He never understood his connection to his namesake. But now, today, he was no longer merely a descendent. He no longer felt like only the man he was in this lifetime. He was no longer merely business owner, Taka, with no connections and no responsibilities beyond making himself happy. Now he was also King Taka Olufemi. And the information in his head was not just images of what he had read. Now they were memories. He felt like he was awake for the first time. He felt the hopefulness of being in the midst of an amazing thing. He felt happy beyond words.

But his wife was standing before him, hurt and scared. His wife! After all these years he finally had another chance and he was dangerously close to losing her, again.

"I understand," he said quickly. "You're seeing all these things you never wanted to see. We're at this place again, aren't we? Please, just hear me for a moment."

"A quick moment," she said, still panting from the onslaught of some sort of panic attack. Her eyes kept darting from his as if afraid to see him, but in the seconds they landed they were raw, wounded, beautiful dark mink brown. She hunched in her labored breathing, as wary as if she expected a blow or a pain so great it would land her in the fetal position. He understood that pain. He understood why she would be afraid of him causing it.

"A long time ago, he . . ." He started and then stopped. That wasn't going to work. "A long time ago I was a king and you were my wife. I bought this pin for you as a wedding gift."

She hiccupped and looked around. "Do you see a paper bag around here anywhere? Where the heck is Skeeter?"

"I had it made especially for you," he burst, bringing her eyes swinging to his face again. "The day we got married was the best day of my life. I vowed to honor, love, and cherish you. I took that vow seriously. But because of my mistake, one horrible day everything was destroyed. And you were torn from my life. You were killed."

"I don't want to hear this," she gasped, quietly. "I don't want to know you, I really don't."

"If you didn't want to know me you wouldn't still be standing there. You wouldn't still be gasping for breath, remembering when the murderers took your breath from you. I wasn't there for you when you needed me. I failed you, I know that. And after you died I had a hard time accepting that you were gone. I didn't want to live if I couldn't have you. So God sent me on a journey and until this moment I had forgotten all of it. He sent me from my home to spend three days with you."

"What are you talking about? I've never met you until today; I'd have remembered." She said it but her eyes darted from his.

He looked at her steadily. "I met your friend, Brenda. I met Gary and Jerome, saw your company, stayed in your apartment, stopped your neighbor from stealing your paper, ate your period chocolate." He gave her a light, tentative smile. Anything to wipe the panic from her face. "You'd remember if it didn't mean having to remember the pain, too. I had three days to win your love but I failed. God took me back home, healed my body, and told me to take care of my kingdom. I spent the next three days burying our people, our things. Burying you, my queen. I traveled to a safe, simple spot, settled, founded a town, married a woman who had lost the love of *her* life, had kids, and began writing journals. And when I was old and my body worn out I told God I was ready to go home. And He said to me, 'Taka, you've got someplace you need to be.'" Taka felt the tears try to start as the memory came back vividly. "There I was on my deathbed and He tells me He is sending me on a journey. Tells me He put a little bit of me in this stone to send out into world as a beacon and a guide. A guide; so my spirit could find you. A beacon; to let you know I was on my way."

He turned the brooch over in his hands. It looked so old. It had lived through many hard years, had somehow traveled the earth and seas and found its way home. Found its way back to the woman who'd inspired it. A piece of him still lived inside, perhaps always would. He reached out to hand it to her. She looked at his hand for a long moment and then, tentatively, accepted it without allowing her fingertips to touch any part of him.

"He told me that someday He'd give me the same face and body, which was a relief because I knew you liked this face and body. I asked Him when I'd find you and He said, 'It may happen tomorrow or a thousand years from now. Whenever it happens will be at precisely the right time.' I didn't want to hear anything about a thousand years but I wasn't going to argue, this time. I was old and sick as a dog but I died with a smile on my face. I left that life happy because I knew I was on my way to you."

She was almost back to breathing normally, now, but still she looked at him suspiciously, clutching the brooch like a lifeline.

"Look," she said, softly, lips bunched like the words were causing her pain. "You seem like a nice man, but whatever is happening here, I don't want that kind of turmoil in my life."

"Is that what your heart is saying?"

"My heart doesn't run me, mister. My head says you're trouble and it's been my experience that my head is right. Don't try to convince me otherwise. Don't try to tell me not to know what I know."

He nodded, momentarily halted by logic. She had always been intelligent. She smelled condescension like smoke from a burning village.

"You're right," he admitted, humbled. "You put yourself in my hands once because your heart convinced you to and I failed you, terribly. I failed myself. I prided myself on being all powerful, all knowing, all seeing; but I didn't see what was coming. And I didn't listen to you or your concerns. Why would I? I was the king who walked with angels, right? You think I'm dangerous and I can't argue with that. Truth is, Taka, the twelfth, is almost as arrogant as Taka, the first. Some things just don't get lost in the wash. But until this moment there were so many things I didn't understand. I understand everything now."

"Like what?" she asked, shyly, as if asking from some deeper place, some rarely touched spot, opening itself up for the first time in, perhaps, a very long time.

"I took it all for granted. I'll never know what could have been prevented if I had been a better man back then but I know how precious every day is. I know how important it is to show your loved ones how you feel. Until the end of my days as King Taka I regretted a lot, but mostly I regretted not taking that horse ride with you that day."

Violet looked down quickly as if in sudden pain, a sob muffled in her throat. He could feel her silent plea for him to stop but he couldn't stop now. He was at that place; the place just on the verge of her soul, the place where he could push through or back off. He wasn't giving up on her this time.

"I'm a better man, today. Better than the king Zahara married. Better than the genie who spent most of three days misunderstanding this woman named Violet Jackson because he couldn't see past his own needs. I'm a better man. I look into your eyes and I see every hurt, every pain you've tried to hide, even the ones you weren't able to. There was a time when I would have said I'd give anything to have you. Today, I would give anything to be with you. I thought there would be more time for us. When you were gone I missed how you would look at me with that mischief in your eyes and tell me how a proper husband should behave; the way you used to speak to me, before people around us told you it wasn't proper to speak to a king that way, even if you were his wife. I missed your beauty and freedom and joy. You were my strength. You were what made me great. My love, when you were gone, I didn't know how to take another step."

He broke off to gain his composure and clear the tears clogging his throat.

"When I came back for those three days and you were different, changed, I thought you were broken. I thought you weren't there. But every day you laid out your pain in front of me, gave me every opportunity to earn your trust again, and I was too self-absorbed to pay attention to how you needed me. You were this new woman, this woman who fought to take care of herself because she knew she couldn't trust anyone else to do it due to the lesson I had a hand in. This woman who guarded her heart because she'd been hurt so many times, and was maligned even for that. This woman who took on the world and fought for a place in it, fought for a name, a reputation, fought like a she-devil when that was the last thing she was. This woman who fought to build her own domain because no one was there for her when she needed them most. This woman who could come home and show her life's work to a grumpy, ignorant stranger and light up with joy so bright it filled the room. This woman who comforted me with her words, who listened to me mourn my wife, who taught me how to drive and fed me, even when she was pissed off. This she-devil who stopped herself from making love with me because she didn't feel right cheating on a man she despised. I waited too long to try to know you, Violet. By the time I realized I was in love with you I was too late.

"God took me back to 1600 and I lived my life as a man who used to be a king; a king who had allowed all his people to perish. I learned all about humility and shame and grace; moving on in pain and making a life where there is none and trying to be the best human being you can when the rug has been pulled from under you. And I changed. I stopped being so concerned about what people called me and spent more time concerning myself with people. I stopped being King Taka long before I died. I finally became a pretty good man. Today, I'm the man Zahara hoped for and the man Violet Jackson deserves. I won't wait until it's too late, this time. I'm not a king or a cartoon character. I'm a man and I want you back. I want to hear your fears so you know you're not alone. I want to know your dreams so I can dream with you. I have cried for you; I have longed for you; I have yearned for you for as long as my soul has existed. I've traveled a thousand lifetimes to get to you, Violet. My arms were made to hold you. My lips were made to kiss you. My tongue was made to tell you what a blessing you are to me and everyone who has the fortune to know you. A kingdom, the world, nothing compares to the kingdom in your eyes. We have this last time to get it right, my love. Please."

She had been trying so hard to keep from looking at him; his height made it easy for her to keep her eyes down. He stepped closer, put one finger under her chin. He liked the feeling of her skin so much he stroked it gently with his thumb.

"Please, don't." She gave a soft plea that told him his touch brought memory. She leaned into it even as her face blanched, blood drained away. Her skin missed him, despite everything. His fingers began to tremble with the impact and his breathing hitched, but he released her as she'd asked. Gone were the days he could take this love for granted.

"You can tell me to go and I will understand," he said, softly. He spoke intimately, hoping his caress of words would reach that special place in her soul. "You've given me two chances already. But I'm asking for a third. You and I could go a lifetime without knowing each other if you choose but that would be a tragedy being that we were made for each other. Please tell me you know who I am, this time? Tell me you'll have me?"

They stared at each other for a long moment. He didn't look away. Her lips pressed together in silent struggle. He could see she was fighting the memories again, fighting the images that had told him his truth a few minutes ago. He could see her struggle, could almost feel her pain. A lone tear escaped her large brown eyes to slowly float down her cheek. In that tear he saw all the years of tears, all the heart-wrenching pain. All these years he'd gone on, searching. Nothing could break his spirit but her. He could feel his soul beginning to crack right now.

She looked at him full in the eye. When her hands came up along the sides of his face he held his breath and kept still, certain if he moved she would bolt. Her fingers touched his skin lightly, running up to his hairline and down along his jaw. Then her thumbs came forward to brush against his lower lip. His lips itched to take her fingers in, to nibble and kiss on them like he longed to do with all of her. But he held still and he held his breath as his heart broke. She was remembering his face with her hands. She was saying good-bye.

His jaw clenched when her hands finally settled again, her eyes searching his. Then she released him, her chin went up and his hopes dashed further. She swiped the tear from her cheek, firmly and decisively and looked him dead in the eye.

"Losing you was worse than losing the air to breathe. Knowing I would never hold you in my arms again or hear your voice or feel your touch. I was dying long before they killed me. You were more than my husband. You own a part of my soul. Without you, there was nothing left to give to anyone, let alone myself. I've been walking through life empty and afraid. No one could fix me, not even you."

Finally, his tears broke free and took her hand, leaning his lips into her palm, kissing it, gently, grasping it with his hand to press his lips there, firmly. "I'm so sorry, my love. Please forgive me. I was too late to save you once and I'm too late again."

She shook her head, confusion on her pretty face. "But, there's never been anything to forgive. It wasn't your fault what they did and it wasn't your job to fix me. That's what I'm trying to tell you. God fixed me. Today, just now, He gave me the strength to fight my fear and remember it all, the good and the bad. And you gave me the motivation. I haven't been pushing you away because I don't want you, it's only because I want you so much! All these years, waking up every day to a world that didn't have you was torture. I was angry at God for allowing me to dream and never giving me anything close to what I wanted. Don't you see? I've loved you all of my life. I loved you as king, I loved you as a genie. I love you right this moment for being man enough to fight for me. I'll love you for eternity, Taka Olufemi: the first or the twelfth. Will I have you? Abso-friggin'-lutely. Do I know you?" Her shy, tremulous smile widened. Her glance became cocky and he thrilled at the familiar glint of mischief in her eyes. "A queen knows her king. And I have to tell you, over the course of four hundred years I have developed a queen-sized appetite to know you all over again. Over and over. And over."

She wanted him. She wanted him!

Taka grabbed her quickly, hearing her squeal of delight and happiness as he swung her around and let out a massive yell of victory. Finally setting her on her feet again, she was almost breathless from laughing and crying at the same time.

"Oh, baby," he breathed, beyond words. He moved forward, feeling the skin of her face with his palms, letting her thick eyelashes brush his fingers, touching her lips with gentle caresses. Then, slowly, he bent to press his lips to hers and the fireworks that exploded between them was shockingly, achingly familiar. He kissed her until they were both dizzy. He kissed her as the memories flashed through his head. He kissed her as dreams of their future began to weave themselves in his mind. And then he kissed her some more, settling into the pleasure with a sigh of contentment.

When they finally pushed open the shop door and stepped outside, the light of a brilliant sunset almost blinded them. The sky was on fire with a mélange of colors as if the sky was a living thing, a beauty that sung the song of heaven above.

"Look, Violet. It's our sunset. It's almost as beautiful as you."

She turned to him, her copper-skinned face so full of the glow of the sun her eyes were like starbursts of topaz within their darkness, her lips slightly parted and the color of berries . . . or Flori Roberts lipstick. She was the most beautiful woman he'd ever seen, today, tomorrow, and always. Her eyes twinkled at him.

"If I'm so beautiful why'd it take you so long to get to me?" At his questioning glance she went on, her shoulders rising along with her hands to the sky in a gesture of exasperation. "Why in the name of all that's holy does it take men so long to come when their women call? I mean, I've been calling four hundred years and a day. As much as I love you, I swear, you travel through time about as fast as you drive a car. I do believe you may have even been going backward."

For a moment he could only blink and stare at her. Finally, a chuckle started deep in the pit of his being. A chuckle that felt warm and at home, that made his mouth open and his soul weep for joy. Violet lips curled and soon she was laughing as hard. With hands clasped, they made their way down the street, with the setting sun warming their path, to their very own happily ever after.

Skeeter finished locking his shop after peering outside and making sure the two crazies were gone. He'd had quite a shock that afternoon and had decided to close early so he could figure out how to get rid of the piece of stolen loot his good-for-nothing cousin had passed on to him. Now he paused as a gentle rumble bubbled under his feet. He cocked his head, trying to identify the sound. Not fierce enough to be an earthquake, not abrasive enough to be the vibration of a passing semi.

Oh well. He shook his head. Whatever it was was kind of pleasant anyway. Comforting and warm. Reminded him of something one of those guys on the nature channel had said once about the contented purr of a great lion. It was the gentle rumble of a king.

A glorious sound, indeed.

The End

Discussion Questions

1. There is a quote that "to whom much is given, much is required." Despite all the blessings he was given, do you think too much was expected of Taka when he was asked to go on after the tragedy?

2. Upon meeting Violet Jackson, Taka immediately thought it was his job to "fix" her but who, ultimately, needed the most fixing?

3. Is it possible to be angry at God and still have faith and love for Him?

4. Was fear the only thing keeping Violet from living a happy life or did she also hold some guilt from the tragedy long ago?

5. In what ways was Taka and Violet's romance symbolic of the relationships of men and women today? Or was Violet's relationship with Jerome more in line with today's unions?

6. Violet seemed to loathe the body weight that Queen Zahara had been proud of. Is Taka fair when he criticizes her for caring what society thinks of her size or is he hypocritical, especially since he has never been at the mercy of society? What are some of the traits of African American women that should be revered but are reviled, instead? How do black men contribute to or hinder our self-image?

7. Violet felt if she allowed herself to love Taka he would ruin her for the inevitable comparison with the lesser man (likely Jerome) she would end up

with. Do women today settle for less because it will be less painful if the relationship ends?

8. Do you have a "Brenda" in your life?

9. Was the Almighty cruel or compassionate in taking Taka back to 1600 AD Africa after his failure to win Violet's heart? Did Taka truly have free will?

10. In their own way, neither Taka nor Violet were able to move past the tragedy at Jaha, but until they were able to do so neither would be able to gain salvation. Is this message overly simplistic or is it helpful when considering how to overcome our own challenges in life?

About the Author

Ava Bleu lives and loves in the Midwest. She enjoys smooth jazz, cuddly dogs, and baked goods of all varieties. You can find her curled up next to her fireplace with a cup of tea or camped out at the local public library.

UC HIS GLORY BOOK CLUB!

www.uchisglorybookclub.net

UC His Glory Book Club is the spirit-inspired brain-child of Joylynn Ross, Author and Acquisitions Editor of Urban Christian, and Kendra Norman-Bellamy, Author for Urban Christian. This is an online book club that hosts authors of Urban Christian. We welcome as members all men and women who have a passion for reading Christian-based fiction.

UC His Glory Book Club pledges our commitment to provide support, positive feedback, encouragement, and a forum whereby members can openly discuss and review the literary works of Urban Christian authors.

There is no membership fee associated with UC His Glory Book Club; however, we do ask that you support the authors through purchasing, encouraging, providing book reviews, and of course, your prayers. We also ask that you respect our beliefs and follow the guidelines of the book club. We hope to receive your valuable input, opinions, and reviews that build up, rather than tear down our authors.

Urban Christian His Glory Book Club

What We Believe:

—We believe that Jesus is the Christ, Son of the Living God.

—We believe the Bible is the true, living Word of God.

—We believe all Urban Christian authors should use their God-given writing abilities to honor God and share the message of the written word God has given to each of them uniquely.

—We believe in supporting Urban Christian authors in their literary endeavors by reading, purchasing and sharing their titles with our online community.

—We believe that in everything we do in our literary arena should be done in a manner that will lead to God being glorified and honored.

We look forward to the online fellowship with you. Please visit us often at *www.uchisglorybookclub.net*.

Many Blessing to You!

Shelia E. Lipsey,
President, UC His Glory Book Club